The Life of a Collective Warrior

CD PULLEY

INSPIRING JREAMS

ISBN: 979-8-218-33099-6(Paperback)
ISBN: 979-8-218-16887-2(E-book)
ISBN: 979-8-9897059-0-0(Audiobook)
ISBN: 979-8-9897059-1-7(Hardcover)
Library of Congress Control Number: 2023923302

Book Cover created by Ravin Phul

Printed in the United States
First paperback edition December 2023

Inspiring Jreams
Columbus, Ohio
InspiringJreams@gmail.com

Contents

Dedication

To my husband. You know who you are!

Preface

The Life of a Collective Warrior came to me in pieces. The first piece was the idea of a young black girl becoming someone she didn't even know existed and not through trauma to herself. The second piece was the idea of a young woman who protects women and children. Finally, the third piece was what would that protection look like?

When I started writing this book, I had no idea where it would go. I knew I wanted to read a story about a black woman that was not about trauma, but about finding out who they are. There are more books out here like that now, but when I started this story in 1990 something, there were not a lot of stories like this one. I also wanted to tell a story about a young black girl with strong family ties. I wanted to tell a story with elements most people do not think exist for people who look like me.

I hope you find entertainment in this book. I hope you find yourself or others you know in this book. And finally, I hope you enjoy reading the story of how this young woman became a Collective Warrior

Chapter 1

When Siobhán called me, I had not been to the Playhouse in a few months. If major decisions needed to be made about the building or if someone wanted to donate money, then I came running. I had to move seven women and their children across state lines and asked if this, whatever it was, could wait, but she insisted it was urgent.

I walked into the red brick building that used to be a department store, past the front desk and our receptionist Jordan. Her hair was green today. The last time I saw her it was yellow. I don't mean blonde--the actual color yellow. She waved and smiled as she spoke on the phone.

I climbed two flights of stairs to Siobhán's office. As I moved down the hall, I passed the student's pictures, poems, and photographs hanging on the walls along the second-floor corridor. In the classrooms, there were a few students and teachers putting things in briefcases and backpacks.

At the end of the hall, I walked into the inner office, past the empty receptionist's desk and a tartan couch. Inside Siobhán's office, I saw my red-headed friend sitting at her desk. Her curls were really something. Remembering back to our first meeting, she had no idea what she was doing with that hair. I don't give strangers advice, yet Siobhán was the exception. Her Irish brogue was strong, and accents always make me feel fluttery inside. Looking at her hair, emerald-green eyes, and alabaster skin, all I could think is that she looked like a damn model.

A young girl was sitting on a couch opposite Siobhán. She had her head down, holding an object in her hand. When I spoke to Siobhán, the young girl didn't bother to turn around.

Siobhán rose from her seat, came out to the inner office, and closed the glass door behind her. We stepped away from the front of the door and she proceeded to inform me about her "Talk to the Public Series." People from the community came to the center and talked about their professions, being in jail, and owning a business. Today the speaker was a woman speaking on the subject of sexual abuse.

I raised an eyebrow and she held up her hand.

"I thought it might be too strong a message for the kids, so I got permission from all the parents. I did it for each of the topics, and parents who didn't want their kids to participate didn't participate.

"And this was working?"

"Yes. I was surprised too. When I saw some looks of recognition today about what she was saying, I knew I probably did the right thing.

"After the talk, the girl sitting in my office," She pointed behind her, "came to see me. She stood by the door and asked:

"Was that lady telling the truth, Miss O'Shea?" the young girl said barely above a whisper.

"Who? Ms. Ankea About what?" Siobhán said looking into the girl's eyes.

"About being touched when she was young, like me?"

"Yes, she was."

"And she is really a doctor?"

Siobhán leaned a little closer, "She's a therapist if that's what you mean."

The young girl paused, "Then, that could happen to me too?"

Siobhán understood now, but she had to be careful, "What could happen to you too?"

"I could be normal like her?"

"You're normal right now, Ledawnia."

"No. I'm like her when she was young."

Siobhán sat the young girl down and didn't say anything to her at first. But Siobhán knew what she needed to do.

"Ledawnia, is someone hurting you?"

Ledawnia kept her head down and whispered, "No."

"If someone is hurting you, you can tell me. You're safe here."

"No. I'm not. I'm not safe."

Siobhán squeezed Ledawnia's hand and turned her face towards her. "Listen to me, I am not going to let anything happen to you, but I need to know who's hurting you."

Ledawnia took her hand away and said, "No one. I will be OK."

Siobhán decided to go another way, "Lee? I think you're scared and that's OK. Maybe others didn't help you when you needed them, but I will. I am not going to let whoever is hurting you get you. You heard Ms. Ankea. She had to tell. You have to tell."

Ledawnia burst into tears and said, "It's...it's...my...father. I don't want him to, and my mother tries to stop him, but he's too strong. Can you make him stop? Can you help my mom?"

Siobhán gathered her in her arms and let her weep for a few minutes. She knew this girl's life was about to change and some of it was going to be hard.

I lowered my head after Siobhán relayed the conversation. I didn't need to know this and couldn't understand why she called me. I loved building the center for the kids, but I was not comfortable being around them. I didn't even know what Talk to the Public Series was until that day.

"I called you Harri 'cause I know you work with people like this and maybe you could be of help. I've never done something like this before except in the classroom. The confrontation with her mother might not go the way things go in a classroom and I already called the police. I just wanted a little backup," Siobhán explained.

Just as she finished explaining, a light-skinned woman with black hair and wisps of grey pulled back in a bun, carrying a little boy on her hip, entered. The woman glanced at the young girl in the office and shifted her glance to Siobhán and me. Her eyes were wild as she also glanced at the exits.

She finally stopped in front of us, out of breath, "Someone called me about my daughter?"

Siobhán stepped up to the woman, "Hi, Mrs. Lancer, my name is Siobhán O'Shea and I run the Playhouse. This is Harrison McCuff, and she's a consultant. We called you down here today to talk about Ledawnia,"

As she explained who we were, I sat down in one of the chairs that matched the couch. I wanted to be able to see all the action without becoming involved and scaring this poor woman any more than she was.

"She doesn't seem to be hurt. I would like to take my daughter home."

Mrs. Lancer tried to move the little boy closer to her, as if we were going to steal him, and kept looking around the entire office rarely looking at us.

"Mrs. Lancer, why don't we sit down," Siobhán offered her the couch.

"Please tell me what is going on. I don't need to sit down," said Mrs. Lancer, her voice rising slightly.

"Ok," Siobhán said, holding her hands up to Mrs. Lancer. "Maybe your son should go and sit with his sister in my office.""No. He is fine right here," as she pulled the little boy closer to her side.

"I promise nothing will happen to him."

The scared woman shook her head no and clung to her son.

Siobhán sighed and said, "Mrs. Lancer, has Ledawnia talked to you about someone touching her?"

"Touching her? What do you mean by touching her?"

"Mrs. Lancer, are you sure you don't want to take a seat?" Siobhán asked again.

Mrs. Lancer was now pacing a little. "No, I do not want to sit down! What is happening?"

I was glad I picked the seat I picked. I could see their exchange and watch Ledawnia's reaction at the same time.

"Mrs. Lancer, Ledawnia says that her father has been touching her."

"What are you talking about? Touching her? No, her father is not touching her. I don't know why she said that to you, but we have to go."

Mrs. Lancer tried to go past Siobhán, moving towards the office. Siobhán blocked her way.

"Mrs. Lancer, we can help you."

"You can't help me!" Mrs. Lancer screamed. Ledawnia turned to look over her shoulder at her mother. Her face was drawn, and her eyes had no tears, yet they were tired and wide. The young girl then turned back to face the inside of Siobhán's office.

I got up from my seat and sat on the edge of the chair while watching Mrs. Lancer and her daughter.

"Mrs. Lancer, I know you're scared. But we can help get you out and he will not find...," Siobhán started to say.

"Don't...tell me that," Mrs. Lancer was crying, "That's a lie. I've done this before. You cannot keep us. I am taking my children home."

Siobhán stepped in front of Mrs. Lancer again, "Mrs. Lancer, I had to call the police. They'll be here soon, and they'll take your daughter and your son. I cannot let you take her home."

"You don't understand. He will find us when he gets out like he always does."

"Your husband will not get out. He'll be in jail for a long time."

"You don't know this. I'm leaving."

Siobhán stood in her way again. Mrs. Lancer was yelling at Siobhán when a man and a woman walked into the office.

"Excuse me. I'm Detective James and this is my partner, Detective Lionel. We got a call about a child?"

"Yes, I called. This is the child's mother, Mrs. Lancer," Siobhán said.

"You cannot take my children!"

While they were dealing with Mrs. Lancer, I stepped away from Siobhán and the detectives. I could hear the muffled arguing as I stepped into the empty corridor and pulled out my phone.

I dialed a regular ten-digit phone number. I waited for what I knew was coming.

On the other end, A female automated voice came on and said, "The number you have reached, 718-555-2692, has been changed. No further information is available. Please make a note of it. 718-555-2692 has been changed. No further information is available." A busy signal then followed.

On the fourth busy tone, I dialed fifteen numbers that unlocked Magus's phone. He picked up on the second ring and said nothing. Every time I called him for information on a client it was the same thing.

"Ledawnia Lancer. I need to know about her, her mother, and her father. I want to know everything."

"I'll call you back in a few hours." And he hung up.

I also called Cara to tell her about my potential client. She told me to let her know about the vetting and keep her informed.

As I ended the call with Cara, I noticed Mrs. Lancer had calmed down. She was holding Ledawnia in a strong embrace against her body, the mother and daughter both sobbing in Siobhán's office. She was a pretty girl with long dark hair in braids with different colored rubber bands to secure the ends. Ledawnia was a little darker than her mother. In fact, I didn't see a resemblance to her mother at all. My eyes fell on the little girl as she bent down to pick up her pink backpack with white polka dots and stuffed a black rag doll in her bag. My heart clenched, and I got butterflies in my stomach. I held the feeling for a few seconds, then heard Ever's voice in my head, and that sent the feeling flying away. I did not want to think about that.

I remained in the outer office while the detectives met with them. After about 20 minutes, they all came out. Mrs. Lancer, her son, and Ledawnia left with the detectives. Siobhán stayed behind.

"They're taking them to the station. Mrs. Lancer doesn't want to go, but they told her they'll take Ledawnia and her son. I'm gonna go down to the station. They're going to need someone, but I would like you to go too, just in case."

"I'm not sure what I can do, Siobhán. I don't really work with kids, but I guess I can find someone if you need me to. Are they gonna pick up her husband?"

"They didn't say. I know this isn't your usual thing, Harri, but I have learned to go with my gut, so thank you for coming down here."

"No problem, Siobhán."

Chapter 2

In the same way Siobhán listens to her gut, I do too. My gut was telling me the police station was the last place I wanted to be, but Siobhán needed me. Upon my arrival, the sergeant at the front desk handed me a badge and directed me to the second floor. As I approached the squad room, I spotted Siobhán sitting in a chair along the wall. When I walked in, the cops yelling at suspects almost drowned out the typing, phones ringing and conversations happening all over the squad room. I could see a holding cell in the back of the room along with what looked to be interview rooms. "Hey, how're they?"

"I don't know. Ledawnia hasn't been in long. They had to wait for a counselor because she wouldn't speak to the police. They weren't sure they could find someone tonight, but they found the lady in there with them. Mrs. Lancer came out soon after the counselor arrived. I'm waiting for an officer to take my statement."

I glanced over at Mrs. Lancer who was standing in front of a glass wall, with the little boy still attached to her side. I suspected she was trying to hear through the glass what questions were being asked and her daughter's answers. I'd never witnessed a person appear worried, scared, and disgusted all at the same time.

A Black officer came over to speak to Siobhán.

"Ms., if you could follow me, please. I am going to take your statement."

"OK. Thank You. Harri. If I don't come back, let me know what happens with them, OK?"

The words made it to my ears, but not my brain. I think I replied, "See you later." But my attention was on Mrs. Lancer. After another five minutes, Mrs. Lancer quickly moved to the door, walked into the squad room, and stood by the filing cabinets next to the interrogation rooms. I'd given her a few minutes, as I assumed it was hard to listen to your daughter go into great detail about her abuse, especially when you were there.

"Hi. Mrs. Lancer? Do you remember me from the Playhouse?"

She glanced at me and looked back at the door where she knew her daughter was sitting, but could not bear to listen to her, "Yes, I remember you."

"Do you mind if I ask your first name?"

She glanced at me for a few seconds, "Mona."

"Is it OK if I call you Mona?" She nodded her head at me. "OK. I want to offer my services to you, Mona. I know you're scared of your husband, but I have people who can keep you safe from him."

"You?" She scanned me from head to toe with the "you're just a woman" gaze. "What can you do?"

"We can make sure he never finds you or your children again. He will never know where you are. No one will."

"Really? Look, I don't know who you are, but if I'm going to hide, it'll be with the police. You're one woman and I don't know you, but I know what he can do to people who try to help me."

"And if the police can't hide you?"

"I'll leave and I won't have to worry about it."

"You just said he always..."

She turned to face me and whispered harshly, "Look! You cannot help me. OK."

That was my cue to stop. I sat back at the desk while Mona fidgeted for another half an hour before Ledawnia came out of the room. We didn't speak to each other or anyone else. I assumed Mona was thinking about her next move and I was doing the same.

When Ledawnia came out to stand by her mother, I saw her doll again and the butterflies returned, but this time it also brought flashes of "her" in my mind. A flash of her brother and her parents' faces popped into my head, and a wave of loss washed over me. I pitched to the left and grabbed the table before I fell out of my seat. A doll just like that was the beginning of the most pain I had ever been in as a young person. I had to leave. I could not help them, but I would find someone who would.

I shot from my seat and ran past Mona and Ledawnia.

I stopped. There was a commotion in front of me. Most people wouldn't even have registered the noises because there was no shouting, but I noticed the air changed. There was the sound of something heavy being dragged and shoes shuffling the floor. There were voices, but the words were not clear. As they got closer the words,

"Take your fucking hands off me. She is a dirty liar," in what I believed was a Jamaican accent.

"Sir, just walk like a normal human being."

"Fuck you."

Turning towards the sounds, my eyes fell on a man in a suit being dragged past the squad room. He had dark curly hair, was medium brown-skinned, and had a smooth complexion with hazel eyes. He was wearing a Tom Ford suit and Ferragamo shoes. When I saw him, he saw Mona. His face went from questioning to recognition to anger and ended in rage. The quickness with which this happened had my stomach in knots. His eyes went dark, and his jaw clenched. There was no mistaking this was her husband. The one she and at least one of her children were afraid of.

I could see Mona out of the corner of my eye. Her body stiffened at her recognition. She moved out of my line of sight. I wouldn't take my eyes off her husband. I moved closer to face him.

If anyone was paying attention, they would have seen what was coming. When he got to rage, he broke from the officers who were dragging him in, even though he had handcuffs on. The room was full of cops, but all he saw was Mona. He ran towards Mona.

All of this happened in seconds, but the knots had untied themselves, and I was ready for him. On my right, I had Mona, who was no longer in my line of sight. On my left, out of the corner of my eye, Ledawnia crouched behind a desk. She was crying. She must have moved there when she saw him.

He was not paying attention to me. He was coming in fast, his teeth bared, and moving to my right toward Mona. The detectives were leaving the interrogation room chatting to each other oblivious to what was about to happen. The cops who lost control of this man were moving towards us.

My advantage was he didn't even realize I was there. As he tried to go around me to reach Mona, I grabbed his shirt and used my other hand to press the pressure point near his clavicle bone. Painful. He stopped, sucked in air, and tried to shift his weight, but instead he fell to his knees.

The police rushed over. As the officers whom he broke away from earlier were pulling him to his feet, the man called Mona and her daughter every filthy name you could imagine while cursing out the officers all in his beautiful Jamaican accent.

When the arresting officers had him on his feet again, he and I were face to face. The darkness had not left his eyes but grew in intensity when he realized I was the person who did this to him and prevented him from completing his attack. He lunged at me, but the arresting officers were on top of their job this time and caught his shoulder and arm before he got too far. He struggled in their grip, spat on the ground in front of me, and called me a piece of shit bitch. I didn't flinch. My eyes never left his, and I smirked. He stopped for a split second and quickly squinted his eyes at me and my smirk. As the police dragged him away, his tirade resumed. The detectives followed the men, leaving Mona, Ledawnia, and me standing in the squad room with all the other cops watching the prisoner being dragged away.

I turned to check on the two of them. Mona had her back against the filing cabinets, shaking while clutching her son close. She didn't even notice Ledawnia holding onto her waist on her other side, sobbing and trembling.

"Mona? Are you OK? Mona? He's not gonna hurt you. He's gone."

She turned her head towards me, but her eyes were fixed on the spot where her husband stood.

"I've changed my mind. How did you do that? He... No one ever... How did you do that?"

Ledawnia had dropped her backpack and was holding onto her mother with both arms. She was crying into her mother's side, not able to catch her breath. Mona looked at her as if she didn't know who the child belonged to. She stroked, rubbed, and patted her daughter's back robotically.

"It doesn't matter how. What do you mean, changed your mind?"

"I want you to protect me and my children. The police didn't even move before you had him on the ground. I don't... He won't find us?"

"No. Never. I'll take you and your daughter somewhere safe for tonight and we'll talk in the morning." As the words left my mouth, I cursed internally because I committed to taking this on with those words. I didn't want to do this. I didn't do kids!

The two detectives returned and stood before Mona and her daughter.

"Mrs. Lancer, I'm sorry about your husband. We have all we need tonight. We're going to write your statements and send the information over to the DA. We'll let you know if we need anything else from you. Do you have someone you can stay with tonight or do you want us to find a shelter for you?"

"I have a place to go," she said looking my way.

"Good. If we need anything else, can we reach you at the number you gave us?"

"Yes."

"OK. We're sorry for what you've been through. Please call us if you need anything. Your husband will at least be in jail until he goes before a judge and we're going to try hard to get no bail."

"Thank You."

I told Mona to meet me out front. I left a message for Siobhán that I had some other things to take care of and would come by tomorrow.

I knew the safest place for them. I called ahead to make sure the house was available and it was. I got on the highway and got off at Kirkville West. We drove for about 2.5 miles and arrived at a blue and white craftsman's house. There were two huge trees in the front covering the windows on the second floor. The bay windows showed lights on in the house, and the porch lights highlighted the flower beds in the yard.

The occupant of the home did twenty-three years in the Marines. He receives a check from the government every month and a check from me.

When we parked the Range Rover in the driveway, a Black man in his mid-forties came to the door to meet us. The entire frame of his body filled the doorway.

"Hello, Grant."

"Harri."

"Few nights. A week at the most."

"No problem. Anything I need to know."

As we walked into the foyer Grant closed the door, "Only if we go past a few nights. This is Mona, Ledawnia, and I'm sorry, what's your son's name?"

Mona hesitated, "Braxton, Jr,"

"Good evening, Ma'am. Welcome to my home."

Mona did not say anything and Ledawnia hid behind her mother. Braxton looked at Grant and tried to grab his nose. Mona snatched his hand away.

"Will we be safe here? Are you staying with us tonight?"

"No Ma'am. My sister will stay with us. You and your family will not be here alone."

"I didn't mean to say...."

"You don't have to explain, Ma'am. She should be here in about ten minutes."

"I'll wait until she gets here," I said.

Grant showed them around the house while we waited for his sister to show. The house had four bedrooms. He showed them the kitchen, the playroom in the basement, and the bathrooms. While he made us all a snack in the kitchen, a woman walked into the house with a boy about seven years old. She was average height, with dull brown hair, and brown eyes. The only descriptive thing about her was a slight droop in her left eye.

Grant introduced her as his sister, Deanna. She clearly was not blood since she was white, but she was family. They were all sitting in the living room. I was standing in the foyer waiting. Deanna was a pro at this.

"A few years ago, I was in the same situation as you. I had a husband who was not nice to me and a child I was trying to protect.

"I had no one at the time. I found Harri and Grant because someone saw I was in trouble and stepped in to help me. When I came to Grant, I was scared, tired, and on the edge. Grant gave me a place to stay and protected me, even from myself.

"By the time I was stable, there was another woman who came here. I helped Grant with her, and I've been helping him ever since. We became close and if it wasn't for my brother, I wouldn't be where I am right now. I live in my own house, I have a job, I am not scared anymore, and my child is happy again.

"So, when he called and told me someone else needed help, I came right over.

"I know you're scared, but being here will allow you to breathe. Nothing bad is going to happen to you here, I promise."

While the two women were getting to know each other, my phone rang. I stepped away from the group and went into the den.

"If you don't have that girl, her brother, and her mother in your possession, go find them...now!"

"It's that bad?"

"It's worse. Mrs. Lancer's first name is Mona, and her maiden name is Montclair. Mr. Lancer's first name is Braxton. I assume he's been beating her since the beginning of their relationship. Calls to the police by neighbors were frequent. There were never any arrests when they lived in the Bronx. Not that there were any in Syracuse either. They moved to Syracuse after their wedding. She got pregnant with Ledawnia early in the marriage. I'm not sure when the abuse started with his daughter. I know Mrs. Lancer left him twice, and he found her both times; once at a shelter and once at a friend's house, whom he beat the crap out of, by the way. Originally, the friend told the police what Braxton did to her and retracted the complaint later.

I remember my reaction being, "Jesus."

"Oh, it gets better. About a year and a half ago, someone called the police to their residence. The paramedic told the police they had to look at the inside of her leg to determine her race because the black and blue marks extended from her face to her legs. The police officer wrote in his report Mona's story was someone broke into the house and beat her. They knew she was lying and could've taken the husband in, but he wasn't there when they arrived, and they couldn't find him. When they found him, he had an alibi for the night of the beating--he was with some woman. They couldn't prove he did it and let him go.

"The mother worked hard not to get pregnant--hence the enormous gap between children. Braxton went with her to a gynecologist appointment. The doctor wrote Braxton seemed controlling, but Mona agreed she wanted to be off birth control. The next thing you know, she's pregnant."

"Jesus, Magus. That's not the worst of it?"

"No, there's more, but I wanted you to know they're not lying and to help them. I have more digging to do. I'll have everything for you in a week or two."

"Thanks."

I returned to the living room, but they had moved to the kitchen. I don't know what happened while I was gone, but Mona was crying and so were Braxton Jr. and Ledawnia. Deanna was hugging Mona tight. Grant was smoking a cigarette on the back porch. He turned as the threshold creaked when I stepped over to the porch. I called him with my finger.

I moved towards the front door, and he followed me. "What's up with the kids? You rarely work with kids."

"I know. She brought back some memories. And her father...Grant, from what I saw tonight, this is not our typical abuse case. There's something else. Please make sure you lose the phone."

"It's that bad?"

"I think so. If there's a problem, you know what to do."

"Yup."

As I walked to my car, I called Cara.

"Cara, the girl, and her family are real."

"You got a full report from Magus already?"

"No, but the preliminary is not good. As soon as Magus sends me the full file, I will let you know."

"Ok. Keep me posted. Hey, you taking this on yourself?"

"I don't know. Maybe," I answered.

"Let me know."

"I will."

Chapter 3

As I drove home, the damn doll kept popping into my mind. With all the activities tonight, there was no time to think about it. Why was this happening when I dealt with this a long time ago? She was the reason I started down this path. Ever told me this was my calling, but this can't be my calling. The responsibility of a child cannot be mine to take on. What I did every day was enough.

I pulled my Range Rover into my three-car driveway. Climbing out of the vehicle, I pushed the button to open the garage and headed through the lifted door to my kitchen. Hunger was not upon me, but I had to eat something, and the leftover stew called to me. I put some in a bowl, put it in the microwave, and started the timer.

Upstairs, I removed my clothes to change into something more comfortable and took a glimpse at myself in my mirror. My smooth mahogany skin was normally radiant. In the mirror, my skin took on a dullness I was sure no moisturizer would brighten.

I headed back downstairs. All of a sudden, she came into my head. I paused in the living room and glanced at the pictures on the mantle. All my family was there, but there was one of her. A picture of her, my grandmother, and I. The bell on the microwave chimed. Warm tears were streaming down my face, and I dropped to my knees on the floor. I couldn't stop it. It all came flooding in.

#######

I grew up in the Wykagyl area of New Rochelle, New York. In the six square miles of my neighborhood, we had a tennis club, a country club, a mini-mall, two lakes, and a few small parks. We were missing a grocery store, dry cleaners, and a bank to be self-sufficient.

They considered the houses in Wykagyl the mansions of New Rochelle. Even with all the space we owned, my father built my mother a cottage on the property for her art. She created art with paint, charcoal, and clay.

My mother hung her art on the walls of the cottage along with pieces by her favorite artists: Basquiat, Keith Haring, Willem de Kooning, and Gordon Parks.

Along with her art on the walls stood her clay pieces in every room of the cottage. Some were bowls, some were abstract, and some were figures.

Mrs. Francis used my mother's charcoal and color pictures to create greeting cards she sold at boutiques and specialty stores around Westchester County.

Mrs. Francis and my mother met at an art symposium. They became fast friends when they learned they lived close to each other. Showing off her art was not something my mother did lightly, but she always said she felt a connection with the white-haired Latino who got her as an artist.

My mother also told me the money she made did not make her rich, but it was enough for her own bank account and to live a bohemian lifestyle.

When I was a kid, I didn't know what bohemian meant, and when I asked my mother, she was happy to pass on her knowledge.

"The bohemian lifestyle means I can be who I want to be without worrying that people are saying mean things about me." She glanced at me, then back to the road.

"You think I don't hear what the neighbors say about me?" as she jerked her head towards her window. We were pulling into our driveway. She turned off the car and turned to me.

I didn't know she knew they talked about her. My mother walked around in her bare feet, in Afghan dresses, her big butt swaying the material as she walked and her even bigger afro. I remember one neighbor saying she couldn't understand how someone so light had hair like that.

"You know why you and I walk the neighborhood barefoot sometimes?"

I shook my head, hanging on to her every word.

"Because I want you to understand those words they say about me are just words. When you are bohemian, you are free, and when you are free, you decide who you are."

She stared at me for a few seconds, "Did you know that the women in our family have had their own money for four generations?"

I shook my head at her again,

"They were bohemians too." I giggled at what she said and because she was tickling me. She told me she never wanted me to change who I was because of what people thought. She wanted me to be bohemian. I tried to live bohemian every day.

"Ask your grandmother about it. She'll tell you," my mother told me as we walked into the house.

My grandmother, Nunu, and I would sit for hours and look at her old pictures. She would tell me these wonderful stories about her brothers and sisters. My mom told me Nunu cried when she saw me for the first time and kept saying the name Holly, over and over again.

Holly was one of Nunu's younger sisters. She had the skin of mocha, with light brown eyes and long plaited braids. While I was looking at her picture, I thought to myself, maybe these were not my father's eyes.

When I asked Nunu about the bohemian lifestyle, she got out the photo albums and told me stories about how Holly always wanted to do her own thing. She would never listen to someone telling her what to do, and it was dangerous to do so. Holly wanted to be free.

She looked into my eyes and told me, "She taught your mother everything she knows. Your mother was strong-willed and wanted to know everything. My sister taught her how to trust what she believed in. And you are definitely her daughter."

My father was a contrast to his Hippie Brown (My father's nickname for my mother). He was dark, tall, and muscular. An engineer at NYU and a professor and researcher at Iona College. My father wore a suit to work every day and didn't own a pair of jeans, but he had plenty of shoes.

Although my father acted embarrassed sometimes by my mother's bohemian lifestyle, he never told my mother to put on shoes or tie up her hair. He would even buy her some of the Afghan dresses she wore. Whenever we were alone, he would always tell me a story about when he and my mother were in college or what they used to do before they had us. And he would always end with "Don't tell your mother I told you that." All I saw was a man who loved a woman. Disparity was love to me.

My parents and their love were my foundation, but they were not my house. My house was my brothers. My brothers looked exactly like my father, but Davis (Day) was a lot lighter than Keenan. Yet, they both had our mother's eyes.

Day was the oldest and the smartest out of the three of us. Keenan and I had good grades, but Day didn't have to study as we did. Keenan excelled in most sports he played. They were both tall and muscular, but Day was not as graceful as Keenan. Keenan played baseball and basketball. Day tried out, but he wasn't good at baseball or basketball. However, he was a pretty good volleyball player.

They were my protectors, but Day was the leader of us kids. Keenan was his second, and I was a soldier. Both my brothers wanted to be teachers; Day, a professor, and Keenan, an elementary school teacher. But they loved cars. When they were both teenagers, they worked in my uncle's auto shop during the summers. The way they worked together; you would think they always loved each other. My parents suspected their similarities were the reason for the fighting.

My mom told me my brothers used to fight as if they were strangers before I was born. It could be the littlest thing to start a fight. My parents tried everything to stop them from fighting: they punished them, lectured them on the importance of family, and spanked them. Nothing worked. My mom told me after my birth, it was like they had signed a peace treaty. They still fought, but there were no physical fights. What she remembered most was not the lack of bloodshed between my brothers after I arrived, but the connection between the three of us.

"I remember the first time I realized what you and your brothers were to each other. It was spring break for your brothers. A lot of kids left town for the break. We didn't go anywhere that year. There was no noise from the three of you in about half an hour. I knew something was wrong. There is always noise in this house. I looked in the backyard, but you weren't there. There was no movement upstairs, and the three of you wouldn't leave without asking me. I walked into the playroom downstairs, and I saw two sandy-colored heads peeking over the couch. I could not see you until I walked in further. You were about three years old; Day had turned eight the month before, and Keenan was seven. Day was on your left, holding your hand. You were in the middle sucking on that damn pacifier I couldn't make you give up. Your head was leaning on Keenan, who was on your right. You sat on the couch holding each other for an hour, watching TV and laughing at cartoons.

"I would find the three of you sitting in that position a lot. You didn't do it all the time, but it was enough. I knew it was something. I asked the boys about it, and they couldn't tell me why they did it. They told me they just do."

I didn't remember being with them in the basement, but I remembered we were always together. Until I was about nine or ten, the three of us slept in the same room most nights. Now that I'm older, I think about that and I can't believe they didn't want some privacy from their sister and each other.

Day and Keenan were where I got my information, my comfort, and shared my joy and my pain. They were my protectors, my confidants, and my teachers. They were my first love.

Each member of my family helped to create the outline for who I would become. The outline was strong and confident and there was no way I would be this woman without all of them. But other people helped to fill in my outline. My real journey into my discovery began when I met her.

Chapter 4

In 1986, when I was six years old, the Corrales family moved in next door to us. My mother was a part of Wykagyl Welcomes, and it was her turn to greet the new family in the neighborhood.

My brothers carried a coffee cake and a casserole, both of which my mother made, as we all walked over to meet the new neighbors.

When Mrs. Corrales opened the door, there were unpacked boxes in the hallway, in the living room, and near the stairs. She invited us in and called the rest of her family. They all arrived, leaving behind whatever move-in project they were working on. When they were standing in front of us, I was in awe. They looked like they belonged in a food commercial.

Mrs. Corrales, who asked my mother to call her Juliana, introduced us to her daughter Jesenia, her son Javier, Jr., and her husband Javier Sr. I remember staring at Mr. Corrales because he was darker than everyone else and I was thinking, "Why does a black man have an accent?"

We stood in the hallway, shaking hands and introducing ourselves before Mr. Corrales invited us into the kitchen. My mother gave her speech about the neighborhood: schools, trash, where to shop, where not to shop, etc. After a good while, the boys went off to the side and talked to JC (Javier's nickname) at the kitchen table, and the adults were standing and sitting at the kitchen island discussing whatever adults talked about. That's when Jesenia told her mom she wanted to show me her room. Mrs. Corrales said sure, and Jesenia grabbed my hand, pulling me upstairs.

Her room still had one unpacked box in the middle of the floor and two by the closet. The rest of the room was completed. She had a Hello Kitty bedspread on her bed and a dresser with Hello Kitty's face on the front of the drawers. There were clothes neatly hanging on hangers and her shoes were on a shoe rack in the closet.

I sat on her bed, not knowing what to say to her. Even at six, her presence drew me to her. My stomach had butterflies and dragonflies floating in it.

She went to one box and pulled out Chutes and Ladders, a Yo-Yo, and a puzzle asking if I wanted to play any games. When I shook my head no, she went to a second box and pulled out the most beautiful dolls. Some were porcelain, some were rag dolls, and some were baby dolls. They all had different outfits, and some of them looked like me. My grandmother made me dolls that looked like me, but I didn't know other kids could have them as well.

She took one of the baby dolls and offered me a black rag doll. We sat on her bed, talked, and played with the dolls.

I recalled she wanted me to tell her about our school, the other kids, and the teachers. She also wanted to know what I did for fun. I asked her about her old school, her friends, and what she did for fun. She did not tell me much except she missed her friends.

When Jesenia's mother came looking for us, we were stretched out on her bed talking about what we were going to do for the rest of the summer. Jesenia begged her mother to let me stay longer, but her mother told us it was getting late, and I had to go back to my house.

Jesenia held my hand as we walked downstairs. As everyone stood in the front hall saying their goodbyes, Jesenia and I were whispering to each other about when we would get together again and what we would do when we saw each other. Before I left, she asked me if I wanted to be her friend. I answered yes before she finished the sentence. My smile was wide and inside I felt like I was doing jumping jacks. Everyone laughed except for us.

Jesenia dropped my hand and embraced me as if I was going to war. It was the most natural thing for me to hug her and for her to hug me.

All night I talked about Jesenia. Day finally told me to shut up, "We get it, you like her." I was excited, but all I had were my words.

About two weeks later, Jesenia and I were spending all our free time together. We swam, went on "camping trips" in our backyard, and created adventures for ourselves. My house would be a cave and Jesenia's house would be the forest. We would even write plays she and I would put on for our families. Most of the play was in our heads. I remember Jesenia would tell me how to wear a costume or how I should play a character, even though we created the play together. When she told me what to do, I would tell her how she should play a character a certain way and she would usually stop. It was a great summer.

Jesenia had little family. She loved coming to my house and being surrounded by all my aunts, uncles, and cousins. Our house was where our family came to meet. Most of my aunts and uncles lived on the East Coast. With aunts, uncles, children, husbands, wives, great aunts, great uncles, second and third cousins, we were fifty or sixty deep for the big occasions and the family reunions.

Whenever Jesenia came over and Nunu was there, she sought her out first. She even taught Nunu some Spanish. My whole family loved Jesenia except for Aunt Jackie. She hated it when Jesenia and I spoke Spanish. My mother kicked her out of the house at one family gathering and told her not to come back until she knew how to act. Aunt Jackie protested to my father, her brother, but he told her she couldn't be disrespectful in their house. When Aunt Jackie came back for a birthday party a few months later, she apologized to my mother.

We would have dance parties, game nights, and movie nights. My cousin Damian always won the dance contests. Game night was always a night of laughter and accusations. And movie night; no one ever watched a movie because of all the conversations going on at the same time. Jesenia told me it was the best time of her life.

At Jesenia's house, the Corraleses spoke Spanish. They tried to remember to speak English when I was in the house, but they didn't always remember. I paid attention to what they were saying, and Jesenia answered all my questions. By the time I was seven, I was fluent enough to hold a conversation with her family. When my brothers made me mad, I would scream at them in Spanish, and I would answer questions in Spanish because I would forget to speak English.

Her house was where they introduced me to empanadas, plantains, arroz con pollo, canicas, and how to dance to salsa. I got so good at playing canicas, I played Mr. Corrales all the time. It was the best time of my life too.

Spanish and family are not the only things we learned from our friendship. The both of us learned a lot of lessons. There were so many firsts between us and issues children should never deal with.

I was the first to get my period at eleven. I wasn't shocked when it happened since my mother always talked to me about sex and my body. I wasn't shocked when it happened, but it was embarrassing. It was one of the few times I didn't want to share something with Jesenia. She came to me at lunch and wanted to know why I was acting weird. I looked at her for a few seconds, and I left the lunchroom. She found me sitting in front of some lockers. I burst into tears when she asked me again what was wrong. She sat next to me and held my hand. I told her I got my period last night, and I didn't want anyone to know. She sat with me for the rest of lunch and let me be miserable. Jesenia told me she was jealous I was growing up without her. I was no longer miserable, yet, my heart did a little flip for Jesenia. I told her my period was the only thing happening to me that wasn't happening to her; I would never leave her behind.

She got hers when she was thirteen. I remember she told me she was not as happy as she thought she would be when she caught up to me.

Jesenia and I also had to deal with ignorance. Our second-grade teacher, Mrs. Wolcott, told us we could not speak Spanish while we were in school. Neither of us knew why we couldn't speak Spanish.

When she went to her mother, who didn't have an explanation for her, her mother went to the principal and the school board, but they had a policy (yes, it was in writing). English was the only language to be spoken in school. While the adults were fighting for us, Jesenia and I decided we would speak Spanish in private when no one was around. Our parents apologized to us, and we all had this long talk about fairness. We didn't have the heart to tell them we were fine with it.

Unfortunately, this was not the last time we had to deal with people who did not appreciate what we were to each other. Since first grade, Jesenia and I were in the same classes, ate lunch together, spent our library time together, and played together at recess. When we were in fifth grade, our teacher, Mrs. Tollin, tried to separate us. She told our parents the relationship we had was unhealthy. She told our parents we didn't speak to any of the other children in our class (which wasn't true. We talked to them; we just didn't like them) and it was not good for us socially.

So, our parents agreed to let them separate us and put us into two different classes "so we would develop relationships with other children." We begged them not to move us. The relationship Jesenia and I had was strange to our parents too. I heard them talking, and they said maybe it would stop us from not having fun with other kids. We did not understand what was going on, but the two of us came to the conclusion we must have done something wrong.

About a month later, all of our parents went to the school and told the principal to put us back in the same class. Our parents explained we were eating alone during lunch instead of socializing. Our grades had slipped, we seemed depressed, and we spent our entire weekends with each other. Mr. Corrales told them it was like watching two siblings who were separated by the State. Our parents told them the experiment was over.

The principal, who had called for Mrs. Tollin, told our parents it was not an experiment. This was their experience as teachers and his experience as a Doctor of Education. My mother told him their experience and his doctorate were making their daughters question themselves and live in a state of depression. They wanted us back in a class together with a different teacher or they were going to the school board, the papers, and then the department of education. We were returned to a classroom together with a different teacher.

Jesenia and I did not know why everyone was making a big deal about separating us. We tried to understand what we did wrong, but we could not figure it out until one boy in the upper grades called us lesbians. Lesbian was an unfamiliar word and when we asked JC about it. We called it leezians. I would have talked to one of my brothers, but neither one of them was home when we got home from school.

When he told us what it was, we went to Jesenia's room and laughed for the longest time. We could not stop giggling. When we thought we might be done giggling, we looked at each other and started giggling all over again.

After that we walked around school holding hands, walking arm and arm, kissing each other on the cheeks (as they did in England; we saw it on some show). Lesbians? It was the stupidest thing we had ever heard. We loved each other, but not like that. She was going to marry Keenan, and I was going to marry JC, not each other.

For years, the two of us described scenarios about what our lives would be like. In our fantasies, our houses were side by side. Jesenia was going to be a fashion designer, and I was going to be a professor. We each had two children, planned to vacation together, and move our parents into a big house we would build next to ours.

One day during our daydreams, I told Jesenia I wanted to marry JC. Jesenia called it gross, that JC was dumb, and she didn't understand why any of the girls liked him? I told her he was cool. She still said it was gross. She in turn informed me Keenan was the guy she wanted. I expressed the same disgust she gave to me about her brother.

Keenan and JC became a part of the life we planned out for ourselves. There was never anyone else for either of us after that. But saying it out loud to my best friend made it more real. After I made this grand announcement, I was speaking less, and my stomach would turn over whenever JC looked at me or spoke to me.

I remembered the first time he hurt my feelings, though. Jesenia and I were twelve, and JC was fifteen. The three of us were in their living room. JC was sitting on the couch reading. Jesenia and I were lying on the floor with our incomplete play. We wanted to include a dance to the story. We both got up and started creating a routine. I was trying to be cool. I was happy he was going to see me dance and how good I was. We were laughing and talking about the moves we wanted to add to our dance routine. JC slid off the couch and asked us why we were so weird.

When JC left the living room, I ran to Jesenia's bedroom. She came in a few moments later. I was lying across her bed, crying my eyes out. She rubbed my back. I told her if I was weird, there was no way he was going to like me. Jesenia might have thought her brother was dumb, but I did not. He was handsome, athletic, smart, and kind. And he thought I was weird.

I cried for a few more minutes. Jesenia told me her brother was stupid, and she dried my tears. Then she told me at least her brother knew I was alive. Keenan barely paid attention to her, and a tear rolled down her cheek. I told her I was sorry, and the two of us abandoned our project and stayed in her room listening to music and talking.

I still think about the feeling of the two of us being in love. It didn't matter if Keenan and JC didn't see us or notice us. Well, it did matter, but it was nice to have someone to share the joy and pain of our first loves.

Chapter 5

My father would never go shopping or sit with me at the hairdresser. Yet we did spend a lot of time together. He said my mother would be better to do those things with me.

My father wanted to do things with me that I wouldn't do with anyone else. He taught me how to fish; both fly and reel. Reel fishing was OK, but fly fishing was my thing. Reel fishing didn't have a lot of finesse to it. Pulling a fish in took some skill and work. With fly fishing, casting into the water took not only skill but artfulness. My mother told me and my father I loved fly fishing more because I always wanted to do the harder activity.

We took trips to the MoMA when interesting exhibits came to the museum. My father and I saw the James Bond exhibit, a collection of Japanese posters, an exhibition of refugees, and an exhibit on China. We also took trips to Central New York where we frequented Harriet Tubman's house, visited stops on the Underground Railroad from Brooklyn to Syracuse, and visited one or two of my father's friends who lived on a reservation.

He never picked anything I wasn't interested in, and I never lied to him about what I liked. My father never took a phone call or even talked about work when we went on our mini vacations. I loved my father for that.

Mr. Corrales loved doing every girly thing Jesenia and I did together. He would attend our tea parties and dress in hats with us. He would offer to act in our plays and whenever Mr. Corrales went to the city for business, he would bring us with him. They weren't shopping trips, but that's what Jesenia and I called them.

The trips started when we were about nine or ten. We would buy little change purses, a shirt, or a poster. When we were older, Mr. Corrales let us pick out clothes and genuine purses. We were rocking FUBU, Enyce, Nike, Mecca, Gucci, Marc Jacobs, Fendi, etc., etc. We were two of the best-dressed students at school. Jesenia and I always chose the same clothes and if they didn't have two, we didn't buy them.

It was May 14th, a Saturday, the day we were going on our most recent trip to the city and I couldn't go. My head was hurting, my body ached, and I had a fever and chills. I remember being pissed at Jesenia for going and pissed at myself for being sick.

But I got dressed and came downstairs to go to the city. I barely made it to the bottom of the staircase and was fighting to stand upright. My mother took one look at me, shook her head, and brought me back upstairs. While my head was spinning, I was fighting with my mother to let me go, and now I was pissed at her for not letting me go. My mother supported me as she took me back to my bed. I believe I went to sleep immediately because I didn't remember going back to my room.

When I came to, I glanced at the clock on my bedside table. I couldn't make sense of the darkness and the time on the clock. If it was dark out, Jesenia should have been at my house to show me what she got us. Even in the state I was in, she would have come to my room and woken me up; my mother wouldn't have been able to keep her out. The clock read 8:49 PM.

Lying in bed, I couldn't hear any sounds. I went downstairs, and Day and Keenan were sitting in the living room. My mother and father weren't with them. Both Keenan and Day were sitting on the couch facing the front door. They both arose from the sofa when I stepped on the squeaky bottom step of our staircase. When they turned around, I knew something was wrong. I knew all my brothers' facial expressions, but I did not recognize the one I saw on either of them. They had me terrified.

I was walking toward my brothers and stopped moving. My mind was trying to put together the pieces of why my world felt wrong. I almost had it, but I was missing something and then the few pieces I had fell apart. I started walking towards my brothers again.

I looked at them, and Keenan said,

"We have to wait for Mom and Dad."

"No, tell me." I didn't even know what I was asking for, but nothing made sense. If he knew what was happening and could make the world make sense again, I needed him to tell me.

Day was the one who said, "There was an accident," and it all slid into place.

I moved for the door, but they tried to stop me. Both my brothers, who were larger than me, moved toward me. Day was grabbing me by my arms from behind and Keenan tried to block the way to the door by holding on to my arms from the front. I kicked Keenan in the leg, and he yelped. He let go of me to grab and nurse his leg. I twisted out of Day's grip and slipped behind and around him before he knew what had happened. I was out the door when Day moved towards me.

When the door shut behind me, I was already running. My slippers came off, tears were streaming down my face, and cold air prickled over my skin making my pajamas stick to me.

I opened the front door of Jesenia's house, as I always did. A police officer was standing in the front hall on the phone with his back to the door. I walked right past him and into the living room. As I moved in, my eyes fell on the couch where Jesenia and I laughed, wrote plays, and practiced Spanish. My mother was sitting farthest from the door, her arm around Mrs. Corrales, rocking her. JC was sitting next to his mother, holding her hand, and my father was sitting next to JC, patting his leg, looking across the living room at the wall.

I stepped to where JC was. "Javier Colon?" That was JC's real name. I called him Javier Colon sometimes because I loved the way it sounded. His full name is Javier Colon Corrales. I was the only one who called him Javier Colon.

He raised his head to expose bloodshot eyes. They were swimming in tears that flowed down his cheeks. His nose was wet around the nostrils with a few drops falling on his perfect mouth. My heart raced as hot tears brewed under my eyelids, and my breath was caught in my chest making it impossible for me to breathe. All the adults glanced in my direction, including the cop from the hallway.

"Que Paso?" *(What happened)* My father put his hand on JC's leg, but JC ignored it.

He stared directly at me and said through his tears and a raspy voice, "Jesy fue asesinado" *(Jesy was killed).*

I knew what he was going to say, but it didn't matter. The sound that came out of my mouth after he said those words came from the pit of my stomach. The voice released was unrecognizable. It was only sound; no words at all. I almost didn't believe it was me.

JC moved towards me. He grabbed me, and I grabbed him back. When he brought me to him, I think I had some of his skin in my grip. We fell to the floor, and I cried half in his lap, my face buried against his stomach. Both my mother and my father tried to remove me, and I wouldn't let go of him. He knew what Jesenia and I were. He didn't think it was weird. Everyone else pretended they were OK with how close we were to each other, but we knew they didn't understand our connection. We didn't have to explain to him why we loved each other.

Jesenia told me once when JC looks at us, he sees the same person. He said the girls he is around scream at each other and fight a lot. We didn't behave like that. He told her our love was not friendship but about finding our soulmate. Back then we didn't know what soulmate meant, but we both knew it was true.

He held me closer, and I cried; and in turn, he cried. In the meantime, my mother took Mrs. Corrales upstairs.

After twenty minutes, my mother finally got me to let go of JC. When I came to my feet, he grabbed my arm while remaining on the floor.

"No nos dejes. Te necesitamos." *(Don't leave us. We need you.)*

"I won't." I started crying again, but I turned back.

"Donde esta tu Padre?" *(Where is your father?)*

"He's at the hospital," JC answered. "They're not sure if he'll be OK."

With that, I turned and let my mother and father take me home.

I slept in Day's room because I couldn't sleep alone, and Keenan kicked in his sleep. Day had to wake me three times because I was crying out. Every time I woke, I cried for a long time. He held me while I cried, and Keenan sat at the edge of the bed, holding my hand until I fell back asleep.

Keenan would return to the floor and go to sleep until I started crying out again. I'm not sure what I would have done if I didn't have them those first few weeks.

When I woke up the next day, I tried calling JC, but there was no answer. I'd assumed he was at the hospital. I tried to convince my father to let me go be with the family, but he said we needed to let them have some time to themselves. I tried to explain I was family, but he wouldn't listen. I didn't know what else to do.

My grief for Jesenia was extraordinary. I thought if I was near the Corrales some of my grief would lift from me. For a week and a half, I couldn't eat; I slept with Day every night and barely talked to anyone.

JC called me from the hospital to tell me his father was awake. My father noted again I should leave the Corraleses alone, but I convinced him to let me go to the hospital. He agreed, but I had to agree if they needed to be alone, we would leave.

Mr. Corrales had been shot in the shoulder, the leg, and his stomach. There were seven bullet wounds. JC told us he was in and out of consciousness, but it was temporary. At some point, he would be awake. I sat with JC in the hallway while my father sat with Mrs. and Mr. Corrales in the hospital room.

"How are you doing, Harri," JC was looking straight ahead, holding my hand.

"I'm fine JC. How are you doing?" I replied as I squeezed his fingers.

"I'm worried about my mom and my father. I can't believe she's gone." JC dropped his head.

The tears were flowing onto my shirt. We sat in the chairs for a few minutes holding hands not speaking. When the tears slowed, I said,

"How is your father doing?"

He paused, "He's alive. The doctors don't know what's going to happen to him. They say we have to wait."

This time I paused, "Who knows about Jesenia?"

"We haven't had time to tell anyone anything. It's just us."

We remained in those plastic chairs outside his father's hospital room holding hands for an hour. Nurses, patients, and patrons walked by us and looked, but no one said a thing.

My father left after about an hour. JC begged him to let me stay for a while. When it became late, I tried to stay past visiting hours, but the nurses wouldn't let me.

Mr. Corrales was in the hospital for two months. I was there as much as my father would let me. After about two weeks, I noticed there were a lot of men around in suits. All JC would tell me was they were friends of his father. I let it go, but I planned to ask him later who they were. No one came to the Corraleses in eight years, including these men. Even as a kid, it was strange to me.

Mr. Corrales couldn't go to Jesenia's funeral. He was in a lot of pain, and the medication they gave him didn't allow him to stay awake for long. I remembered being hurt he couldn't go to the funeral. He would want to say goodbye to Jesenia. I asked JC if they should wait for his father, but his mother decided they needed to say goodbye to Jesenia.

The service was a wake. There was no church service and no burial. The suits, my family, and people from school were the attendees there. The oddest thing was the lack of family I saw on the Corraleses' side. I was always asking Jesenia about other family members. It was odd to me she didn't have cousins, aunts, uncles, and grandparents. She would tell me it was just them and there was no one else. I accepted what she and the rest of the family told me.

I walked into the funeral home with my brothers. There were flowers on either side of her casket. Some were on the floor, some were on the casket, and some were on stands. It was a closed casket since Jesenia was shot in the head.

Some people were already sitting in the pews. Others were standing in line to pay their condolences to the family. Everyone else was passing the coffin, touching it, and looking at the framed class picture from the year before. The shirt she wore that day was one of her favorites. Light blue with little pink polka dots.

They were saying their goodbyes to my friend, something not within my power to do. Being that close to her, knowing my friend was inside the box with a bullet in her head made me queasy and angry. That coffin was not my friend, and I would not pay respects to it.

I believed going to the wake could help me deal with the grief of Jesenia's death, but all I wanted to do was climb into the coffin with her.

JC was standing in the receiving line, shaking hands and listening to people tell him how sorry they were for him. I didn't need to wait in line. I was family, and there was no need to console them. There was no consoling them because there was no consoling me.

After the wake, instead of helping me deal with Jesenia's death, depression crept in on me. Jesenia was in my mind all the time and it always ended with her death. I couldn't access the good memories. I went to talk to JC, who was spending some time at home with his mother. I held off as long as I could to talk to him about his sister's demise, but I needed to talk to someone.

I went into their house as I had done hundreds of times in the past, and I saw boxes all over the front hall. Some boxes had tape on them, and some were still open, waiting to have more belongings added. The pictures once hanging on the wall were gone. Some furniture shifted against a wall, and rugs were removed. It was like I was six again, except Jesenia was not there, and they were moving out instead of moving in. I wanted to cry and scream at the same time. They couldn't be leaving me.

"JC, what are you doing?!" One guy in a suit moved towards me and JC told him it was OK.

"Harrison, what are you doing here?"

"I came to talk to you. Why are you packing all your stuff?"

"Dad has to go to another hospital to rehab, and we don't know how long he's gonna be there. It could be two months or two years, so we're going with him."

"You were gonna leave without saying goodbye?! How could you do that?!"

JC looked around. Everyone in the room was watching. He pushed me onto the porch. "Stop pushing me! How could you just leave?!"

"Shut up, Harri!" he growled after he shut the front door.

I was stunned. He had never spoken to me like that. I shut up.

"I don't have long." JC was looking back at his door. "Me and mom have to leave. There may still be people out there chasing us. You're not supposed to know this, and your parents and brothers don't know. You can't tell them. Ever. I'm telling you because you cannot contact us. You have to let us go."

"What's goin' on JC? I can never see any of you again?! How am I supposed to let you go?!" I was choking on my tears.

"Shhhh," he said pulling me close. My face was against his chest, making his shirt wet from my tears.

Whispering, "No, not til we're safe, and I don't know when that'll be. You have to keep this to yourself, or we could get killed. Do you understand?"

"No. I don't understand!"

"I know, but I need you to trust me, Harri, and do what I'm asking you. I'm telling you this because you loved Jesy, and you loved us. Please."

I pulled back from his chest and gazed into his brown eyes. "I won't tell anyone, JC. I swear on Jesenia. But who are the guys in the suits, and who's after you?"

"I can't tell you that, Harri. You have to know that if we had a choice, we wouldn't leave you."

"I'll miss you so much JC."

"I'll miss you too."

We stood on his front porch and stared into each other's eyes. Then Javier Colon Corrales kissed me. Not a peck on the cheek or a brief kiss on the lips. He gave me my first real kiss. Full on the lips, soft but strong. He held me like my father held my mother when he thought no one was watching.

I moved my hands from my sides to the middle of his back. When he adjusted his body closer to mine, his tongue touched my lips. I could feel his chest against mine, and I gasped with his mouth over mine. JC slipped his tongue in. My hands were sweating against his shirt and there was wetness between my legs.

He pulled back and gazed into my eyes again. I wanted to tell him I loved him, but I couldn't get the words out--what if he didn't feel the same, and the kiss was just to say goodbye? He grabbed my face toward him kissed me on the forehead and hugged me again. He let me go, turned, and went back into the house.

I stood frozen on the porch, taking in what took place with my heart racing in my chest. Did that actually happen? I wanted to go back into the house and have them take me with them. I wanted to go home and scream into my pillow. But I remained frozen. I would have talked to Jesenia about this, but she was gone. I was losing my only connection to her, which was keeping my mind together, I think JC loves me, and he is leaving me. What the fuck was I supposed to do with all of that? I just went home.

Chapter 6

A few months after JC and his family moved, I was going to school every day and interacting with my family, but I wasn't present. My grades slipped, and I could not focus on anything for more than five minutes.

I would cry for no reason, anything anyone said to me made me want to punch them in the face and I thought bad people were lurking around every corner when I went anywhere. Someone had taken away Jesenia and her family and there was nowhere to direct any of those emotions.

I was having these dreams about some phantom person killing me and Jesenia. The dreams were real to me. When I awoke, I could not remember where I was. I would search for Day or Keenan for a few seconds. They were not there because I was sleeping alone again. Day told me they would stay with me as long as I wanted, but I told him I was coming to terms with Jesenia's death, and I could sleep alone again.

After Jesenia's death, my mother invited family over to the house more often. Before the death of my best friend, we would have a function for birthdays and holidays, but now, they were coming over just because it was Tuesday. I tried to interact with the family when they would show up, but I could only do it for a few minutes, and I would have to leave.

My grandmother was still living with us, and although she was one of my favorite adults in the world, her allowing me to cry in her lap was comforting but not helpful. I knew she knew what I was feeling because she lost her sister, but it wasn't enough to help me get past my grief. My parents decided I needed to talk to someone.

The first and the second therapists I saw told my mom they thought I was grieving a lover and asked my mother if Jesenia and I had been intimate. Fucking idiots. I talked to three more therapists after the first two. Although they tried to help with my grieving, I could see it in their eyes and hear it in their tone; they were thinking the same thing as the others. It was middle school all over again.

The therapists didn't understand my relationship with Jesenia, I couldn't tell anyone what JC told me, and I didn't bother to tell anyone I was in love with a boy whom I may never see again.

When my parents decided on no more therapy, my grief and loss hung around my neck, strangling me. I no longer had hope I could work through them. My parents were great, but they didn't know what to do with me. Even my brothers were not an option. They tried talking to me, but what did they know.

This went on for about three months. Then one morning, I found some notes Jesenia and I had passed back and forth in middle school. One of them mentioned getting married, how much Jesenia loved Keenan, and how much I loved JC. Another letter mentioned where we were going to live and what our children would look like. Still, another mentioned a new play idea. I remembered every single thing about those notes; where I was when I wrote them, where we were when we gave them to each other, and where we were when we talked about them. Every word of those notes stabbed me in my heart with love and loss.

I went downstairs for some water as my mother passed me in the hallway. She asked me if I was OK. I whispered yes. She said, "What?" and I turned around and said,

"Damn Mom, I said I'm all right. Leave me alone. You can't freakin' help me."

She didn't say anything. She slapped me across the face. I distinctly recall my head shifted to the left and my braids swung around my head and smacked me in the face on the right.

"Who the hell do you think you're talkin' to? I know you're in pain because that baby died, but don't you ever talk to me like that again!"

By this time, my father and Keenan were in the hallway. I was holding the place my mother slapped me, glaring at her and just waiting.

"I have let you walk around this house feeling your pain and trying to come to terms with your world without Jesenia, but if you think I'm gonna stand for that shit, you are out of your goddamn mind."

My father tried to grab my mother's arm, but she jerked away from him, almost hitting him in the process.

"Get off of me Davis. Enough. I want to allow her to grieve, but she is not going to behave like this, and you are not gonna let her." She turned back and pointed at me.

"And you. If you snap at one more person in this house, you are going to join Jesenia, now get your ass upstairs."

I didn't try to explain or apologize. My mother would have killed me if I had opened my mouth to say one word to her. As I walked upstairs, my father told her she was being too hard on me, and my mother told him he could kiss her ass; she was not letting me get away with that.

My heart ached for what I had done. Even though she was yelling at me and had given me that slap, I saw the look in my mother's eyes; it was disappointment and sorrow. I cried in my room for my grief and for making my mother feel bad. Everyone in my family had done nothing but be there for me, and I was treating them horribly. And even at that young age, I knew I was doing it because they would let me.

I came downstairs a few hours later. My mother was in the kitchen cleaning the lunch dishes. "Mom," I said, barely audible.

"What?" She didn't even turn around.

"I'm sorry for what I said. I..."

She spun around to face me, "I don't care, Harri, I just want to know you're gonna be OK. You have no idea how hard it is to watch your child in pain and not be able to help them. But I won't allow you to forget your training girl."

"I don't know what to do, Mom. Jesenia's gone and JCs gone. I miss them so much."

I ran into my mother's arms, and she hugged me. When she stroked my braids, I burst into tears. I remember I cried harder in my mother's arms that day than I had since Jesenia died. Almost everything came out of me.

She let me cry for a few minutes, "I don't think you just miss them, Harrison, you're angry too. You're grieving for the whole family. You're sad, pissed, depressed, and lonely. You're about to be fifteen, and you don't know what to do with what's going on inside you. It's the reason I thought you needed to talk to someone. Along with all your regular girl teenage crap, you have this too. It's a lot to handle. But I think I might have a solution for you."

She took my head from her chest, held my face in her hands, and wiped away my tears with her sleeve.

"I wasn't sure if this was the right thing for you, but after today, I think this might be the answer. I found this boxing gym that will work with girls."

"What? Why a boxing gym? How's that gonna help?"

"You need to release your aggression, your anger, and your pain, Harrison. You can't keep all those emotions inside, and you won't talk to a therapist."

"I will talk, Mom, but they read me all wrong. They all think Jesenia and I were lesbians."

Smiling, "I know they do, and I'm sorry. You need to learn to channel your energy. You might get a better handle on your feelings. I just want you to try it and see if it helps. Besides, this is our fault. We know who you are. Alternative therapies should have been our starting point. We would have saved a lot of money."

"I'll try, but I don't know anything about boxing."

"I know, but he's willing to teach you all about it. Just keep an open mind."

"When do I have to go?"

"Saturday morning. He's expecting us at nine."

We hugged and talked some more until dinner. I told my mother I was in love with JC. She said she knew, and I started crying again. She told me about the first boy she ever loved, who didn't love her back. His name was Marcus Reynolds. I thought my father was the first boy my mother loved.

My mother was thirteen, and one of my mother's friends found out Marcus liked her, too. They were hanging out and someone saw him with another girl. She confronted him, and he told her it was his cousin. It happened two more times. She told me she was no bohemian back then. When her sisters found out what was going on, they beat the black off of Marcus Reynolds. My mother said she felt better he had a fat lip and a cut over his eye, but she was still heartbroken. It wasn't exactly my story, but I knew my mother understood the heartbreak.

That night, lying in bed, all I kept thinking was why would I want to box?

Chapter 7

I didn't know where my mother met James Evers. When I tried to find out, she told me he was a friend of a friend. I didn't think she was telling me the truth, and James Evers gave me the same answer.

The gym was located off North Avenue on Union Street. The building was brick, there was a sign posted on top of the building that said Evers Gym in Black letters and it shared a parking lot with a hairdresser. There was also a laundry mat and a dog grooming business. The rest of the street was residential.

When I walked into his gym, I wasn't sure what to expect. There were three boxing rings, an office towards the back of the gym, a locker room, five punching bags hanging in different parts of the gym, and tons of old fight posters and pictures of past fighters.

Sweat and blood hit your nostrils as soon as you crossed the threshold. All three rings were in use by at least one person. There were guys everywhere who were boxing, exercising, or getting ready to do something. My mother and I were the only females in the gym.

When my mother and I walked in, James Evers came right over to us and introduced himself. He was a tall white man with sky-blue eyes, jet-black hair cut in a military hairstyle, broad shoulders, huge arms, his chest pushed against his t-shirt, and a soft voice. I never heard an adult speak so softly, and his speech pattern was weird to me. After a few days of speaking with Mr. Evers, it was a slight accent I was hearing.

I never saw the ring the first day. Mr. Evers made me punch the heavy bag, jump rope, and run around the block. He examined my hands, and barely spoke during the hour I was there, except to give me instructions. And when I finished, he said,

"I think you'll be OK in the ring. You have some nice moves and seem to know where your body is."

I had no idea what he was talking about. I thought who doesn't know where their body is? Where's the boxing? But my mother wanted me to try, and I wanted to try to give her some peace.

My mother came with me to the gym every day at first. The men would stare at us. Some sneered when we walked in, and others made side comments about what we were doing in the gym. Others glanced at us and went back to their workouts, and still others didn't even glance our way. My mother was excellent at recognizing not being wanted. She also knew how to change those feelings if she wanted to. And soon after invading their space, she fed them.

She discovered athletes who train like these boxers ate certain foods to keep themselves fit. She would bring chicken and tuna sandwiches, fruits, vegetables, peanut butter, and boiled eggs, and once a week she would bake something sweet. After being fed three or four times, the men at the gym forgot we were invading their space. My mother soon knew all their names, what they liked to eat, who was related, who had family, and why they wanted to box. For some of the men, she was their confidant. So, while Mr. Evers was teaching me to box, the men in the gym had adopted my mother.

Mr. Evers had all these philosophical views about fighting. He wanted every-one who came into his gym to be responsible for every action they took. He told every member his philosophy and made sure each one of us understood what he expected of us. We each had to repeat back the Evers Gym Creed: *Through our own power and ability, we must strive to be courageous, honest, sincere, compassionate, courteous, loyal, and honorable. When we cannot, we must fight to be so.*

For Mr. Evers, boxing was not about teaching people how to stand, how to throw a punch, and how to take a punch. For him, it all began with teaching the mind how to think about life. The philosophy was so ingrained in most of us, you could hear the other boxers speaking this philosophy while they trained. It was a part of the culture in the gym, and everyone was expected to comply. After everyone learned Mr. Evers's philosophy of boxing, the real work began.

I knew nothing about boxing. I did not know there were two different stances (or what a stance was) or that punches had names. I thought people were in a ring hitting each other. Mr. Evers explained things to me, and even if I had lots of questions, he answered every one until he was sure I knew it. Of course, my brothers taught me how to fight, but I didn't know anything about jabs, a cross, or a hook. How would I know how important my chin was to me staying on my feet or how important it was to be focused on the ring or how much I needed to learn balance for my footwork? I was learning a new language with my body.

I was a fourteen-year-old girl coming into my body and my first time in the ring with Mr. Evers. I was all over the place. I learned quickly, but it wasn't easy. For instance, when learning how to throw a jab, you had to hold your fist up by your chin and throw your right arm out straight while turning your wrist, so the bottom of your wrist was pointing at the ground when the punch landed. All this while making sure your shoulder was up to help protect your face until your hand came back to protect it.

In the beginning, I didn't remember all those things and got caught off guard a couple of times. I became a skilled fighter, but in those first six months, I got knocked out once and had a black eye twice. My mother told me I had to quit, but she retracted that decision and said it was a part of boxing.

I mentioned that Mr. Evers spoke softly, but that was only part of how he spoke. He never yelled. Ever. His first response was to talk to people, but he always did it in a calm voice. It was hard to be around someone who did not allow his emotions to control him. It made you look at yourself when you lost your temper.

I was with Mr. Evers for about four months before he put me in the ring to fight with an actual opponent. Mr. Evers told me once he had never taught anyone like me before. I thought he was talking about me being a girl.

One day I came out of the locker room, and it'd appeared as if everyone stopped working, staring at me as I walked to the ring. Some were even standing at the ring with arms crossed, whispering to each other.

I asked Jeremiah, one of my friends in the gym, "Jeremiah? What's everyone looking at?"

Chuckling, "They're not looking at anything. They're waiting for you."

"Waiting for me! Why?"

"Most of the guys in here are students of boxing. You don't fight like a girl. You fight without fear and with a style that shows your knowledge of boxing. When they watch you, they are soaking up knowledge."

"I am not special, Jeremiah. I just do what Mr. Evers tells me to do."

"I know. It's what most of us do, but you catch on differently than most of us and you are a girl. It's fascinating."

It was intimidating, but Mr. Evers couldn't care less about my feelings. He wanted me to train. It never occurred to me at that young age that anyone was paying attention to me let alone that I was good. Mr. Evers didn't tell me that. What could I teach any of these men when some of them have been boxing almost longer than I'd been alive? Then I saw them mimicking some of my moves. Jeremiah told me the way I moved was like someone born to box, and most of the guys never saw that in a woman.

My mother told Mr. Evers what I was going through, but I didn't think he knew how much anger I had inside of me. When I felt the power behind my punches, I put everything I had into it. But there was no focus. I cried in the ring twice, but Mr. Evers didn't care. If you were not hurt from a punch, he wasn't interested. He told me to dry my tears and go back to my training.

Once I learned the basics of boxing, Mr. Evers taught me how to channel my anger and use it in my boxing. He told me I needed to make my emotions an extension of my body. I used my anger and grief and focused on releasing it through my punches. Every punch was me hurting the people who took away part of my family. I felt like I was gaining a handle on my grief and working through my emotions about Jesenia. A dear friend helped me realize I needed more.

Maurice Evers was the oldest son of James Evers. He was 25 years old when I met him and always had money but no job. Back then, I didn't know why I hadn't questioned that.

You would never know Mr. Evers and Maurice were related. Maurice was the opposite of his father. He had brown eyes, light hair, and darker skin than his father. He had high cheekbones, a broad chin, full lips, and towered over his father. Everyone said he resembled his mother, who died a few years before from breast cancer. Her picture hung in Mr. Evers's office where it was placed alone on a wall directly behind his desk. On more than a few occasions I'd glanced at the picture and noticed Maurice resembled his mother.

He had two brothers and a sister and none of them were the same shade. Whenever I saw them all they reminded me of was a Crayola crayon box.

Mr. and Mrs. Evers came to the United States from Colombia when Maurice was seven. Both Mr. Evers and Maurice spoke fluent Spanish, and it amazed them both when they learned I could do the same.

Maurice was the first person outside of my family I talked to about Jesenia (If you didn't include those stupid therapists). Mr. Evers talked about my grief in general terms to help me gain control of it. We never talked about Jesenia or our friendship.

I knew what I said about Mr. Evers's demeanor, but according to Maurice, Mr. Evers was wary of everyone. He told me I was a tough girl and not because I beat people up or tried to show my strength in the ring; I was fearless and he had never met a female who was as audacious as I was. He told me that was why his father liked me.

One day, when I was on my way home, Maurice stopped me in the parking lot to say hello. We chatted about insignificant things like school and whether I had a boyfriend and then he asked me,

"Why do you want to be a boxer?"

"I don't know. My mom thought this was an alternative to therapists and might help me work through my feelings. Not sure I want to be a boxer."

"What feelings would you need to get out in a boxing ring?" Maurice said.

I didn't say anything. No one had mentioned Jesenia's name to me in months. I thought about her all the time, but no one was talking about her. I wasn't even sure I wanted to talk about it.

Maurice said, "I'm sorry. I didn't mean to get too personal."

"No, it's OK." I put my bag on the ground next to his car and leaned against it.

"It's just that no one has asked about this in a long time," and I told him the story about Jesenia. I left out the part about JC and the family having to go into hiding, but I told everything else.

"I'm sorry Harrison. I think no one's asked you about it because they think boxing has helped you get past what happened and maybe you don't need to talk about it. Have you changed since you started coming here?"

"Yeah. I guess. Boxing helped me to get my anger out."

"Don't hold that in. You need to talk about her and tell someone how you feel. You can't grieve in that boxing ring. If not your family, then find a friend who'll listen."

"I don't really have any friends. I know people, but not like Jesenia."

"They're never gonna be like Jesenia. You have to open yourself up again, Harrison. Don't hold back because you're afraid and think you have this place to comfort you. Find some friends. My father would tell you the same thing if he knew."

"How did you get so smart?"

He chuckled, "Life. And I lost my mother. I know how grief feels and what it does to you and the other people around you." He kissed me on the forehead and went into the gym. I remembered at the time I wasn't expecting him to kiss me. I watched him go into the gym and he didn't turn around to smile at me or check to see if I was still there. Then I thought maybe that kiss was an "I care about you" kiss and not a romantic kiss. It's not like I hadn't noticed how hot he was, but I didn't think of him in a romantic way. And I didn't think he thought of me like that. It still made me smile as I went to the bus stop. He was the first person in a long time to care for me who wasn't in my family. It was nice.

Before I go on, I have to come clean about Maurice. I didn't tell the whole truth about him. About a year after I met Maurice, I asked him what he did for a living, and he told me he was into sales. He never lied to me before, so I accepted what he told me. Plus, the women I saw him with never resembled the hookers (they hate that word, by the way) on TV. I had no frame of reference. I believed him and thought he was just a whore. To me, he was no different from Keenan, who slept with a different girl every month. Day and I used to call Keenan's room Sodom and Gomorrah.

I found out by accident. I was in the Hollow (a housing project) one day, visiting one of my newfound friends I'd met. (Ever told me I needed to learn to relate to people? Maurice was right). We were leaving her apartment, and two of Maurice's girls were coming out of another apartment taking money from some guy. There were about two or three more male voices in the background. The ladies took their money as well and left.

I thought to myself there was no way Maurice would date a prostitute, and why would two women that he was sleeping with be around each other? When I exited the apartment building, I noticed Maurice's car parked and the women got in. It was all starting to make sense. It all fell into place.

I wasn't shocked really, and it didn't change my opinion about Maurice... well, it did change. I didn't know why I wasn't shocked. It always seemed that Maurice was a little off, but I never felt I was in danger, so I placed it in the back of my mind.

I asked Maurice if my findings were right, and he told me the truth. I immediately turned on him. I didn't mean to, but I've been a feminist since I was twelve. I asked him how he could exploit women, and he didn't have an answer for me. He walked away and had some of his ladies talk to me.

They told me they didn't feel exploited, that Maurice protected them, and he loved them. Most of them worked high-end clients, and the ladies I saw were on the street. I told the ladies that this relationship was not love. They called me a kid and walked away.

When I saw Maurice again, he was angry. He told me I didn't know what I was talking about and who the fuck was I to tell his ladies he didn't love them. I was just some stupid kid who thinks she knows everything. I told him I didn't think I knew everything, and it wasn't my fault a kid had to tell him he was full of shit.

We didn't speak for a while, and then he came to me and apologized.

"Look, Harrison. You were right, OK. I am using them, but they're using me too. I don't force anyone to work for me. They make money, I don't beat them, and I treat them like ladies and not whores."

"That's bullshit, Maurice, and you know it. Those women are objects to you. If that's how you see them, how do you see me?"

"You're different. So is my sister. The two of you are not like these women. I don't see you as the same as them."

"You know that's the same thing white people do to minorities, right?"

"It's not like that."

"Really? You're seen as the good guy because you live in the suburbs, and someone living in the Hollow is bad. It's the same thing you do to women: 'These are the good women, and these are the bad women.'"

"You don't understand, Harrison. And you're 16! Who taught you this stuff?"

"My mother. No. I understand perfectly. Does your family know what you do? Does your father know what you do?"

He didn't say anything at first. "They know what I do. They don't speak to me because of it, but I can't do anything about that. Ever doesn't like it either, but my father can't say much to me about what I do."

"Why can't he say anything about what you do?"

"Nothing. Don't worry about it. Look, I just wanted you to understand where I'm coming from. If you can't be my friend, I can understand that." He then walked away.

I loved Maurice and knew he would die for me, but I also knew he didn't see me. I was his little sister who he put in a box and kept there. He took me out when he wanted to play with me and be my brother, but I wasn't real. Because of this, I held back a lot of myself from him after that day. My first complicated relationship.

Chapter 8

Later on that year, things changed for me. I was no longer the girl who boxed in the gym. Mr. Evers let me be a part of the gym. Mr. Evers gave me jobs to do. I worked with incoming boxers on their conditioning; I helped him clean the gym at night, and he gave me a desk in his office. No longer a boxer only, it was my gym too. The guys in the gym changed my name to Miss Harri instead of "The Girl."

I would spend two hours at the gym after school. When I was working there, the hours changed from two hours to four hours. My homework was completed there, and I sometimes ate dinner there. My mother was against this at first but allowed me to continue since I was getting As.

I've already mentioned the people who helped create who I became. Losing Jesenia and meeting Mr. Evers was a big part of my identity, but what happened at the gym when I was sixteen put me on a path to who I would truly become.

I was finishing the books for the day. Mr. Evers was cleaning in the gym. The squeaky hinge we have to oil every few weeks alerted me that someone came in. I rose from my chair to look through the glass from the office door. It was late and people didn't come to the gym that late. I saw Mr. Evers, who was standing by one of the boxing rings putting away equipment, glance in the direction of the door. I had my hand on the doorknob and was about to go out when I heard someone say,

"So, I'm not good enough for your gym?" in a deep voice.

I took my hand off the doorknob and remained in the office. Worry knotted inside as his booming voice filled the gym. I knew the voice. Mr. Evers had thrown him out two months before because of his "incessant bullying." Mr. Evers didn't respond to what the man said.

"Don't you hear me, Ever?" (I have no idea what happened to the "s" at the end of Mr. Evers's name, but everyone called him Ever. I couldn't do that; my mother would have killed me).

In that always calm voice, "I hear you, Lyle. What are you doing here?"

"What am I doing here? I'm here to show you how great a boxer I am." I could see him through the glass now. He was taller than Mr. Evers and a bit broader than him. His hair was slicked back, he had a bulbous nose, small eyes, and a scar on his right cheek. There was always talk he was using steroids, while others thought he was just an asshole.

"I already know you're a good boxer. This is a wasted trip."

"No, it's not wasted. You haven't seen what I can do, and I think you should know what you gave up."

"I did not throw you out because of your lack of boxing skills, Lyle. I threw you out because you were mean and a bully."

"You piece of shit Ever! This is a boxing gym, not a kindergarten classroom! We're supposed to be men in here!" Lyle yelled, slapping his chest.

"That doesn't mean you have to be mean."

I saw a second man move around to Mr. Evers's right. He must have come in with Lyle. He was shorter than both of them, but he looked as mean as Lyle and was about the same size as him. Mr. Evers never looked at the man, he kept his eyes on Lyle.

"Yeah, well, you're gonna find out how mean I can be."

Lyle lunged at him, while the other guy came at Mr. Evers from behind. I was going to run out (as if I was going to do something) and I paused. Before Lyle could get to him, Mr. Evers had his friend in a chokehold causing him to fall to the ground. It happened fast, and Lyle faltered. He recovered quickly and started going after Mr. Evers again.

When Lyle was in front of Mr. Evers, he swung like a boxer would, but Mr. Evers didn't box him back. He was blocking his swings, but not with punches. Mr. Evers was shifting his weight and blocking Lyle's fists. He wasn't hitting Mr. Evers, and he was falling all over the place.

Lyle let out a yell. It was more a battle cry than a yell, and he tried again to swing on his opponent. Mr. Evers grabbed Lyle when he was close enough by his shirt and took hold of his arm with the other hand. He swung him around. Lyle's back was to Mr. Evers' front and he got him in the same chokehold as his friend. Finally, Lyle was on the floor too.

As soon as Lyle was out, Mr. Evers came to the office door. My heart stopped in my chest as the door opened and froze as our eyes met.

He moved past me and headed for his desk. Picking up the receiver of the phone, he dialed and waited.

"Mr. McCuff, this is James Evers. No, no. Harrison is fine. She is standing right here with me, but I need you to come to the gym. Something's happened."

There was more to the conversation, but I wasn't listening anymore. "What just happened" is what was running through my head.

He hung up, and he called the police. After he hung up with the police, I was going to ask him a question, but I didn't know what to say.

"Harrison, are you OK?"

I nodded my head because no words would form in my mind. This was not fear, just a lack of comprehension of the events. Boxers don't move like Mr. Evers moved. That was not boxing.

"We're going outside to wait for your parents, OK?"

I nodded my head again. He took my hand and led me outside. A cop car pulled up about two minutes later. Mr. Evers left me standing by one of the trees outside the gym while he moved away to talk to the cop. A few moments after that, my parents arrived. My mother ran to me and hugged me.

"Harrison, are you OK?" My father was by her side. As they were grilling me, an ambulance showed up along with two more cop cars.

"Yes."

"Did they hurt you?" My father asked.

"No."

Mom released her hold on me. "What happened?"

I looked into her eyes, "I don't know."

As soon as I said, "I don't know," my father walked over to where a police officer was speaking with Mr. Evers. My mother hugged me again, tighter this time, as we walked over to the police, Mr. Evers, and my father.

The paramedics were bringing Lyle and his friend out of the gym. They were groaning and about to be waking up. The policeman asked Mr. Evers what he did to them, and Mr. Evers said he just knocked them out. We had to wait in the gym because the police wanted to talk to me too since I was a witness. We all had to go to the police station to make out reports. Mr. Evers told the police that wasn't necessary because he did not want to press charges. The police took our statements, had us sign them, and left. I kept my story as close to Mr. Evers as I could. I didn't want to explain what I saw, and I didn't know why. Then my father turned to Mr. Evers.

"What the hell happened here tonight, James?"

"It was someone who I asked to leave the gym a few months ago. He was angry."

"I know that. I heard what you told the police. I want to know why my daughter is in that state?" He pointed at me, and they both glanced at me in my mother's embrace.

I forced myself to say, "Daddy, I'm OK."

"No, you're not. Did they hurt her? Was she in danger?"

"Davis, you know I would never let anything happen to your daughter. If anything happened to her, it would be because I'm dead. Do you understand me, Davis? Dead," again in that calm voice.

My father said nothing. He just glared at Mr. Evers. "I know you care about my daughter, but she's my daughter. She could have gotten hurt here tonight."

"I know, but I wouldn't have let that happen. I understand your fear and anger; I have children too. This is a safe place, Davis."

My father again said nothing; he just stared at Mr. Evers. He finally turned to me and my mother and walked us to his car.

I couldn't sleep. I kept seeing the fight in my head, fascinated by the moves and the fact that Mr. Evers could do it. He moved so fast and with such confidence. I was just trying to understand.

Chapter 9

I finally woke up the next morning like I normally do. My mother was already up, beginning her weekly cleaning.

She turned as I was passing her to go out the door, "Harrison, where are you going? You need to eat something."

"To school," I yelled back as I was putting on my jacket. "I'm gonna eat at school today."

She was by the door. "Don't you want to take a few days? Last night was a bit of a trauma for you."

I picked up my bag and turned to her,

"Mom, I'm all right. Nothing happened to me. Besides, I have to go to school, or I can't go to the gym. That's one of Mr. Evers's...."

"You're not going back to that gym."

I put my bag back down. "What?! Why?!"

"It's too dangerous. I don't want you there anymore. It was wrong for me to give you so much freedom with that gym anyway. You're a young lady and shouldn't be around all those men all the time." She walked back towards the back hall.

"Mom, what are you talking about? You love the gym and the men at the gym. You have to let me go back." I pleaded as I followed her.

"I won't risk the safety of my daughter. You're not going back there."

"Mom?! I need to go back. I love being there. They helped me."

She turned to me. "I know that, but I don't want you there, Harri. That's it. We're not talking about this anymore. You come home after school."

I couldn't believe it. How could she do this to me? I stood there for a few seconds and turned around, walked back to my bag, picked it up, and slammed the door as I ran out.

I didn't speak to anyone on my way to school, at school, or during lunch. All day long, all I kept thinking to myself was "It's not long enough. I need more time with them. She can't do this to me."

I'd never thought about the role the gym or the people at the gym played in my life until my mother took it away from me. If I didn't have them, what was I supposed to do? The gym and everyone in it were a part of me.

After a month, I couldn't take it anymore. My mom was being irrational, so there was no reasoning with her. A couple of times I tried to raise the subject of the gym, and she wouldn't even talk about it. A solution to this evaded me. I finally spoke to Keenan and Day, and they told me I should talk to our father.

I went to my father one night while he was working in his den, "Dad, I need to talk to you about something if you're not too busy."

He looked up from the computer screen at me, "I can take a break if you need to talk. Come in."

I came in and sat in one of the black wide leather chairs in front of his desk. I always felt small in those chairs, even as an adult. His desk was also black, as were the bookshelves on all the walls. All the pictures he had on the walls, were of family. He didn't even have his diplomas on the wall.

He looked into my eyes and said, "What do you want to talk to me about? What's going on?"

"Mom still won't talk to me about going back to the gym. I've tried to approach it a few different ways and she won't listen."

He interlaced his fingers and put his hands on the desk, "She's scared, Harri."

"I know Dad, but I need to go back."

"Why, Harrison?"

I sat forward in my seat, "When Jesenia died, the gym was the only place that gave me solace to what was going on inside me. I was lost without her." I put my head down for a few seconds. "I didn't think I would want anyone to be around me again. I didn't know I needed them. Being a part of a group that is supportive, and you can be supportive of helped me."

"I can understand that. I did see a very quick change in you."

"Then will you help me? I want to go back."

"Aren't you scared?"

"No, Dad. It's the only other place outside of this house that I feel safe."

He pondered my request and finally said, "OK. I'll talk to her."

I jumped up and ran around his desk. I hugged him tightly, "Thank you, Dad. Thank you."

I didn't explain everything to him because I was afraid he wouldn't understand. The adrenaline rush from boxing was no longer there. My free time used to be filled with something that gave me joy and purpose. I was on edge without boxing and was sad my friends were disappearing.

Although Jesenia never left me, she became more of my focus. For months there were no dreams of Jesenia and her death, but with no gym, I was being killed with my best friend again. Plus, my body was losing some muscle tone and there was a difference in the way my body moved. I used to run to the third floor of my school with no problem; now I couldn't walk those flights of stairs without wheezing at the top. I needed the gym.

My father waited until they were alone in the kitchen after dinner that night. Instead of going to my room, I waited on the stairs, listening to what my father was going to say to my mother.

"Keisha, we have to talk. You have to let Harrison go back to the gym."

"Davis, I'm not letting her go back there. It's dangerous."

"You can't keep her locked up like this. She loves that place because of you. Hell, you love that place. I know you're scared, but you cannot do this to her."

She raised her voice, "I don't care, Davis. She is not going back, and that's it."

My father raised his voice,

"No, that's not it, Keisha! You gave her that place because she needed it, and she still does. I know you know our daughter is special. She's not a regular kid; she never has been. You've watched her fight. You've watched the way they all respond to her. You can't keep her from them. She'll hate you!"

My mother's voice rose higher, "I said no!"

My father yelled even louder, "I...said...yes!"

My mother didn't say anything, and neither did my father. I could imagine her staring at him, "Davis?..."

"No, Keisha. I know, because of what happened you think something bad could happen to her, but our daughter could die on the way to school or going to the store. Do you think I like this? I wanted to kill James that night. It wasn't his fault, but she's my baby. I want her to stay here, but that's not what she needs, and it's not who she is. And James Evers would never let anyone harm our daughter unless he was dead. If she wants to go back and thinks she can, let her."

"You think just because he said he would die for our daughter, it means something? I heard him."

"No. I don't think it means anything. Those are just words, but he's done nothing but watch over our daughter for an entire year. You were there, Keisha. Does it seem to you like James would let anything happen to her? We can't protect her from everything."

"No, we can't, but we don't have to put her in harms way either." She sighed, "But I know James won't let anything happen to her. I don't like this, Davis. What if it's a gun next time?"

"Look, Hippie, you raised that girl like this. She's gonna get there because she needs them, and it's what she wants. Can't imagine where she gets that from. She'll be OK, Keisha."

Neither of them spoke for about ten seconds. "I'm just scared for her. I never thought of that place as dangerous."

"I know. But everywhere is dangerous. You know she needs this, Keisha."

"Fine. She can go back. You hear that girl? You can go back!" she yelled.

From the stairs, as I hustled to my room, I yelled back, "Thank You!"

Chapter 10

When I went back to Evers Gym, all the boxers were waiting for me: Mac, Bobby, Denver, Jeremiah, and the rest of my gym. They exchanged hugs with me and expressed how happy they were I was back. Maurice was there with one of his girls. I hugged him the tightest. He told me he missed me, and the gym wasn't the same without me there. After my welcome back, I went to the office. Mr. Evers was sitting at his desk with his back to the door. I knocked, and he turned to look back at me.

"So, you made it back. Ready to box again?" turning back to what he was doing.

"No, I'm here to learn what... I... saw... a... month... ago." The last few words dragged out, and my voice became quieter. Where did that come from? I wasn't planning to say that at all. I hadn't even thought about what I was going to say, except I missed being there. Mr. Evers turned around fully. "What are you talking about?"

"I...I... saw what you did when Lyle was here, and I want to learn."

"You already know how to box. You don't need to learn anything else? Besides, that was nothing."

"It wasn't nothing, Mr. Evers. When I woke up the next morning, I realized that I understood why you made the moves you made. I didn't know they were coming because I didn't know what the moves were, but when I thought about the sequence of your moves, I could understand why you did them. And I don't need to learn, but I want to."

He looked at me for a long time, "Harrison, can you see a punch when you're in the ring fighting?"

"I don't know what you mean by seeing a punch."

"Yes, you do."

"No. I don't."

"Harrison, when you're boxing, I see you anticipating your opponent's moves. It's the same thing you just described to me about the fighting you witnessed."

"That's because I've studied how my opponent fights and what they do in certain situations. I can't see the punch. Watching you fight was like watching your fight film. I was just replaying the moves in my mind."

"What if you closed your eyes with a studied opponent? The opponent threw a punch. Would you know what punch they would throw and where?"

"I don't know. I don't think so."

"I think you can. This is not about boxing Harrison. This is about instincts and about quiet."

"Quiet?"

"Yes, quiet." Mr. Evers stood from his chair, walked past me, and into the gym to one of the rings with me on his heels. He moved around the ring and boxed with me.

"When you box, you're not thinking about killing the person in the ring with you. You're thinking about your movements and their movements. You're thinking about how to win." He paused and stood in the middle of the ring.

"When you're in the ring, I bet your vision gets narrow and all you can see is your opponent and the ring. You probably don't even hear me when I'm yelling instructions to you."

I didn't know what to say. He wasn't exactly right, but he was pretty close. If I watched tapes of my opponent before a fight, I could anticipate their moves, mostly. It wasn't foolproof, but it worked enough that I had a good record. If I didn't watch the tapes of my opponent before a fight, after the first round I could figure out their strategy. As for my vision in the ring, it didn't narrow to my opponent. It narrowed to the four corners of the boxing ring, including my opponent and the ref. The crowd was not in my field of vision, and I couldn't hear Mr. Evers. That's why my record was twelve and two.

"That's kinda what it is. What does this mean?"

He exited the ring and walked back to the office. "I don't know what it means. I recognized it a long time ago, but I ignored it. Harrison, what I did the other night is not something to teach you." He sat back at his desk as I stood in the doorway.

"Why not?"

"Because it takes a long time to learn, and it's not an art that's taught anymore."

"I'm only sixteen, I have time."

"It's not just about the time."

"Coach, please."

"What is this really about, Harrison?"

"I know I'm supposed to learn this. I feel it."

"What do you mean you feel it?"

I thought about my answer, "It wasn't just that I could see the reason for the moves. When I thought about what you did, I could see myself doing the moves. You know I love boxing, Mr. Evers, but I want to know what you know. You didn't even hurt those men, and they were out."

"What do you mean you could see yourself doing the moves? You never saw them before."

"I know, but it felt... I don't know how to explain it. It was like I recognized the moves... I know it sounds stupid."

"It doesn't sound stupid," Mr. Evers whispered. I remained standing in the doorway while Mr. Evers sat at his desk; neither of us uttered a word. We just listened to each other breathe.

"I know you're supposed to learn it, too. I've been avoiding it for a long time, and if Lyle and his friend never came to the gym that night, you wouldn't know anything about this."

I stood staring at him. It was the first and only time I saw him wrestle with something. It scared me and made me rethink learning this.

"This is not like anything else you've seen or been through, Harrison. We'll no longer box except to keep up your skills. We will spend all our time learning this art. And this is something you'll need to keep to yourself. You can't tell anyone. I will talk to your parents."

"Why?"

"Because no one can know this art is being taught."

"I can keep a secret, Mr. Evers."

"I know you can. You have to understand, Harrison, this art is very intense and soul-moving. You'll have to be dedicated. You're gonna be tired, both mentally and physically. You have to find a way to keep going. You can't quit, Harrison. Are you sure you want to do this?"

"I have to do this, Mr. Evers. I won't let you down."

"I know you won't, Harrison, but I want you to think about what I've told you. You know me as a coach, and if I say this is difficult, it is. You have to be sure you're prepared for this. You think about it, and we will talk again after the weekend."

I was not happy about him wanting me to wait, but he was insistent. Besides Mr. Evers wouldn't exaggerate how difficult this was going to be. Taking time to decide what I wanted to do was the next logical step.

The way Mr. Evers talked about this being a secret, I was scared. Lies did not go over well in my family. It was not a part of my relationship with them, but I knew they would not understand this was a need. Disrespect of my parents was not an option, but neither was walking away from this.

When I made my decision about being trained in this art, I told Mr. Evers my concerns. I told him I was worried about how hard this was going to be, my fear I could not do it, and I did not want to lie to my parents.

"Harrison, if you are having doubts about this, we don't have to do it."

"Mr. Evers, I want to be sure I can do it. I don't want to let you down."

"Harrison, only you know that. You know what I am expecting of you. If you don't think you can do it, don't do it. And we will not lie to your parents."

He called my parents, and they came to the gym. He told them he needed to talk to them about something new I wanted to learn, but he needed their permission, and he wanted to show them what it was. When they arrived, he took them to the new training area, which was another gym downstairs. The entire floor was covered in mats. My parents had to take their shoes off to look around. There were pictures of men and women doing martial arts on the walls, along with swords and grappling sticks. Weight benches and weights were scattered across the room. My mother looked around and initially said no. My stomach dropped.

They talked about it for a couple of weeks and even talked to me. My father had one question for me,

"Why?"

"Well, karate is cool and it's something different from boxing. I want to expand my fighting skills."

"Is that right? You've been boxing for a year, never mentioned karate, and you want to expand your fighting skills? Tell me the real reason."

Damnit, "I didn't want to bring this up again. When I saw Mr. Evers take those men with the moves he used, I felt safe and thought if I knew those moves, I could further defend myself."

"And you didn't tell me because?"

"I did tell you, Dad. I just left out the part about seeing Mr. Evers do the moves."

He pondered while looking at me, "OK. I believe you."

"Mom?"

"I don't like it. I don't think you should be learning anything dangerous."

"But Mom..."

"Mrs. McCuff? Why don't you come to the gym and see for yourself what I'm teaching her? You can get a feel for it. If you don't like what you see, we won't do it."

"What!" I scoffed.

"That sounds like a great idea.

My mother came to the gym a few times to watch me learn. Mr. Evers regretted inviting her. She stayed longer than he expected and he had to change our lessons. He was teaching me the fundamentals of karate. After a month my mother was satisfied, and she stopped coming to the gym.

And thus began my training in Senshijutsu. One of the first things Mr. Evers made me do was learn the history of Senshijutsu and its founder Hajime Ino. I moaned and groaned, but Mr. Evers would not let me learn anything until I knew the history of the art and the people who lived it.

Chapter 11

Even after I learned about the creators and designers of Senshijutsu and learned what my predecessors had to go through, I still could not grasp the concept that the preparation would be unlike anything I had ever known. My training included my body, my mind, and my spirit.

Mr. Evers's first lesson for me was meditation. We sat in the basement after hours on fluffy mats. Mr. Ever taught me breathing techniques to settle my mind and my body. We spent a long time working on finding my quiet place and clearing my mind.

I sat in the basement of my house, a clearing in the woods, my room, and even in a quiet room at Iona College. No matter where I went, my errands, or what I wanted to do would pop into my mind. Mr. Evers told me I needed to keep practicing, and I needed to think of nothing. I didn't know how to think of nothing. It took me three months to figure out how to clear my mind and meditate.

After I learned the basic concepts of meditation, Sensei taught me Tai Chi as a way to harness my quietness and steady myself. With Tai Chi, I could meditate for hours. I found myself to be a lot calmer and able to make better decisions. My change in self-control was a signal to Mr. Evers that I was ready to learn the true concepts of Senshijutsu.

He didn't think working with certain weapons and combat would be challenging for me. Becoming a master was not about how well I wielded a knife or knocked someone out. It was about becoming a master of every discipline of Senshijutsu.

When Mr. Evers taught me disguises (we didn't learn impersonation), he told me for a disguise to work, changing how I looked wasn't enough. I had to become the person I was trying to be. These kinds of lessons were difficult for me at first because I believed if I resembled someone else, or changed my voice, I could deceive anyone.

He had me go to the mall and other public places to watch men. I had to pay attention to their interactions with other men and women, how they ate, how they shopped, how they talked, and how they moved. I sat at tables or followed them around to witness their interactions. I had to learn the differences between how older men acted and young boys or young men behaved. It took me years to get it right, but my initial findings were good enough to trick civilians.

My first test in disguises was with my brothers. For three months, I practiced changing my voice, wearing men's clothes, wearing different wigs, changing my teeth, and adding padding in the places I looked like a woman. The Adam's apple was Mr. Evers's idea.

I walked around New Rochelle to see if anyone recognized me or gave me the impression I was not a man. No one did. Even though I built some confidence from my outings around town, my stomach still had butterflies in it when I went to play basketball a few months later.

Even if there is no snow on the ground, it's not a good idea to play basketball outside in the winter. Luckily, the YMCA lets people play pick-up games. There were already six men on the court I was standing in front of. Two of them were my brothers.

I planned to ask if I could join a game. With more people, there was a risk of being recognized as a woman. If my brothers did recognize me, they probably would have been too embarrassed to mention it was me and would've let me play and questioned me later.

I held my own on the court. Keenan talked to me afterward, trying to find out where I was from, and even told me he and the rest of the guys got together every Friday night if I wanted to come by.

As I dialed Mr. Evers, tears fell on my cheeks and my tracksuit.

"Hello"

"Mmmrr...Evvers..."

"Who is this?"

I stopped, took in air, and let it out slowly. Tears were still falling, "Sensei, it's me. Harri."

"What's wrong?

"I fooled them. They didn't know it was me."

"Harrison. Hang up the phone and come to the gym. Don't come in. I will come out to you."

I finally stopped crying by the time I got there and could tell Sensei everything. He let me be happy for half a second. He told me because I had fooled my brothers and some guys on a basketball court didn't mean other people wouldn't notice things my brothers missed. I still had a lot of work to do to feel cocky about anything.

All of my lessons were like this. When I was learning about water, I learned new breathing techniques which allowed me to be in the water longer than I ever had before. But it wasn't about swimming or holding my breath, it was also about having five pounds of supplies on my back, not panicking, being able to float, dealing with the cold water, diving, and wielding weapons underwater. And even when I became good, Sensei would tell me I needed to learn more. Nothing was ever perfect in his eyes. There was always something more to learn with Sensei.

To be a Master, all that encompasses Senshijutsu, had to be who I am; I could no longer be Harrison McCuff, a young high school girl who enjoyed boxing, loved her family, etc., etc. Senshijutsu had to be my first identifier. Otherwise, it would be a simple hobby I did on the side. No Master of Senshijutsu practiced the art for leisure. Senshijutsu must be present in every situation, no matter how small or intense. Still, these concepts were not the hardest for me to learn.

I could learn all the skills and techniques I wanted, but if honor, loyalty, compassion, or courage were not a part of who I was, being a master would elude me. And Sensei tested me every chance he got.

In the beginning, I didn't know I was being tested, and I failed. A lot. I remembered a messy incident when a girl about my age was sent to confront me when I was in the mall. She bumped into me as she walked by. I was going to say excuse me, but before I could,

"Watch where you're going bitch"

"Excuse me?"

"You heard me." She put both her hands on my shoulders and shoved me.

When I righted myself, I punched her. She punched me back. I saw her ponytail and went to grab it and punch her in the face, but security was there by then. They pulled us apart, and a few people were standing around looking at us. We both got thrown out of the mall.

When I arrived at the gym the next day, Sensei questioned me about the incident.

"Why did you fight the young lady yesterday?"

"How do you even know about it? What, are you following me?"

"You didn't answer my question."

"She started with me!" I yelled. "What was I supposed to do, just stand there?"

"No, you were supposed to find another way to diffuse the situation."

"Why would I learn all of this if I'm not supposed to defend myself?"

"You're not learning it to defend yourself. That's not the purpose of Senshi-jutsu, and you know it. You are learning to serve others. Did you ever think that perhaps the young lady was having an issue and needed help? Your first response should not be to fight. Think about the situation first and then react. That is where the compassion and honor come in."

"Sensei, she put her hands on me first. I did think about it. I thought she put her hands on me first, and I'm gonna bust her ass."

"And there was no other way to handle that?"

"No."

"You are a fast learner, Harrison, and I know you understand the lessons. There was nothing you can think of in our lessons that would have put you on a different path?"

He looked me in the eye and crossed his arms. There was no smile, smirk, or even a lifted eyebrow.

I sighed and dropped my head low and took in what he said to me. "I'm sorry, Sensei. I wasn't thinking."

"I know. You need to learn how to control your emotions, and I need to better prepare you."

After that incident, my training included more lessons on meditation. The more I meditated, the more focused my mind became. Before I took action, I was thinking about what could happen. There was a lot less reaction without thought. It helped a good deal when keeping my grades at As and Bs while in training.

In my senior year of high school, I decided to stay in New Rochelle and continue my training in Senshijutsu. I applied to Iona College in New Rochelle and was accepted. My mother and my father were pissed. Because I was such a good student, I could have gotten into any other school—-better ones at that. I had applied to other schools and was accepted. However, I told my parents I wanted to study social work, and Iona had one of the top programs in the country.

My mother hoped I would go to college where my father and I met, but I told her this was what I wanted. I don't think she believed my explanation, but neither she nor my father challenged me on my decision. They could have refused to pay, but if my goal was social work, what were they going to say?

I, on the other hand, told Sensei the truth.

"The three years of training is good, but it's not the entire program, and I want it all. My training can't continue if I go away to school. Traveling back and forth from school would not make me a Master."

He thought about it for a few days and told me, "Your parents are correct. You should go away to school."

"Sensei?"

He raised his hands, "You are excellent at this art. You've made progress I didn't think was possible. I want to continue teaching you."

I jumped up and down. He raised his hands again.

"Harrison. I will only agree to this if you are a 4.0 student every semester. If your GPA drops, training will end. Do you understand?"

"Yes, Sensei. I understand."

Chapter 12

After four years of learning Senshijutsu, my whole life and mind-set changed. I believed everything I needed and wanted was in New Rochelle. Sensei knew better and during my second year of college, he told me I had to leave.

Sensei and I were standing in the gym after it had closed. I was helping him clean.

"Harri, it's time for you to leave."

"OK. Why are you rushing me? I'm going as fast as I can."

"That's not what I mean."

I stopped wiping the bags, "What are you talking about?

"It's time for you to leave New Rochelle. I don't have anything else to teach you."

I walked over to where he was standing by one of the rings, "What are you talking about, I know there's more for you to teach me."

"No, there isn't, and even if there was, you have to leave. It's time."

"What do you mean it's time?", raising my voice.

"You're supposed to be doing something else. The skill level you have is too high for you to end your life here in New Rochelle. You stayed here to attend school, and I knew it was the wrong choice back then. You need to be out there," he said in that infuriating, calm voice.

"How do you know what I need? I need to be here with you and learning!" I was hysterical at this point.

"No. I can see in your eyes you know I'm right, Harrison. Apply to go to another school next year. It's November. You have time to apply somewhere else and get in for next Fall. I want you to finish school."

My eyes fill with tears, "Sensei, did I do something wrong?"

"Harri, you know that isn't it."

"I don't want to go."

"Yes, you do. You're just afraid to leave because your parents, Maurice, and I have been allowing you to stifle your potential. We've let you stay in our lives for us and not make you leave for you. You want to leave."

I stared at him. I didn't know what to say,

"I don't know where I'm supposed to go! I'm supposed to go, but I don't know where Sensei! How do I know where I'm supposed to go?" choking on my tears.

James Evers did something that he never did again. He came over to me and wrapped his arms around me. Wrapping my arms around him, I sobbed into his chest. After two minutes, he released his arms from me and insisted I leave.

I gave a nod with my head held low and left—left him and the life I once knew. Yet, my whole world was Senshijutsu, my family, and the gym. My whole life was in New Rochelle. I didn't want to know anything else.

To add to my pain, we lost Nunu at the beginning of the year. Even with all my training, I always found time for my Nunu. There was no way I would have been able to train for three years if I wasn't involved in the family. Everyone would have known I was hiding something. Everyone has to attend family dinners or parties unless they are sick, or it has to do with school. I would not have been able to use the school excuse too many times.

It was easier to have my training scheduled around my family visits, which included visiting Nunu. We still watched TV together, went out to dinner, and I described pictures in her albums so she could tell me the stories behind them.

At the reading of the will, when the lawyer read, "... and the rest of my assets I bequeath to my granddaughter Harrison McCuff on her 21st birthday" all eyes in the room fell on me, including my parents. There was no explanation, and I knew my face told them this wasn't what I'd expected.

The other grandchildren received money, but my inheritance was considerably larger, and they were giving me side eyes and scowls. The only person who knew how any of this happened was the old, white-bearded lawyer who sat behind his desk reading the last will and testament of Abigail "Nunu" Lafayette.

On my twenty-first birthday, the lawyer phoned me and instructed me that I needed to come to the office and come alone. I traveled back to New Rochelle and upon arriving at his office, he left me alone with a tape from my grandmother. He wasn't allowed in the room while I watched the videotape.

On the screen, my grandmother, with her dark olive skin and hair in a bun, sat in a high-back chair and said goodbye.

"Hello, Harrison. If you are watching this, I am with my sisters and brothers right now. I am sorry I had to leave you. I made this tape for you because I wanted to tell you why I've done what I've done. I know the rest of the family may not understand, but that's OK. They don't need to, but I need you to.

"I left this money to you not because you are my favorite. I do not have one. I left it to you because there is something you are going to do. I don't know what it is, I just know it will be great. Money gives you choices and whatever God put you on this earth to do, I want you to be focused. You can't be focused if you are worrying about paying your rent."

I did not know at the time how true the statement she made was.

"I know it's a lot of money, but your grandfather and I liked to save, and I was a very smart businesswoman." I didn't realize I was crying until tears hit my hands.

Nunu told me more than that, but I'm not allowed to reveal the contents of the video. I wasn't allowed to tell anyone the contents of the video. So, I have to keep the rest to myself. Sorry.

Over the next few weeks, my sensei would not see me. He wasn't at the gym when I'd go by and would not answer the phone when I called.

In the meantime, I applied to schools all over the country: LSU, University of Arizona, University of Miami, Syracuse University, Brown, Cornell, and

Princeton. I was accepted by all. I needed to talk to Sensei about where I should go but couldn't find him.

Instead, I used what he gave me and meditated. I decided on Syracuse University (I just kept seeing orange and blue). As soon as the decision was made, sensei called and asked to see me. This was in March.

"I've been calling you for weeks, and when I came to the gym, you weren't here."

We were standing in the middle of Sensei's gym. No one was there. It was early Sunday evening.

"I know. I've been busy."

"Why did you want to see me? Where is everybody?"

"I heard you're going to Syracuse University. I think that's great," Sensei was taking off his shoes. I took mine off too.

"Yeah, I'm ready."

"Well, I think it's time for your last lesson with me."

"Ok. What's the lesson."

"We're going to fight. That's your last lesson," he stood facing me.

I chuckled. "A fight with you? That's not a lesson. You and I have fought before."

"I know." He stood there looking at me and then he lunged forward and hit me in my stomach. I had no time to react. I couldn't imagine he was going to hit me so hard. The blow knocked the wind right out of my body. I staggered back and looked at him, my eyes wide. I struggled to catch my breath while holding my abdomen. This wasn't how we fought in the past.

When he came at me again, I moved out of the way, landed on the floor, and swept his legs from under him. I was on top of him before he could stand. I punched him in the face twice. He flipped me off of him. I landed on my stomach. I was on all fours before he was on top of me. He had his arm around my neck, lifting me up to my feet, choking me. I elbowed him in the solars twice, but he wouldn't release his grip.

I gave a hard stomp on his foot. He let out a howl, yet he wouldn't let go. I had one more technique to execute before losing consciousness; I raised my arm behind me, placed my finger in his eye, and stomped on his foot again. He loosened his grip, which was all I needed. I got a hold of his arm, came out of his choke hold, swung around him, kicked the side of his knee, which gave out, and punched him in the face again. This time he went down.

I don't know how long we fought. I was terrified but had no time to be terrified. I was fighting the hardest I had fought in my life. I had to beat him. I had little time to think, but I remember how afraid I was Ever would hurt me or I would hurt him.

The fight ended when Ever and I ended up on opposite sides of the gym, panting. I was crouched, my fists up, blowing out air, but Ever stood upright and put his hands to his sides. He glanced at me with tears in his eyes. There were none in mine. Tears rolled down his cheeks. He closed his eyes, and he bowed to me. I came out of my attack stance, bowed to him, put on my shoes, grabbed my jacket, and left the gym.

When I got outside, Maurice was leaning against his car, waiting for me. He didn't say a word to me, just stared at me without moving. As if he had come out of a dream, he strolled over to where I was standing to help me walk. We got into his car, and he drove me to the hospital.

I didn't know how I looked, but my adrenaline was wearing off, and pain rushed to my limbs, back, and face. I didn't think anything was broken, but I was also sure I had cracked a rib. I recall being pissed at Maurice because if he was waiting for me, he must have known this was going to happen, and he let it.

"Listen, Harri. I didn't know what was happening. Ever told me to be at the gym tonight and wait for him outside, but he didn't tell me why."

I kept my sentences short, to control my pain, "And you just did it."

"Yes. My father doesn't ask much of me and doesn't say too much about how I live. What the hell happened?"

"Not now."

I was happy he was there because I couldn't think and he helped me develop a story to tell my parents.

When my parents arrived at the hospital, Maurice told them he was driving by the high school and three girls were pounding on me (one of Maurice's girls drove my car to the high school and dropped it off). He told them I got the girls good, but I was pretty beaten by the time he got there.

"Davis, call the police. Tell them to meet us here."

My father stepped away to call the police. I could talk in longer sentences. They were giving me drugs for the pain. "Mom, I don't want you to call the cops. I don't know who they were and I'm sure they are gone now."

"I don't care. Call them Davis."

My mother, of course, wasn't having it. Nonetheless, my father called the cops despite my protesting. The cops took my information, a description of my attackers, and said they would look into it. Lucky for me, they didn't seem to push.

I was right about the cracked rib. With my clothes off, my entire body resembled a rainbow. I could move, but I didn't want to. Every movement brought pain to a leg, an arm, or a side, whether it was standing, bending, walking, or peeing. Even opening my mouth sent a shock to the nerves in my face.

Maurice phoned me two days later and told me I had broken two of Ever's ribs, fractured his foot, he had nerve damage in one of his arms, and had a slight concussion. They were unsure if a scrape on his eye would heal all the way. I hung up. I wasn't holding back; I'd hurt him badly. Ever, on the other hand, held back. If he had used his full power, I'd be dead.

Ever never called to check in on me how I was doing. It angered, disappointed, and hurt me. When I lost Jesenia, he gave my heart a home. He opened up my mind to the endless possibilities of myself, and he gave me the skills that were the basis for what I would ultimately do with my life, but at that time, I didn't think I'd ever forgive him for what he'd done to me.

As I healed and prepared to make my way to Syracuse University, I became nervous and excited all at the same time. My brothers took me to visit the campus. Main campus had a mix of modern and old buildings. Most of the older buildings looked like mini castles. You could immediately tell those from the more modern buildings who did not have spires on them. Main campus also held the library, fraternity row, and a short distance from main campus were restaurants and bars.

All the rumors I heard about the snow in Syracuse were real. We went in March. There was two feet of snow on the ground, and the snow was still lightly falling. The weather channel said it would snow for the next two days, and when it stopped snowing there would be another two feet of snow on the ground. Even with all the snow, the campus was beautiful.

I said goodbye to my friends at school and my family at the gym and proceeded in August to make my way to Syracuse.

We were packing the van, and I was making my third trip with my television set and my duffle bag with some of my Senshijutsu tools. On my right, I saw movement and looked up at Ever standing in front of Jesenia's old house. He stared at me, with his hands in his pockets, and smiled. He took his hands out of his pockets, put his hands together, and bowed to me. I choked back a sob and bowed to my sensei. When I rose, he was walking away, and I had to grab onto the side of the van. My head was clear, and I wasn't running on emotion or adrenaline anymore. I understood.

Maurice was the first one out of the house after Ever walked away. He caught me crying, holding on to the van. When I saw him, I flew into his arms, and he dropped the suitcase he was holding. I kept saying over and over, "Tell him I love him too. Tell him I love him too, Maurice."

He gave my body a squeeze, "I will Harri."

Chapter 13

None of the students had a clue who I was before arriving in Syracuse. This was something I had to remember. To everyone here, I was Harrison McCuff, a student and not a boxer or student in the art of Senshijutsu. My guard wasn't as high, but I had a hard time getting out of fighter mode. To me, it seemed better to be someone other than me while around new people in an area that was foreign to me.

Due to my junior status upon my arrival, I had the option of living off-campus. Before I left for school, I posted in the school paper I was looking for a roommate. Polly called me in answer to my ad. We were not on the phone long before we were talking about Syracuse, boys, the other ladies she lived with, and boys. There were four roommates, but one of them left school, and they needed another fourth. Polly and I made a date for me to visit. I went to visit them before the summer break. There was no snow on the ground in Syracuse. People were not bundled under coats, hats, and scarves. The trees had leaves, and the sun gave the city a bright glow. Unlike when I came to visit when a grey hue was the backdrop for the city.

Polly opened the door and she looked nothing like I thought she would. In my mind, she was light, big, and pretty. She was light, thin, beautiful, and had the blackest hair I had ever seen.

As soon as I walked in, they all wanted to hug me. We went to Acropolis to eat. They told me about where they were from and their majors. I told them what it was like living downstate in such a small city. They even took me to places not on the official Syracuse University Tour. We got to know each other, and I liked them. I hoped they liked me. We were both right.

My three roommates and I lived together in this great house. I never lived with anyone besides my brothers—let alone other women--I wasn't sure what to do. Although I decided to give this a real chance, at first, my training made them potential targets. It took me a while to trust they were three girls going to college and learning about life.

Noises made me jump from my sleep. When people walked by me or us, I was checking their movements, and my workouts were every day. After a month, my training subsided. I was sleeping through the night (mostly), I wasn't watching everyone's every move all the time, and I let my body rest.

I even started going to parties with my roommates Jolene, Nina, and Polly, joined a few clubs (Social Work Undergrad Association, African American Student Association, etc.), and thought about pledging to a sorority. It was a wonderful organization, but it wasn't for me. The ladies were OK, but with everything I had been through and the things I'd seen, sorority would add nothing to my life. Besides, Jolene, Nina, and Polly were plenty for me to handle.

Jolene was a white girl from Whiteface, Texas (yes, that is an actual place). I didn't know they made white girls that looked like her. She was not fat, but she had big thighs and a big butt. And she was proud of it.

She was the first person to go to college in her family and one of the few people in her town to leave Texas to go to college. She was naïve about what was going on in the world when she first arrived. Her town was extremely small, but she was not stupid. She learned a lot in the two years she lived here and was no longer the small-town girl she was when she arrived.

Jolene knew Polly. They were roommates in their freshman year. Polly was from Syracuse. Her mother made us food all the time. It was as if I was home with her fried chicken, potato salad, sweet potato pies, green beans, macaroni and cheese, and even collard greens. It wasn't my mother's, but it was damn delicious.

Polly had a boyfriend she'd had since high school. He wasn't in college. He worked at the post office.

And then there was Nina. She came from Darien, Connecticut. A tall, blonde beauty who came from money. She drove this badass 1998 BMW M Roadster. It was candy apple red with a brown leather interior. It was sweet. She had another car we rode around in, a 1998 SAAB 9000 CSE Turbo. She loved that car more than the roadster. The SAAB drove better than the BMW, which was why Nina loved it more than the other vehicle.

Their other roommate Lisa had a death in the family in the middle of their second year and decided not to come back to school. That left a spot for me with my new friends.

I had never met a woman who could have any man she wanted until I met Nina. I didn't know what she was doing, but I knew guys were at our house all the time for her. At first, I thought it was the money, but a lot of the guys had their own money. It was her. She was what they wanted.

Nina knew we were all interested in how she got these guys to follow her around like sick puppies and had no problem telling us everything.

"They just really like me."

"It's more than liking you, Nina. These guys are drooling over you," said Polly.

Nina laughed, "It's because of what I'm doing to them."

"What are you doing to them?" I asked.

"I've had threesomes, I've done DP."

"DP?" I asked.

"Double Penetration. It means that I have two guys penetrate me. One in my vagina and one in my ass."

I thought to myself, "I didn't know it had a name."

"There's a few of the guys who want to be dominated, which I'm good at. I also like being submissive. But I only do that with one guy. I don't trust the others. And, I have no gag reflex."

"No gag reflex?" I questioned again.

"Yeah, I can get a whole dick down my throat without gagging on it. A lot of people can't do that."

She wasn't embarrassed about it and talked to us all the time about it. My two sex teachers: porn and my roommate, Nina.

It was one hell of a year and allowed me to be free and young like everyone else. Sorry to say I didn't think about my training again. I didn't box, didn't practice any of my weaponry, I didn't even meditate. My skills were in there, but I buried them almost in my feet so they wouldn't interfere with my new life. My tools were buried too. They were far back in my closet; I couldn't see them even if I wanted to. It was the first time in five years someone wasn't watching me, and I took full advantage of it.

I began drinking, smoking marijuana, and going to any party I was invited to. I didn't have to think about anyone, I didn't have to worry about training, and I could do what I wanted without eyes on me. I loved my life before and wouldn't change it for anything, but this was outstanding.

Plus, I found boys! I had a few dates while I was learning the ancient Japanese art form of Senshijutsu. I liked boys, but there was no time for them in high school.

I tried to date once and Ever knew right away I wasn't focused on my training. He was right because the guy was hot; Kenneth Jordan. Oh, man. Chocolate skin, chocolate eyes, 5'10", and all muscle. He was a running back for New Rochelle High School's football team. I even considered letting him be my first. I wasn't ready for that, but he was the first boy who pursued me.

We went out for about six months, but when my training started suffering, I had to give him up. When we stopped dating, there were no tears or feelings of loss. I realized the feelings that were supposed to be there, those butterflies in your stomach when you like someone, were not there for me. I didn't want to give him up at the time. The fact that someone liked me made me feel sexy and wanted. But I had to let him go, and I'm glad I did.

In college, I met some guys, but there was nothing there. They didn't do it for me. They were cute, some were funny and a lot of them were smart, but it just didn't seem to be what I was looking for.

In all fairness to the guys, I was chasing the feeling I had with JC on his porch. He was on my mind a lot over the years after he left and that kiss we had. That kiss was the perfect storm: He was cute and older; I was young and in love; he was leaving; I was staying, and I had never been kissed and he knew it. I was bound to feel that way again. When you experience the perfect storm and have solid relationships as examples of what you should look for, I couldn't settle for anything less than the feeling I had with JC.

One thing that didn't change was going home to see my mother. I had to. When we lost Nunu, my mother realized how little of her older family she had left. My father had some aunts and uncles around, but Nunu was one of the last of her family. I think my mother needed me even though she didn't want to admit it.

When I went home, I spent a lot of time with her. My brothers weren't around much, and I knew she needed something to focus on. She had my father, but focusing on him wasn't the same as her children.

I was surprised no one asked me about Ever's Gym. My brothers told me later my parents thought I had given up on boxing and martial arts to pursue other things like boys. I laughed hysterically.

I told my brothers that wasn't it at all, but not to tell my parents. I told them I needed to take a break and so did Ever.

It was a good first year. I had friends, I had my family, I got an excellent GPA, and no thoughts of Senshijutsu.

Chapter 14

We were all busy in our last year of school. Our schedules were not as synced as they were before, but we saw each other occasionally. There were a lot of days when one of us had the house to ourselves. Today was my day and I was going to have the house to myself for a while since one of my classes got canceled.

I parked my Jetta a few houses from our house because our driveway was full. As I was walking towards the house, I noticed some guy standing outside. It was a jolt. Everything I had pushed to my feet and forgot came rushing back into my head with a snap. I stood frozen. I realized I was holding my breath, trying to remember my training. I headed back to the car before the figure caught sight of me. The need to be cautious was high, yet I couldn't shake the sense I knew this individual. There was something familiar about him, but he wasn't anyone I recognized.

I started the car and drove past him, watching out of the corner of my eye. The guy had black hair and a full beard. He wasn't giving off a dangerous vibe, but I wasn't confident in my ability to assess the situation yet.

I needed to know who this guy was, and the only way was to approach him and be prepared to fight. I parked the car again and reluctantly walked towards him.

"Can I help you?" keeping my fists balled to my sides as I approached him.

"Yes, you can, Harrison. You can give me a hug," he said.

My stomach did a flip. "JC!!!!" I ran to him, jumped into his arms, and dropped my bags. He gathered me into his arms and held me tight.

"What are you doing here? Why are you here? How are you here?" practically jumping up and down.

"I came to see you. Stand still," he was laughing and trying to hold me steady. His large hand touched my face and held it gently. "You look great, Harri."

My stomach was doing somersaults, "I can't believe you're here. I have so many questions. Come on," I commanded, pulling on his arm toward the front of the house.

He gathered my bags from the ground while I dragged him toward the entrance.

When we got upstairs, I peppered him with questions. He held his finger to my lips.

"Don't talk, just listen. I will explain everything, OK? First, for the last seven years, I've been living as Andre Colon. I love that you called me JC. I haven't heard that name in a long time. It's also good to see you again, Harri. You look exactly the same, just more filled out," he said, as his extraordinary eyes blazed and glowed while glancing me over.

His lingering eyes were making me giggle. Around fourteen I hit puberty, but when I was sixteen, all my parts came into full view of the world. I was 5'6", and slim, but my hips and breasts were anything but slim. I had put on some weight because I wasn't working out, and I am sure I lost some muscle, but I still looked amazing.

"Before I tell you the story," JC continued, "I want to tell you I've really missed you, and thank you for not telling anyone about me and my family. Jesy would be proud of you if she could see you." He stroked my face again and held my eyes with his for a few seconds. The old feelings were resurfacing again.

"When we left seven years ago, I couldn't tell you the whole story, but some things have changed for us. You were the first person I thought about when I realized we were safe.

"My father was a police officer in Tucson, Arizona. He worked undercover for three years in a drug cartel running out of Nogales, Mexico. They thought they had enough evidence to arrest the people who were working at the top of the cartel in Arizona and Mexico. So, they raided the Arizona house, and they arrested my father with them. My father wanted out of the cartel and police work. I don't know exactly what happened, but those three years changed my father somehow. They faked his death instead.

"He was gonna stay in Tucson, but his bosses decided it was too dangerous and sent him to New York to start a new life. This was never done before. Because the drugs were being brought into the country, this was a federal case. They went around the feds, got my father and us out, and no one ever came looking for us. I found out later, my father stuck around long enough to testify against these guys.

"We moved to New Rochelle, changed our names, and lost contact with everyone we knew. My real last name is Zayas. The rest of my name is real.

"My mother knew about this, but my sister and I didn't know when we moved. They had to tell me something 'cause I was a little older. My parents told us our father quit being a cop and wanted to get a new start. They said we couldn't contact our family because the new job was top secret, and we couldn't tell anyone. We were used to this with his undercover jobs, so we knew how to be quiet. When I was about fifteen, my father told me what happened. He was going to tell Jesy when she was older, but he never got a chance.

"The day they went to New York City, someone recognized Dad. He recognized the man and tried to push Jesy out of the way, but it was too late. There were two of them and they both were shooting at my father and Jesy. He tried to protect her, but Jesy was dead, and he was dying.

"When my mother found out what happened, she called his old captain immediately. No one knew where we went, not even him, so he knew something was wrong when he heard my mother's voice. When my father woke and saw his old captain, he started yelling the names of the men he saw. The captain called the federal authorities.

"The feds were pissed because they were not included in the operation and because they had to come in and clean up what Arizona did. The lead agent didn't even know how to hold anyone responsible because it had never happened before. The agents in charge at the local offices in Arizona and New York met to discuss what to do with everyone involved. They decided we had to leave New Rochelle.

"The men who my father worked for were still alive, and they needed us under protection. They weren't happy about it, but they did it. This meant we would have to leave my friends, my mom's friends, and you."

He grabbed my hand and paused for a few seconds. "I was so pissed at my father for a long time. When we got to Wisconsin, I started hanging out with these guys in my neighborhood who helped me get into trouble. My father tried to talk to me about it, but I would just blow him off or tell him all of this was his fault. He felt guilty. He wouldn't say anything. When I got arrested for the second time, my mother stepped in after my father tried to talk to me again and I told him I didn't have to listen to him. My mother came into my room, slammed the door, grabbed me around the neck, and pushed me against the wall. She told me if I didn't start showing my father some respect, I didn't have to worry about jail because she was gonna kill me. I'm sure you remember how my mother was when she was angry. This was worse than that. She was gonna hurt me if I didn't get it together.

"But the damage had been done. My father felt the need to make up for what he'd done to the family. I'm sure he was already thinking about going after the people who killed my sister, but me behaving like an asshole helped him make the decision.

"He told Mom and me he was probably gonna get killed, but he couldn't sit around and allow these men to live, and his daughter was dead. My mother pleaded with him, but he wouldn't listen. I apologized for my behavior and told him none of this was his fault. He told me what he had to do was not about what I had done. A little bit of him died each day over the last five years that those men were still alive. He had to do this.

"My mother could have called the feds, but she was afraid the feds would lock him up and she didn't think he could survive it. She couldn't call his old partner or his captain because we couldn't risk letting our location out. We knew there might be spies anywhere.

"My father didn't have to worry about the men from Mexico because the cartel broke apart a few years before. The only people left were the men in Arizona. My father told me the men he used to work for were brutal men and wouldn't stop looking for him because of what he'd done. My father wanted to kill the two guys who killed Jesy. He knew the head of the family in Arizona would still be alive and might still look for my mother and me, but we would still be under federal protection, so he was OK with that. We weren't OK with it, but my father didn't care what we thought at that point."

JC was fidgeting now, and I saw tears forming in his eyes. He paused again holding my hand tighter in his.

"I don't know how he did it, but he found the two men. My mother thinks he used contacts he had a long time ago. The men were not alone. And my father was right. The men he went after killed him, but before they killed him, he made sure he killed the men who killed his daughter."

JC was sobbing. I didn't know what to say or do. All the conversations I had with JC in my head, this was not the story he told me about what happened to my best friend. I held him and let him cry.

When he pulled away, I said, "I can't believe this was your life."

"I can't believe it sometimes either and I lived it," as he wiped his tears.

"Are you out of danger?" I took his hand into mine again. He placed his hand over my hand.

"Yeah. After my father killed Jesy's killers, the Arizona family started falling apart. Not only did they have the authorities after them, but other groups wanted to take over their interests because they saw their weakness. And in that business, it's usually a violent end. A lot of the men who were after my family were killed and the rest are in jail. The cartel broke up a year ago, but I needed to get my head together before I came to see you."

JC wiped his eyes again, "So, that's my story, and I don't want to talk about it anymore. I just needed you to know why we left. I thought about what you were doing and where you were all the time." He was caressing my cheek with the knuckle of his forehand. "Now, I want to talk about you, Harri. What have you been doing besides going to school?"

"Me? Well, I've been...wait a minute? How did you know where I was?"

"I called your mother."

"My mother didn't tell me you talked to her!"

"I told her not to. I wanted to surprise you. Now come on, I want to hear about what you've been doing since I left."

I took a deep breath and told him about my life after he left New Rochelle. I left out everything having to do with Senshijutsu but told the rest of my story until I got to SU. After we talked about me, we talked about Jesy. We both cried and laughed over his sister and my best friend. It was nice talking about her to someone who knew her.

When we continue to live when we lose someone, we think about them every day, but as time passes it becomes harder to remember their voice, their face, and what you did. It is easier having someone who knew them; who loved them as you did.

It was also nice to hear about things I didn't know about. Like when Mrs. Corrales told Jesenia we were spending too much time together and she wanted Jesenia to spend less time with me. Jesenia had a fit and refused to talk to her mother. She stayed in her room and would only come out to eat, go to school, or go to the bathroom. I recalled the time because I hadn't seen her for three days. His mother finally gave in, and Jesy and I were hanging out again. It felt really good to talk about that particular moment.

When we stopped talking, laughing, and crying, we were both sitting on my couch staring into each other's eyes. I'm not sure what made me do it, but I climbed into his lap, faced him, and placed my mouth hungrily onto his. I felt the same feelings I had when I was fourteen years old. My entire body heated up about ten degrees, my legs became weak, and my panties were wet. At fourteen,

I hadn't a clue what my body was doing with my first kiss and why it was happening to me. I knew now.

My hands were in his thick, black hair. His hands were on my ass, on my back, and in my hair. His beard and mustache were ticklish against my lips and chin. I thought they would be scratchier.

I'm not sure how long we were kissing, but I knew what I wanted. I pulled back. He tried to pull me back to him, looking at me with his eyebrows furrowed. I hopped from his lap and held out my hand for his. He rose from the sofa, placed his hand in mine, and we walked upstairs to my room.

I closed the door and started to remove my clothes. I had my shirt off, standing in my bra and pants when JC placed a restraining hand on my arm. His hands relaxed, and he lightly took my hands. He led me to the edge of the bed… He knelt in front of me,

"Are you sure about this, Harri?"

I gave a slow nod.

"We don't have to do this right now. We can wait."

"I don't want to wait, JC. I've been waiting for this since I was fourteen."

He smiled and kissed me with a hunger that belied my outward calm. Standing to his feet, he started removing his clothes.

When I tried to stand, he pushed me back onto the bed. I watched as he took off his shirt. He had been working out and he had been in the sun. His chest had some hair across it that went past his breasts and ended in an uneven V above his navel. He removed his pants, and my heart raced. He peeled off his underwear and revealed his dick to me, which was semi-hard already. I didn't know where I was supposed to look or what I was supposed to do.

When JC was finished, he stood me up and helped me out of my pants and my panties. He put his hands behind me and unhooked my bra. He kissed me on the forehead and took it off and let it fall to the floor. He stood in front of me, gazing into my eyes. I was exposed and open. I tried to look away, but he placed his hand under my chin, turning me toward him.

I reached out to feel between his legs. It was the first time I'd seen an actual penis up close or touched one. I didn't even know if I was doing it right. It did not feel the same as a dildo. It was warm and soft, and my touch was making him moan.

He raised his left arm and used his left thumb to rub over my right nipple. I closed my eyes and grabbed his right arm.

He leaned over and whispered in my ear, "Are you OK?"

Unable to speak, I nodded my head.

JC was squeezing my bud now. Moving his right arm to my back to hold me up, he continued massaging and squeezing my nipple.

I could feel my wetness dripping between my legs. He stopped and kissed me. He took my hand and led me to the bed, ordering me to lie down, and then he lay next to me.

"God, you are beautiful," looking down at me.

I smiled at him. Being with him was the feeling I had been waiting for. The touch of his hand made my skin feel like his hand belonged there. An electrifying shudder reverberated through me, and heat rushed from my face down to my feet. I was hot, and I kept feeling myself drip between my legs.

I touched his face,

"JC?"

"Yes, baby"

"Do you have...?"

"What do you need, Harri?"

"Do you have condoms with you?"

He smiled and laid down next to me, "I was so excited I didn't think about that. I didn't bring any with me."

To know he wasn't expecting sex or anticipating sex with someone else made me happy.

"Don't worry, I know where there are lots of condoms. You stay here."

"Tell me where they are, and I'll go get them. You stay here."

I put my hand on his chest, "No, I'll do it."

I rushed to Nina's room to steal a few from her drawer. As I was heading back to the room, I realized I didn't know what to do. Was he going to expect me to know what to do? Did he want to have sex with someone he had to teach?

I climbed into bed with him. He kissed me on my lips and my neck while he caressed my stomach and my nips. My abdomen was doing flips, and my heart was crashing against my chest.

He began caressing my breasts and then squeezing one of my nipples again. He moved his mouth to my other nipple. I moaned and squirmed, then moved my hand between his legs. I wanted to be a participant and not just a recipient, but I was fumbling and didn't know how I should hold it. I started stroking him as Nina had instructed. His moan against my breast made his lips reverberate against my nipple. It sent little shocks straight to my clit.

His hand left my nipple and traced from my breastbone down my stomach, past my navel to the top of my mound, leaving a trail of fire as he went. I let out a gasp and moaned when his fingers parted me and grazed my clit and stroked my opening. My hand was the only hand that had been between my legs for this purpose. JC's hand was bigger and knew what to do. He used two fingers and dragged my juices to my clit and did this squeezing-rubbing thing. I tried to duplicate this later and could never get it quite right.

He whispered in my ear,

"My God, you are so wet, Harri. Is that all for me?"

"Yes," I moaned back. I actually recalled thinking in an instant, "This is why Nina was a slut."

With his hand still between my legs, JC used his other hand to roll my right nipple between his fingers and put his mouth on the left, caressing it with his tongue. My hand was in his hair, holding him against my chest, while I moved my hips to receive more pressure from his fingers. He placed one finger slowly inside me while continuing to rub my clit.

With all these sensations, I was unable to think straight. My eyes were closed, my mouth open, panting. I was grabbing onto the bed and holding his head against me. My orgasm was starting, but this was different. It was coming from far away and building from my abdomen. The first sound I made was high-pitched and shaky.

Then I was calling for him, "JC. Oh, God, JC."

It felt like I could not stop coming, and I was going to float away. As I was coming down, I let go of him. He rose to look at my face while he smiled at me. My breathing was labored, and my heart was beating against my chest.

"Are you OK?"

I had a hard time gathering the words, "Yes, JC."

"We can stop."

"No, I want more."

He chuckled. "You do, huh? Well, aren't we greedy? OK. I have some more for you."

He moved down my body, leaving little kisses on my breasts, my stomach, and my thighs. I had only heard about this and seen it in porn. They did not do it justice.

JC kissed both my labia and then began sucking on them. It was a weird sensation. It felt great, but I also felt too sensitive. He licked my slit with the flat of his tongue. He opened me with this tongue and licked the opening to my pussy. My hands were in his hair again. His tongue was exploring inside my walls. He moved to my clit and lightly touched his tongue to it.

I threw my head back and my eyes rolled back into my head as he took my whole clit into his mouth and suckled it gently. He placed one finger inside me and then another. I took in air when he added the second finger. My cunt felt too tight for two fingers. He went slowly, but I felt like I was being stretched.

He waited for me to stop squirming and moved his fingers again a little faster. It was a little less uncomfortable. He increased the speed on my clit as well. I could feel another orgasm coming. This one did not feel the same as the last one. I felt it coming, but it felt like it was coming from everywhere. When I came, I screamed Javier and not JC. I kept his head pressed against my clit. I didn't want it to stop. Unwillingly, I let go of his head.

JC got up to put on the condom and whispered in my ear,

"Are you ready for me?"

I answered back, "Yes," not even knowing if I was ready or not.

He entered me a little at a time. I bit my lower lip so I wouldn't cry out.

I think JC knew because he would stop,

"Are you OK, do I need to stop?"

"No, I'm OK"

He started again and moved slow. I held on tight and tried to relax. He asked again if I wanted him to stop. I shook my head. I was afraid I would moan in pain if I opened my mouth, but I loved him so much for asking. Once he had it all in and we were pumping together, it didn't hurt as much.

JC raised one of my legs and went deeper inside me. I grabbed his back and dug my fingers into his skin.

"You still OK, Harri?"

"Ahh, yes, JC."

JC lifted my other leg and started pumping into me a little faster.

"Tell me if I need to stop, Harri," he whispered.

"Oh God, Javier. Don't stop."

"I won't baby. God, I'm so close. I wanna come so bad."

"Javier?"

"I love when you call me that. God, Harri, I'm gonna come. Fuck. Yes, Harri. Jesus, yes."

Listening to him call my name and come inside of me, I could feel another orgasm approaching causing me to brace myself by wrapping my legs firmly around his waist.

We both lay there holding each other after our orgasms. JC looked into my eyes and his mouth covered mine hungrily. The strong hardness of his lips sent new spirals of ecstasy through me.

"I've been in love with you since you were thirteen. I didn't think I would ever see you again. That kiss on my porch was everything to me."

"Yeah, well, I've been in love with you since I was seven." I started tearing up.

"What's wrong? Are you in pain?"

"No. I just didn't think this was ever going to happen. I think I've been waiting for you."

JC laid down and pulled me onto his chest. We lay together, not speaking, just caressing each other. We fell asleep, and when we woke, it was dark outside.

I heard the door slam and one set of feet on the stairs come up and then go back down.

I stared at him for a long time. He looked the same to me but with more muscles. I couldn't believe he was here, and he was in my bed. I wanted to tell him everything, but I couldn't. He didn't need to be a part of this after what he'd been through.

JC stayed in Syracuse for a week, even though a job was waiting for him in Boston. I showed him around Syracuse and the rest of his time was the two of us having sex.

When he left for home, we talked on the phone all the time, and we would visit each other at least once a month. During the holidays, the two of us would go to my parent's house in New Rochelle. He would sleep at a friend's house, but we saw each other every day. We got to know each other.

A sense of remorse came upon me that I was holding this piece of myself back from him, but I had to hide that part of my life. The only people who knew about Senshijutsu were Ever and Maurice. However, after all these years, no one knew who I really was and what I could really do. I always knew, even though Ever never directly stated it, I was keeping people safe by not telling them. Even with that, the time with JC was the happiest of my life to this day.

Chapter 15

My mind was made up, I decided I was going to stay in Syracuse to attend grad school. The social work program was one of the top programs in the country.

When I was in my second year of graduate school, JC asked me to come and live with him in Boston. We were in my room, and he was packing to go back home after spending a week with me and I was putting away clothes I just washed. I stood in front of my closet, stunned. I wasn't expecting him to ask me to move in with him or to leave Syracuse.

The last year and a half with JC filled me in ways I never knew were possible. I knew JC and his family since I was a child and it seemed like we just picked up where we left off, but there was so much to learn about each other. We were not the kids we left behind on that porch. We had both grown into young adults with thoughts, feelings, and ideas of our own. I watched him with my family, visiting with his mother, arguing with him, making up with him, and living with him sometimes. It was the first time since Jesenia died that I felt like a small piece was put back onto my heart. But it wasn't enough.

For two and a half years, I had been living like a normal person; not seeing the world through the eyes of a warrior. I was just a young lady going to college and falling in love. But JC brought the warrior back into me. I don't know why he was the trigger, but being with him, I realized I'd been neglecting who I was.

I wish I could tell you I resented being a warrior, and I didn't want the warrior to be my life, but that would be a lie and not my story. Yes, I was doing things during those years that had nothing to do with anything Ever had taught me, but when the warrior came back, I realized I missed it. I missed who I used to be.

With my back to him, "I can't do that JC, I'm in school."

"You can go to school in Boston. There's Harvard, Boston College, Wellesley..."

I turned to face him, "JC, I can't go with you. I have to stay here."

JC moved closer and put his hands on my hips, looking into my eyes, "Harri, you know I'm in love with you."

I put my hands on his hands, "I know JC. I'm in love with you, too. I don't think I'll love anyone else the way I love you, but I can't go."

"Por que?!!" (Why?!!!) he took his hands off my hips.

Por que hay algo que se supone que debo hacer aqui)"Because there's something I'm supposed to do here. I don't know what it is, but it's here that I have to do it."

"What the hell are you talkin' about?"

"I don't know, JC. I just know I have to be here."

"How do you know that if you don't know what it is?!" he said, throwing his hands up.

"I don't know! I feel it inside me!" I moved closer to him, "You being here has been the greatest thing that has happened to me since I met Ever. When I came to Syracuse, I got taken off my path. I wasn't seeing things clearly. There's something here for me to do. I don't know what it is, but I have to do it alone."

JC, stood staring at me for a moment and then said, "I'm not gonna see you again, am I? I don't understand anything you're talkin' about, but I get the feelin' that I'm not gonna see you again. Are you in witness protection? Why can't I help you?"

I gave a slight smile. "No, I'm not in witness protection. and no... you will not see me again. You can't come back here to me... I won't be here."

"Harrison?..."

I held my hands up. "JC, I think what I have to do is going to be hard and ugly and will mirror what you've gone through over the past eight years. You cannot go back to that." I held up my hands again to stop him from interrupting me.

"You helping me would mean going back to a life you just left. I know you want to, but I can't. You need to live, JC. I've lived my life the way I wanted to so far. You haven't, and I won't cause that."

His eyes were swimming with tears. "Harrison, I want to live my life with you. Please don't send me away. I need you. And I don't want to live some life that does not have you in it."

I was now choking on my tears. "I know. I love you, JC. This is the hardest thing that I've been through in my life, including losing Jesy. But I have to do this for you because I love you."

"You're not gonna tell me what you have to do, are you?"

"No. Even if I knew what it was, no. Please go back to Boston. Fall in love, get married, and have babies. Be happy."

Through a cracked voice, he said, "Harrison…"

"JC, please. Let me do this. The same way I had to let you go all those years ago, you have to do the same."

"You can't send me away and ask me to just love someone else. Is that what you're gonna do? Find someone else?!"

I placed my hand on the side of his face. "No, JC. I will not find someone else. I'm asking you to do this because I want what is best for you. And I want you to be happy without me."

"You can't ask this of me!"

"Yes, I can! The same way you asked it of me all those years ago. And I did it. You have to go, JC."

I knew JC did not have all the information, but I could not drag him into this life. I knew it would involve my skills, which meant it would be dangerous. It wasn't that I didn't think JC would understand, but I couldn't have him get hurt.

The one mistake people who are in dangerous lines of work make is believing they can live a normal life and do their dangerous job. I would rather see JC happy with someone else than hurt with me.

JC stood looking at me. He turned and grabbed his bag from the bed and started putting clothes in it. I didn't move from my spot. I watched him pack his clothes as he mumbled to himself, he didn't understand. He stopped and turned to me.

"This is bullshit, Harri! My issue was different from yours. Fuck what am I talkin' about? I don't even know what your issue is. Why can't we fight this together?"

"Because you can't. You can't be a part of this JC. You have to go. I don't know what else you want me to fucking say."

"You know what I want you to fucking say. I want you to tell me what is happening."

"I can't do that."

"Fuck!"

"JC, please."

"You know what, I'm not going."

"Yes, you are. JC, I am drowning, but I can't keep you."

JC put his arms around me. My face was pressed against his chest.

"Harri, I can't do this. Please don't make me do this."

Tears were streaming down my face, making his shirt wet along with my face. I pulled my face away from his chest and looked at him. Tears were streaming down his face. His eyes held a sadness I had forgotten he had. A sob caught in my throat.

"JC, I'm sorry."

He closed his eyes, and we stood there with his arms still holding me. He kissed me on the forehead, turned, and went back to packing his bag. I put my hand out to grab the dresser. He didn't say anything else to me, and I stood there while he got his things together.

When he was done, I watched him walk out my door—never seeing him again. I then crumpled into a pile and cried for three days.

After JC left, I knew it was time to go home. I needed to get my warrior back. I didn't feel like doing that. I was heartbroken. The only pain that even came close to it was when JC left me on the porch. The fucked-up thing was this time I left him, and I still felt like shit.

I knew Ever was the only person that could pull me back. He would not let me wallow in my pain. He would make me use it, and that's what I needed. I needed to find my way back and see if what he taught me was really still inside me.

My ex-roommates and I were searching for dresses for a party we were going to. I had no desire to go to this party, but they came for a visit and said I needed to get out of my head. They also told me they were going to tie me up and drag me there if they had to. It had been two months since JC left.

We were walking through Carousel Mall. The three of them were talking about the party. My mind was not on this party. I was trying to figure out how I could get out of this party. My pace was a step behind my friends. I noticed this guy walking towards us with a woman. They looked familiar, but my mind was so clouded. Then he spoke,

"Harrison."

It was Maurice. Candy was with him. When he said my name, my feet wouldn't move from the floor, like they were stuck. In my head, I said to myself, "It's Maurice."

I ran to him, threw my arms around his neck, and he almost fell over. When he righted himself, I burst into tears.

"Harrison? What's the matter?" He tried to push me away to look at me, but I wouldn't let him go. I couldn't tell him. It was easy to tell my roommates because they didn't know the whole story about JC and me. Maurice didn't know the whole story either, but he knew me.

My friends were staring at me confused about the two individuals that stood before them. I introduced them all through my tears. Candy gave me a tissue during my introduction. I explained Maurice was like a brother to me, and Candy was his wife. Everyone said hello or shook hands.

Maurice was glancing at this watch, so I knew he needed to go somewhere else. I wanted to know what he was doing in Syracuse and how long he was going to be in town.

Candy was talking to my friends. Maurice was looking at me.

"Don't want to talk in front of them?"

"It's not just that, but yes."

"OK. Why don't we go to dinner tonight."

"Yes. Text me."

We hugged. I hugged Candy, and I joined my friends.

"So, where do you know him from?" Nina asked.

"It's a long story I might tell you guys one day."

"Didn't you grow up in the suburbs? Rich suburbs?" asked Polly

"Yeah, I did."

"Then where on God's green earth would you meet a pimp?" We all stopped and looked at Polly.

"How do you know that?" I asked in a whisper voice.

"He is?" both Nina and Jolene asked at the same time, looking at me. I was still looking at Polly.

"I grew up in the hood. I recognize a pimp when I see one. Not judging, just wondering."

"Another time, I will tell you guys about Maurice. Just not now."

"OK, but we will come back to this," said Jolene.

Maurice and I met at a place in the mall and sat at a back table.

"You look really good, Harrison."

"Thanks, Maurice, but what the hell are you doing in Syracuse, and where's Candy?"

"No. We are going to start with why you were crying as soon as you saw me?"

I sighed. "I'm sorry. As soon as I saw you, all the emotions about breaking up with my boyfriend hit me."

I gave him some of the story about JC and me. I only gave him the highlights of the story JC told me, but I told him about what happened when I was fourteen and what was happening now.

He rose from his seat and wrapped his arms around me. I teared up a little and then pulled myself together.

"Do you want to talk some more about this?"

"No. There's nothing to say. My heart is broken and there's nothing I can do about it. I know I made the right choice, and I would make the same one again if I had to do it over, but it hurts so bad," I dabbed at my eyes with one of the napkins. "But I do want to talk about you. What are you doing here, Maurice?"

"I'm not in Syracuse. I'm living in Cicero. I told Candy I wanted to talk to you alone."

"Cicero?! Why would you be living in Cicero?"

"Well, things were kind of drying up in New Ro with the town going to hell, so I thought we needed a new start?"

"In Cicero?"

"Yeah, Cicero! You would be amazed at how easy it is to get into the game there. Not a lot of competition and lots of horny rural men."

"You can't make any real money with just the men in Cicero, Maurice. I'm not that naïve girl anymore. How long have you been here?"

"About eight months."

"Maurice, why didn't you call me?"

"I didn't want to disturb your life, Harri. You seem to have a good thing going here."

"You've been watching me? For how long?"

He shrugged his shoulders, "A few years."

"Years?! Why?"

"Just wanted to make sure you were OK. Ever did too."

"So, you both have been hiding in the shadows? Why didn't you tell me you were around?"

"Because we weren't around, and we didn't want you to know. We knew you wouldn't like it."

"You're right, I don't like it."

"Yeah, well, we don't care. We both love you, and we needed to know that you were OK out here. Stop getting so mad, Harri. We weren't following you around. We checked in now and then."

"Fine. I'll let it go," then I switched gears. "So you gonna tell me how you're surviving? I know it's not off of sex in Cicero."

"Not really. I mostly work in Syracuse, but my base is in Cicero."

"How do the other pimps feel about that?"

"I wouldn't know. I try not to get in their way, and they stay out of mine. And that's all you need to know."

"Maurice? You're a new pimp coming into their territory. Even I know they wouldn't just let you come in like that."

"When did you get so smart? Look, I still do the high-end. I try to stay away from the street stuff. That's what most of these pimps are into. Besides, I have connections here that you don't need to know about, so don't ask," he said, putting up his hand to stop any more questions.

"Fine. How's Ever?"

"My father's fine. You should call him."

"I plan to. Does he know where you are?"

"Not really, but he could find me if he wanted to."

"Is this it? Are you gonna be here?"

"Yeah, this seems to be it."

I thought I was going to have to go to Cicero to see Maurice, but he worked out of a bar near downtown. Everyone who was a patron of the bar knew what was going on, but no one cared or made an issue of it. They came in, drank, danced, and partied, and paid no attention to the girls going in and out of the back area. Somehow, having Maurice in Syracuse made me feel a little safe. I was glad he was here, but I wasn't going to tell him that.

Chapter 16

Thanksgiving was more hectic and crazier than most holidays for our family. The entire family gathered in one place. That year it was in New Rochelle, and it was as nuts as always.

That year's seating arrangements had to be redone because my Aunt Pat wouldn't sit next to my Aunt Lola, one of my cousins on my father's side had to be separated because one of my cousins owed the other one money, and my uncle George, who showed up drunk, fought with his daughter's boyfriend. When the dance party started, everyone loved each other again, at least until we picked a winner.

It was perfect timing. I could visit with my family and check in with Ever. It was time. I didn't know exactly what it was time for, but I could feel it inside me. Something was about to happen, and I wasn't ready.

The Tuesday after Thanksgiving, I went to the gym. I was going to call, but I was afraid he would tell me he didn't want me to come to the gym. I knew it was irrational, but Ever and I had had no communication in two years. When I came home while dating JC, I did not see him. My mom would always ask why I wasn't visiting Mr. Evers, and my response would be he was busy.

When I entered the gym, Ever happened to be in the ring. I went into his office and sat at my old desk, waiting for him.

"Hello, Harrison. How are you?"

I stood to my feet, "I'm fine Ever. And you?"

He strolled over to his desk and sat in his seat facing me. "Have you seen Maurice?"

"He told me you didn't know where he was.""I can find him if I need to. How is he?"

"He's OK. Why?"

"He had some people after him here. The game was tight, and some people tried to take over what was Maurice's."

"Didn't you help him?"

"He wouldn't have wanted me to do that. So, I didn't," He stared at me for a few seconds, "How's your training going."

I dropped my head low. "I'm not training, Ever. I have no one to train with."

"Plus, it feels good to be a regular person, right?"

I looked him in the eye. "How d'you know that?"

He smirked. "Because I know you. You would never complain about your situation, but you wanted to be a regular kid too. The first chance you got, that's what you did. And you should. But I suspect that's over. You need to train, Harrison."

"I know, Ever, but what am I supposed to do?"

"You can start training with me again when you're home, and I'll get you some jobs when you're ready."

I sat in my seat again. "Jobs? What jobs?"

"Jobs where your skills will be used and honed. You weren't ready before. This is how you will train."

"You can do that?"

"Yeah. Just haven't till now. Mostly because of what I was afraid of for you."

"What are you talkin' about?"

"Harri, you know the story of Senshijutsu and Hajime Ino, but you don't know my whole story."

"You told me your story."

"No, I didn't tell you everything. The art was important, not me. I should have told you years ago, but I wasn't sure you wanted this life, and I didn't want to influence your decision. Now that you're back, I need to tell you everything."

"You know, my father was stationed in Japan, and I lived there most of my childhood. My father moved to Colombia, and I lived there until I came back to the United States with Josephina. What you don't know is I learned Senshijutsu when I lived in Colombia from a disciple of Hajime Ino.

"When I arrived in Colombia, I didn't know what my father did for a living. The only thing I knew was he was in the army. We started going to this beautiful house. It was bigger than any house I had ever seen. It was on acres and acres of land. There was a pool, a huge backyard, lots of rooms, and two kitchens. We ate dinner with the people who lived in this house. I even played with the children who lived in this house. We kind of became a part of the family. They treated me as if I was one of their kids. My father didn't seem to mind.

"They discharged my father from the army, and we became permanent residents in this house. I still didn't know what my father did, but I loved being in that house. Mr. Delgadillo's children became my brothers and sisters. I loved them and would do anything for them.

"I tried to ask my father once what he did for a living. All he would tell me was he was a private contractor. When I tried to get more information about what a private contractor does, he got angry, and I dropped the subject.

"The Delgadillos were a part of the legacy of Hajime Ino. The head of the household, Roberto Delgadillo, taught me Senshijutsu. I went through a very similar training to your training, but I didn't have school to focus on or my family as you did. I trained for six years from when I was about ten or eleven. When I finished, I was a trained assassin. I didn't even know what that was, really.

"I was seventeen when he sent me on my first job, which was to steal something; a statue from this guy's house. From that day on, I worked for the cartel. I did their odd jobs.

"The Art of the Warrior was not supposed to be used to make us into assassins or thieves; the purpose of the art was to make us warriors and protect others. I found out what it was on my own, and it was not easy. No one wanted to talk about it, but I did find out. And I found out they were misusing Senshijutsu and me.

"I was young, so deep in, and had a father who was proud of what I had become. I didn't know what to do to get out. I couldn't confide in my brothers and sisters because they were a part of the life too. My brother Manuel took over the business when his father died.

I did finally find my way out with the help of my brother. I knew I couldn't stay a part of that life if I wanted to raise my son. He saw more than he should have, and I couldn't allow it. Plus, Josephina was not going to stay with me if I stayed in this life."

"She knew what you did?"

"Yes. I told her everything. She grew up in that life but knew she didn't want to stay in it, so I had to find a way. I don't want what I had for you, Harrison. You do not have to become what I became. You can help people and do better than I did."

"Where was your father? Couldn't he stop them?"

"He didn't want to stop them. He liked the level I had achieved in the cartel. It gave him status too. My mother couldn't help me either. She wasn't a very strong woman."

"I don't know what to say. How did the cartel feel about you leaving?"

Ever looked me in the eye, "I never really left. I go home now and then. But we have family here in the U.S." "You still do jobs for them?"

"Not really. I just help them out sometimes with surveillance. Manuel died some time ago. The people left in the organization don't see me as a threat anymore. I'm old now."

"How could you work for them?"

"No one gave me a choice, Harrison. But that does not have to be your life. You are choosing whether you want to do this and how you want to do it. I did what I needed to do, and I guess, so will you."

"I guess. What will these jobs be? Am I going to work for them?"

"No. They don't know you exist. You will work for people who are in trouble. Nothing like what I did. When you go back to Syracuse, I'll set up some work for you. You can work the jobs and determine if this is the life you want. I want your life with Senshijutsu to be different from mine. In the meantime, you need to get back to training. You can start today. Come back when the gym is closed."

I stood and turned to him. "Thanks Ever."

"You don't need to thank me."

"Yes, I do, and you know I do. You didn't have to tell me that story and I would have stayed..."

"Don't. We're here now. We don't dwell.""Yes, Sensei," I gave him the respected bow.

"Ten o'clock. Don't be late and bring aspirin. You're going to be in pain."

Chapter 17

Working out with Ever again showed me what being a regular person could do to a warrior. Every muscle I had hurt that first night. I could barely walk into my parent's house after three hours of training. I didn't even take off my clothes. I climbed into bed and when I woke, I noticed I had on one shoe.

By the end of the week, I was at the same level as my seventeen-year-old self. And by the time Christmas break was over, I was back to where I was before I left for Syracuse. I didn't have too much to do for my mind to reset, but my body would not cooperate. Thank God for the Christmas break.

My family hadn't noticed any change in me. They'd assumed I was working out again, which meant I was focused.

When I returned to Syracuse after Christmas break, Ever found some "jobs" for me. He wanted to make sure I sharpened all my skills, so my jobs were varied. They included security, surveillance, tracking, and setting up harder jobs for my non-existent boss.

Yes, I pretended to be the "secretary" of a thief and an enforcer. Most men, even though we were moving into the next century, didn't want their organization to be seen as weak by hiring a woman. So, I lied. I told them my imaginary "boss" sent me to scout things out and then "he" would come in and take care of the rest. They, of course, never saw "him," which made "him" more believable.

I had one or two women clients, and they had the same problems with me as the men did. One of my first jobs was for a woman looking for her son. Even though Ever gave me the information about the woman, I checked her out myself.

After watching for a few days, I found out she had an ex-husband, two more children, and a routine. She didn't have any enemies. There were no real issues within the family except for the missing son, and to me, she appeared to be a good mother. I showed up at her house a week after her initial call.

When Mrs. Talbot opened the door, her eyes were wide, she was looking me over and her mouth was slightly open.

Glancing behind me,

"Yes, may I help you?"

"No, I'm here to help you. I believe you're looking for someone?"

"You're the person who's going to help us?"

"Yes, I am. May I come in?"

She moved to the side, and I walked into her house. It took me forty-five minutes to get to her huge house in Skaneateles. I knew she was a lawyer in Syracuse, and her ex-husband worked in the mayor's office. They were big money, and I was receiving a lot of money for this job.

As we walked into her living room with three couches and two chairs, "Will your ex-husband be joining us?"

Before she sat on her huge couch, she stared for a few seconds and then sat down, "Um...no my ex doesn't know I called anyone." All of her furniture complimented each other. Things didn't necessarily match, but you could tell a professional had been in this room. I sat on her other huge couch, "I understand your ex-husband and a couple of PIs looked for your son with no success. Is that correct?"

"Yes. But you're just a woman and a small one at that. You're going to have to go into another world."

I smiled, "You're free not to take my help, but because the men couldn't do anything doesn't mean I can't. I'm the best. The amount of money you're paying, you won't get anything less than excellence. The money you paid those men was a waste; I'm not."

"How are you going to find him?"

"Tell me what's going on first, and then we can talk about what I'm gonna do."

She paused, "My son and my ex-husband are very much alike. They look alike, walk alike, they even speak alike. They are essentially the same person. I think that's why it was so hard for my ex-husband to accept him. My ex did not reject my son, but it took him a while to come to terms with who my son is. By the time my ex-husband got over his issues, my son was gone.

"The last few years have been hard for us. Lewis is seventeen, but our trouble started when he was fourteen. He was hanging around some older kids. They were into drugs and had access to anything. My ex and I were going through a divorce, and we didn't notice what was going on. Of course, this is my fault because he was living with me."

She pulled a tissue out of her dress like magic and wiped her eyes before she continued, "When we realized what was happening to our son, we got him into rehab, but it didn't work. When he came out, he continued to do drugs. No, that is not entirely true. He stopped for a while, but I don't think he ever completely stopped. I tried to keep him on a short leash, but he wouldn't listen to me. I tried sending him to his father, but that was worse. He's been to rehab three times in three years. When he went to rehab the last time, he was smoking crack.

"After Lewis came home, he changed nothing. I tried to make his father more involved, but Lewis wouldn't even talk to his father. I knew something was wrong because Lewis always came home." She pounded her fist on the arm of the soft sofa. "I thought he went to a friend's house, but when he didn't come back after a few days. His father and I called around and none of his friends would admit to seeing him. That was about eight months ago.

"We called the police, and they couldn't find him. My husband got some phone numbers for private investigators from a friend. We called three. We only had success with one PI. He found out Lewis was in Syracuse, on drugs, and involved in some pros... prostitution ring. When he got close to finding him, some men put him in the hospital."

Her eyes were swimming in tears and the tissue she had was now a tight little ball.

"His brother and sister keep asking us where he is, and I don't know what to tell them except he's in trouble, and Daddy and I are trying to find him. I just want someone to find my son and bring him back to me! Can you do that?"

"I can, but you need to understand something, Mrs. Talbot." I sat in a chair next to the couch she was sitting on. "I can find your son, but he will not be the son who left your house. If what you're telling me is true, your son is gonna need rehab and lots of counseling."

"I know. We can find him a place."

"No, you can't. The place you're going to send him, Mrs. Talbot, will not help your son. I have a place that he can go, but you need to understand, he'll be gone for six months to a year."

Her eyes widened and her mouth dropped, "A year?"

"Yes, and you can't contact him for the first month. This rehab is very effective and has a low recidivism rate. I know you've been dealing with rehabs for the last few years, but they were all bullshit. Ninety-day rehabs don't work and most of the ones you probably sent him to are not effective either. All they do is clean the drugs out of your system, and that's only the first step for addicts. Can you and your husband live with this?"

"I don't know. I want to see my son and I'm sure my ex would too. We have been dealing with my son's addiction for three years and if this can be the end of it, I want to try it. That is what you're promising, right?"

"No, I'm not Mrs. Talbot. Your son has to want this for this to work, but this is your best chance. I do promise I will find your son. After that, I can't say what will happen."

"Have you encountered this before? Do you know anything about this life he's into?"

"I've heard rumors of it in Syracuse. I know where to look."

"How will we contact you?"

"You won't. I'll contact you if I need something. I need a picture of your son."

"Do you want the contact information for the private investigator we used?"

"No, that won't help me. Whatever they found out is worthless. I'm going to start from scratch."

"Are you sure you can handle this?" she asked as she handed me a picture of her son.

I stood to my feet and glared at the wary woman, "Look, Mrs. Talbot, although we've been having a conversation here, you've been looking at me like I'm an intruder in your home. Your husband and all the men you hired couldn't find your son. I know what I'm doing, but if you feel more comfortable with a man, then please hire one. I have other jobs."

"I'm sorry. I didn't mean to do that. I just didn't know women did what you do."

"They don't usually, but I do. I get results, Mrs. Talbot."

"I apologize. Please help me find my son." She said grabbing my hand.

Unfortunately, she wouldn't be the last sister I would have to convince to let me do my job.

After I met with Mrs. Talbot, I went to the North side and met with someone I was sure knew all about the sex trade in Syracuse.

I arrived at a nondescript house on Van Rensselaer Street. A huge man answered the door. That was the only thing descriptive about him. An average white man except for his four hundred-pound body.

"What can I do for you?" He said after he let me in.

We trekked through a long hallway to a kitchen where I could see pot tops bouncing or releasing steam. Tomatoes, basil, and garlic filled my nose, and saliva collected inside my mouth. Those were the only parts of his house I had ever seen.

"I need to know who's running gay prostitutes in the city?" I sat at a plastic wooden table that looked like it belonged to the people who lived in the house forty-five years ago.

"You go big, dontcha?" with his back to me while he stirred whatever was in one of the two enormous pots on the one stove.

"Do you know?"

"You're the second person to ask me about that this week."

"Who was the first?"

He stopped stirring. "Well, she asked about girls. You're asking about guys," He went back to stirring.

"Who's she?"

He turned around. "This young girl who thinks she's a detective. Her father works maintenance at the police department. When she's investigating, they give her some space to do it."

"So, what do you know?"

He turned back to his pots. "I know a lot."

"Are you gonna tell me?"

He turns back around and holds out his hand. "You know the price."

"How are you still here when you're available to the highest bidder?"

"Not everyone knows what I do and the people who do aren't talkin'."

I smirked at the large man before retrieving a large manila envelope from the inner pocket of my jacket. Two thousand dollars is a lot of money, but he's never failed me. I gave him two thousand dollars,

"OK. What do you have?"

"There's a tiny business with men going on. It's on the East side."

"Where?"

"It's a house on Canal Street. The woman who runs it is Taylor. You're never gonna get past her. She runs a tight operation."

"Don't worry about that. Who can tell me how the operation works?"

"I know someone, but he won't talk to you. I'll find out and get back to you."

He got back to me within two days, and his source told him Taylor had men standing guard inside. Most of the sex workers were strung out on heroin or cocaine. Any drug that kept them compliant while they worked. Some of the workers were young. No services were performed at the house. It was a place to check in with the money they made and where they rested while waiting for their next john.

All their cash was handed over to Dame Taylor, and no one held out on her. The source also stated although she bought them clothes, and let them have free time, it is rumored, she was sleeping with a few of them, it is also rumored she abuses them, will give them to anyone willing to pay, and is making a lot of money.

Taylor Mitchell was not what I thought she would be at all. She was average height, she had a flawless dark-skinned complexion, and when she walked her feet were gliding like she was walking on air while still commanding the sidewalk. Her clothes hung on her frame perfectly, and they looked expensive. I think I was expecting what I was told about her workers.

She always had someone with her, and she kept a low profile, even when she went out. From there I focused on the house, watching who was coming and going. Little by little I analyzed each individual's patterns.

I studied the layout, the guard's movements, and who the other men were. I would have to go in to remove Lewis, which meant a fight and possibly killing people. I didn't want to kill anyone, and it would be hard to do this alone. So, to avoid all of that I took Lewis on the street.

I followed the young man who was with a client at a motel outside of Syracuse. I knew a car would be at the motel to pick him up and either take him to a new date or back to the house. When the car arrived, I was waiting for the driver to get out of the car. I crept behind him. I smacked him across the back of the head. He fell to the ground, holding his head. He tried to turn his head, and I hit him again. I put him back in his car.

Lewis came out of the house carrying a bag, walking to the car he believed was waiting for him. When he put his hand on the door handle to the back door, I stepped forward and used my rag and chloroform to put him out. I placed him in my van, and we drove away.

I took him to my friend Victor's house in Chittenango. He was on vacation and wouldn't even know we were there. When Lewis came to later that morning, I explained who I was.

"Hello, Lewis."

"He scooted back to the headboard, "Who the fuck are you?"

"My name is Tara. I was hired by your mother to find you."

"Maybe I don't want to be found. You can't keep me here."

"I actually can, and I'm sure you didn't want to be found. Your mother needed to know you were OK."

"Well, you can go back and tell her I'm fine and take me back to my friends."

"Those people are not your friends, and your mother wants to see you."

"I'm not going back."

"You're right. You're not. You're going to rehab."

He tried to move off the bed. I pushed him back to the bed. He tried again, and I pushed him back again. He glared at me. He started yelling.

"HELP. Help me! Help."

"Stop yelling. That is not going to help you. Lewis, I know you're scared and probably really pissed off, right?"

"Fuck you, you fucking cunt."

"I am going to get you clean."

"I don't want to be fucking clean. I like my life. Fuck you and my mother. Let me out of here."

He got off the bed and tried to rush me. I pushed him to the side, and he fell into the dresser.

"You bitch!"

He lunged at me again, and I threw him back onto the bed. When he tried again, I pushed him back again, but I got on top of him and put his arms in restraints. He tried to kick me a couple of times when I put his legs in restraints.

Lewis tried screaming again and I gagged him. He was crying and fighting, but he finally fell asleep. When he woke up a few hours later, he struggled a few times but gave up fighting.

The next night, Lewis fell ill.

"Tara, please. I'm so sick. I just need a little."

I walked over to the side of his bed. He was sweating and his skin looked pale. "Lewis, I know you're hurting. It is going to pass, but it's going to hurt."

"Please, just call my mother. Tell her how sick I am. She will tell you to give me something."

"She might, but that's not what you need. I'm going to take you somewhere where they will help you."

"I can do that. I can go, but I just need something. I will go, I just want one more hit. And can you untie me please?"

"No, to everything. I'll be here. I know you're not hungry, but I will be here when you are."

I gave him nothing. I'd seen it before, and I knew sooner or later the pain was going to overtake him. I had never been through it myself at the time, but I was told it hurts like a bitch until that shit seeps out of your system. And how long it took depended on the drug and how long the person was an addict. By the next night, Lewis agreed to go to rehab. Upon his arrival, he was in tears due to the pain he was having.

I came back and gave his mother an update.

"I found him as I told you on the phone. He was combative like I told you he would be. He is at rehab, and they are getting him started with his recovery. Please remember, Mrs. Talbot, you cannot call Lewis for a month."

"I remember. Did he ask for me?"

"He did ask for you. While he was coming down and after going to rehab. His head is clearer. Also, let your ex know he can't speak to him either."

"I understand. How am I going to repay you for this?"

"You already have by paying me. Plus, this is not done yet. Your son still has to make it through rehab and even then, he is going to need support."

"I know, but the fact I know where he is, and he is relatively safe is more than I've had in eight months. Thank you."

Lewis stayed in rehab for eight months. His withdrawal lasted two weeks. Although Lewis left rehab before a year, his counselors felt he needed more time but could do the time outside of the rehabilitation center. He attended all his therapy appointments while in rehab, was open about his feelings and history with drugs, and took responsibility for his actions.

His release was conditional on spending five months in a halfway house in Vermont. He did every day of his time there. When he was released, his parents decided it wasn't a good idea for him to come home to his old friends and familiar bad habits. Lewis said it was the first time his parents had agreed on anything in five years.

Lewis also wanted to go to school. His parents agreed again and told him no. They wanted him to have some more sober time before he added something to his plate. He was not happy about it, but he did as they asked.

Eventually, they let Lewis go to school in Vermont. He spent four years there, and I think he is still there. Lewis had one slip in his first year of school, immediately called his father who came to Vermont and went with him to NA meetings. He never slipped again, finished college, and is working for a production company in Vermont. Lewis was one of my first successes.

They never saw me again, and I never saw them.

Chapter 18

Along with locating the lost, Ever had me doing security jobs. The jobs were evaluating an existing security system and pointing out the holes. I would sneak into their compounds, disarm their men, and even kidnap some clients while they were away from home. The men they had for security were always amazed and pissed. Once, Ever called me and told me I needed to be more subtle. I laughed hysterically, but I told him I would try. It wasn't my fault they hired shitty people. And I wasn't trying to embarrass anyone; I wanted to have a good reputation.

After I pointed out their problems, I would demonstrate how to fix it. Those security jobs were the only jobs I ever took where they paid me directly.

Ever was comfortable enough, on the completion of my security work, that he sent me on surveillance and tracking jobs. It was the easiest of all my jobs. The job involved me tailing the subjects to wherever location they were headed, recording what they were doing and if they were doing it with another person, and reporting back to the client with details. The subjects or their companions never knew I was tailing them. It was amazing to me how many people don't pay attention to their surroundings. I was a smallish black woman, and no one paid any attention to me as long as I carried myself as if I belonged where I was.

What I enjoyed most about the job was now and then I had the opportunity to wear "costumes." For instance, I dressed as a street walker for the Lewis case. I dressed in a business suit to blend in with Wall Street investors to catch a sneaky broker who was ripping his clients off. There was also the time I was a street vendor surveying a runaway girl.

The surveillance took more time than the tracking. People tend to believe all I do is follow someone for a week and memorize their routine, but surveillance was not that easy. You have to follow them for a few months to find their pattern (if they have one). If they don't have one, you have to figure out what you can from their movements, predict their next move, and, develop a plan from there.

All the clients I worked with while I was doing surveillance and tracking became impatient. Still, everyone loved the results I gave. My motto to my clients was, "If you want it fast, you won't find them, and I <u>will</u> get caught." I never changed my method. Instead, I managed their anger and kept doing my job.

The assignments I took were preparing me to determine if this was what I wanted to do. After about a year of these jobs, it was time to decide what I wanted.

"You've been going on jobs for a year. Is this the life you want?"

"This is what I need to do. And yes, I want to do it."

Ever smiled, "I thought so. You are a natural, Harrison."

I smiled, "I feel like I know who I am."

"Good, 'cause I think it's time to send you on more rigorous jobs. I know you can handle it. You'll start protecting people."

Preventing men from killing each other took a lot of planning and a lot of waiting. It worked like this: I would receive the name of a client and question the client and the staff to find out how they lived. The questions were invasive and always made everyone uncomfortable since they were always men, and they wouldn't want to tell me the real shit happening when it came to their sex lives. Why were their sex lives important? Because the sex people have explained a lot about them and how they lived. Discerning their environment, who they lived with, the job they had, and the people they associated with was not enough. What people did in the dark was who they really were. So, when we got to the sex part, I always had to look them in the eyes and say,

"I have seen and heard every kind of kink you can think of and even a few you haven't. You are not going to shock me, and I'm not gonna judge you. But I need to know."

Every once in a while, there was some asshole who would try to shock me with something I hadn't heard of, but I never let it show. As a part of what I did, I had to know what the perverts and freaks were doing, so, when I say there is nothing that shocks me, nothing does.

Once I had all the questions out of the way, I would start watching. If I knew who was after my client, I would watch my client and the person after him. I have to say I'd only encountered a couple of professional hitmen in my time. Most of the people I'd encountered who believed themselves assassins were amateurs, and I always saw them coming.

I never had the chance to catch the professionals. What was played on television was not real. Professionals were never caught for the most part and those who worked for the government weren't ever snagged; they were killed. We were an elite group; none of us knew the other.

My third protection job was working for a guy who was a witness to a mob hit. He was smoking a cigarette in the alley when the hit happened. The two men who killed the mobster shot at my client and tried to chase him down. It was obvious how sloppy these guys were since the target was able to slip away.

The problem was all this took place outside a restaurant where the employees knew who my client was. The two men came back a few days later and were given the man's name and where he lived. After finding out some things about his life, I did some surveillance on him along with the mobster.

My client, let's call him Fred, had no wife and no children. I had to keep him safe. His only living relative lived outside the U.S., so there was little chance of them becoming a part of this. Plus, my client was such an asshole, I doubted his relative would've cared.

When I arrived for our meeting, the client looked at me, his eyes grazing over my body and behind me. He frowned when he saw no one behind me.

"What the fuck is this? Who the fuck are you?" said Fred. Three bodyguards were standing around the room.

"I work for Mr. Lang. He is in charge, but I do the inside work and he works from the outside."

He chuckled and some of the guards laughed. "What the fuck are you going to do to prevent my death? You are one person, a woman no less, and you look like you couldn't fight one of these guys," he chuckled again.

"Look, Mr. Fred, you contacted us. If you don't want me here, you can take your chances with people who aren't as good as us," I stood while looking around the room. "I have other jobs," I turned to make my way to the door.

"Wait, I want to talk to your boss."

I stopped and turned, "Fine."

I dialed my boss's number (Ever). I put him on speaker.

"Mr. Lang, our client wants to talk to you."

"What's the problem, Mr. Fred?"

"The problem is you sent me some woman who doesn't look like much of anything."

"Mr. Fred, you paid me a lot of money. Do you think I would send you someone who can't do the job? You are free to fire her if you want, but I suspect my colleague could take out any of the men you have standing in the room with you right now."

All the men started laughing, including Fred.

"Tara, please tell Mr. Fred about the men standing in the room with him."

"The man standing behind him has a nine-millimeter on his hip. He won't get it out before I put a bullet in him. He keeps massaging his hand. The guy by the door hasn't been paying attention to anything we've been doing. He has a gun in his shoulder holster and one on his ankle. I would shoot him first 'cause he would never see it coming. The guy standing behind me and to my left has been checking me out this whole time. He doesn't have guns, he has knives. Two at his back and one in his right shirt sleeve. Once I take out the three of them, our client would be next."

No one said anything. They were all looking at me. Fred with his eyes wide and the guards with their eyes narrowed.

"Hello?" Mr. Lang said.

"Never mind," answered Fred. "We should be fine."

"You sure you don't want a demonstration? I can't be sure she won't kill your guards, but I'm sure she wouldn't do the last part."

"No. We're good."

"Good. Don't fucking call me again unless she's fucking dead." And he slammed the phone down.

I rented a penthouse at this hotel where there was one way in and out. There was one woman allowed on the floor, and I vetted her myself. We paid a lot of money for no one else in the hotel to give a shit about who we were. I made sure no one saw us come in and out and the client wore a disguise, as I did. There were a lot of rumors about who it was in the penthouse, and most of the staff thought it was a famous, well-known celebrity. I was sure we would be safe there for a while if he did what he was told.

My client's family had a lot of money. His grandfather was a gambler and a bootlegger, his father was in real estate. His father was as much of a criminal being as a real estate man as his grandfather was as a bootlegger.

My client wasn't a criminal. He was just a rich douchebag with a huge chip on his shoulder. He inherited everything he had and worked for nothing.

After the killing, when the men tried to chase him, Fred's driver had to drag him in the car. He was going to explain to them he didn't care about the guy they killed and throw some money at them.

During my research, I found this was not the first time he was in trouble because of his attitude toward the world. A few years ago, he tried to beat up a seventeen-year-old kid over a poker game. The kid's father came looking for him, and he tried to bribe the man while telling him his son deserved it. The guy broke three of his ribs, his nose, and fractured a few fingers. His uncle (his father died a few years before) hired bodyguards to protect his nephew from himself after the incident. He wasn't confident his nephew would stay out of trouble, even with the mob after him. That wasn't the issue. The issue was the mob would not stop coming after him, even with the bodyguards.

Everything was going great. I was watching everyone, including the mobsters, and I had a routine. My client decided he wanted to change things around.

"Tara, I would like you to get me a woman."

"I'm sorry, what?"

"Not that I want you to get me a woman, but I want a woman."

"This is not a good idea when we are trying to lay low."

"So, I'm supposed to never have pussy again?"

"I'm trying to keep you safe. Pussy is not my concern."

"Well, it's my concern. It's been a month. How long am I supposed to hold my dick?"

"You can hold it as long as you want, but inviting someone here you don't know is not a good idea."

"I'll know her. I'm not an idiot. Pierre will send over a regular."

I shook my head, "It doesn't matter if she is a regular. They can still get to her."

"You are too paranoid. And this is what I hired you for. You are supposed to keep me safe while I go about my life. So, keep me safe."

"Mr. Fred, in keeping you safe, I have to minimize any threats, and I can't do that if what you are worrying about is sex."

"I don't care. I want it. I'm just letting you know, not asking your fucking permission. Make it happen."

I located the service he frequently used. They usually sent over one of three girls but could send anyone based on availability. It didn't matter who they sent because he knew all the girls.

This time, the girl who showed up wasn't someone he recognized. The owner called my client before the girl arrived and informed him he was sending a new girl. His regulars were busy, and she was his type. It was too coincidental and sounded like bullshit to me.

When the girl arrived, I talked to her before I would allow her to go into the room with the client. When I told the five bodyguards I didn't trust this girl and didn't want to let her go back to our boss's room, I got,

"You want that dick for yourself, dontcha?" said Tommy.

"No, she wants the girl for herself?" said Stan.

"I knew a woman couldn't do this job without falling in love," Brett chimed in.

"I'm sure he would have both of you. Let's ask him," said Stan.

The other geniuses, who didn't make any comments, told me I was overreacting as they were laughing at the comments being made.

I turned my attention back to her and told her she had to take her clothes off before I would let her go back there, which started an argument between me and the other bodyguards. While we were arguing, the elevator dinged. I was the only one who recognized the sound. I turned toward the elevator.

I was facing one of the bodyguards, who had a submachine gun on his arm. I cut the strap with a small knife I carry on a key ring, went down the hall to the elevator, and as soon as the letters PH lit up above the elevator carriage, I pulled the trigger. The other bodyguards ran over to me, but it was already done. As the doors opened, two guys and two guns fell out of the elevator. There was a third guy, but he was sitting on the floor against the back wall in his own blood.

I threw the gun at the bodyguard who I took it from. I rushed over to the girl, who was in a state of undress, grabbed her by the neck, slammed her up against the wall, and told her to tell me everything that led her here. She said they would kill her. I pulled my gun out, held it up to her head, and said in a normal-speaking voice while looking directly into her eyes,

"I am not these men. You are going to tell me what I want to know, or I will put a bullet in your head."

She refused again, I turned the gun toward her right side and shot her in the leg while covering her mouth when she screamed. Those men who made fun of my cautiousness stood with their mouths gaping and staring while I interrogated this woman.

"Now, I'm going to take my hand away and you're gonna tell me what I wanna know or the next bullet goes in your head."

I took my hand away. She peed on herself and told me,

"S...s...some men c...came to see Pierre today. I...I...I don't know what," she stopped to catch her breath. "I don't know w...what they talked about."

"What did the men look like?" I asked.

"They looked like people you don't fuck with," she was crying and holding her leg.

"And then?"

"Then Pierre told me I...I...I was coming here. Th...the men who came to see Pi...Pierre drove me here."

I told her to put her clothes back on, I tended to her wound, and then took her somewhere safe.

Mr. Fred wasn't happy about what happened because he wanted to have sex, but he was also pissed at his lax staff.

"What the fuck? I could have been killed tonight. None of you thought it was important to make sure who she was?"

"Boss, you saw she was a new girl, and you still wanted her," said Tommy.

Mr. Fred ran over to him and pushed him in his chest. Tommy fell back. "Don't tell me what I wanted. I know what I wanted. Why didn't you think about ME?"

Tommy lowered his head.

Mr. Fred looked over Stan's head and pointed at me.

"You are in charge of security."

He walked back to his room, "Get the fuck out," and slammed the door when they all filed out.

I knew what kind of man my client's nemesis was, but I was going to reason with him first. When I went to his house for the first time, I asked myself "Why do people hire bodyguards?" They were useless unless they were at my level or higher.

I instantly found the holes in his security (which, by the way, are complacency and ego), crept into his house, and went right to his room. He was asleep and didn't move an eyelash when I came into his room.

He eventually woke up, and I talked to him in the same voice I used for the prostitute. I told him I could get him anytime I wanted, and I wanted him to leave my client alone. He laughed at me. Told me my client was a dead man and so was I. I saw him reaching before he thought to do it. As soon as the gun came from under his pillow, I was there to take the gun from him and point it at his head. He held up his hands. I took out the clip and cleared the chamber. I gave him back his gun, but not before I smacked him across the head with it, knocking him out.

I wasn't very hopeful my talk would stop the chase. It didn't surprise me when he made another attempt on my client. (He was going to church. I tried to tell him God would understand until the threat was gone, but he didn't listen). I used the rest of my knowledge about the mobster to end this job.

I could have started with this, but it's exhausting to have to use people's lives against them. It was much easier for them to be afraid of you or reconsider their decision on their own. He wasn't cooperating. I made a fascinating movie about my new friend, where he was the star along with some young men just past jailbait.

When I went to his house again, I found he had beefed up security. It was harder to enter the house, but I was able to do it. When he returned home that night, he stayed downstairs for two hours and then went to his room. I was waiting for him. As soon as he walked in and closed the door, I turned on the TV, and my movie started. This wasn't a single movie, but a triple feature. The movie showed him in three different movies with three different young men.

In one movie, he was engaging in anal sex. He was the bottom, and the young man was the top choking him. In the second, his hands and feet were tied behind his back, and he was kneeling, giving a blow job to a beautiful blonde. In the third, it was pretty boring; he was getting whacked off while they watched porn. There were clips from all three movies playing in fifteen-second intervals.

While he watched, I said to him,

"You will stop bothering my client. I know no one in your organization knows about this, and you can <u>never</u> let them find out. I will not tell anyone. But if anything happens to my client, the world will know. My client is leaving, and he will not say a word to anyone. He just wants to be left alone."

"I can't let him live. I don't know what he'll do in the future, and I can't risk it."

"He will not talk, but that doesn't matter. You can't touch him if you don't want this out. And don't think of going after me. I have a contingency plan if anything happens to me."

He didn't respond. He sat on his bed and placed his head in his hands. He picked up the crystal clock I saw on his nightstand the last time I was there and threw it against the wall. His team tried to enter, but he locked the door and told them everything was OK (If it was me, I would've broken the door down anyway. Shitty bodyguards). He turned to me, called me a fucking bitch, and told me to get the fuck out. At his request, I did what he wanted and left.

My client moved to the Bahamas somewhere on one of the islands. He probably could have stayed in the States, but his uncle said he couldn't risk his nephew wouldn't get into more trouble. I knew he had to go because as long as the mob didn't see him, our friend could save face by not killing him. Once my client left, we didn't have to worry about his would-be killer.

His would-be killer was gunned down two months later.

Chapter 19

While completing my master's degree, I made a few friends, but there were two people who became lifelong friends.

When my undergraduate work was finished, Jolene, Nina, Polly, and I tried to call and meet each other. After a while, I had to let them go because of the work I was doing. It was too dangerous to have those kinds of ties that weren't close by. The three of them had moved away either for a job or to go to school in another city.

Around this time was when I met Siobhán O'Shea and Patty Huntley at a party off campus. Siobhán was DJ'ing. I knew her from my social work program, but we never talked that much. When I walked into the party, Siobhán was taking a break standing near her turntables. When she saw me, she waved me over. She introduced Patty, who was in the fine arts program. She had a short magenta pixie. It was a lovely color against her medium brown skin and her brown eyes.

We had a quick conversation and Siobhán went back to spinning records. Patty and I hung out and got to know each other. Her Brooklyn accent was so great, I wanted to jump in her mouth. We were all tipsy when the party was over.

Patty's place was the closest. The three of us stayed at her place. You would think we went right to sleep, but drunks never believe they are as drunk as they are. The three of us sat on her couch and her living room floor and talked.

Siobhán told us stories about her early days in Ireland, Patty talked about her shitty boyfriends, and I talked about growing up in New Rochelle.

The next morning, we woke to all three of us holding our heads, groaning, and laughing at how awful we all looked. I noticed when the two of them were hungover, their accents would come out. Siobhán's Irish accent was like a song to me. Patty's Brooklyn accent was also like a song on a different key.

Patty made us all some coffee. We sat on her window box seat. We sipped coffee and looked out her window.

"I think we need some food in us," said Patty.

"Oh God, no," said Siobhán. "I could not eat a thing."

"Don't worry. I'm not making eggs. I'm going to make something solid. Harri, what do you want?"

"I could eat some pancakes and bacon."

"How do you know I have bacon?"

"I saw it in your refrigerator."

Patty chuckled, getting off the box seat, "OK. I'll get started."

We ate pancakes and bacon. Siobhán only ate pancakes. We spent the day together in our borrowed pajamas, watching movies and cartoons.

After that, we saw each other every day or talked on the phone. Our graduate programs were demanding, but our connection was solid. I shared more with those two ladies than I had with anyone since I arrived in Syracuse. My guard was still up, but I opened myself to them about Jesenia. Jesenia's name had not been spoken since JC, but my life had changed so much that I felt I could open up a bit more. I needed to talk about her. Goddamn, I still missed JC.

Right before I graduated from Syracuse with my bachelor's, I had the idea to open a center for children. I wanted a place where kids could go after school to do their homework, play sports, and meet with tutors. My vision was to rent out a small space, as I wasn't sure how the children would participate. As my idea grew, I knew I needed to locate a place in a central location, large enough for my rapidly growing dream and for children to get to easily.

I chose a place near downtown on the south side. I had the money, needed permits, and the old Sears and Roebuck building needed a lot of work. The city wanted to view my plans before they sold me the building, and even then, they didn't want to give it to me. No one would tell me why, but a friend who worked in the building office was asked how a young black woman had this kind of money. She told them to ask me. When I hired a couple of lawyers, they stopped blocking the sale. After the lawyers, it took me another six months and the building was mine.

My Nunu was right. I was going to do something great, and the money did give me choices. Over the years, I had always wondered how she knew. I didn't even know, but she knew I was going to be in this position. I will never thank my grandmother enough for allowing this to be my life.

By the time I finished my master's degree, the center was open. Siobhán and I named it The Little Red Playhouse. One of the last things we did before we opened the Playhouse was paint the outside of the building, facing South Salina Street, red.

The grand opening was in early August before college started. Members of the community showed up to the event. Mothers, grandparents, fathers, and lots of children. The police chief, city council members, community leaders, and the mayor also came to the event. I don't think they understood what we were doing because they were amazed by our little project.

When we had the grand opening, my parents were proud.

"Why is Siobhán the one out there in front of the cameras? This wonderful place is all you."

"Because, Mom, I don't want to be the face of this Playhouse. If I was out there, the focus would be on the rich black lady who built a place for poor kids instead of what the Playhouse can do."

"I guess you're right, but you deserve your shine."

I chuckled, "Mom, you deserve your shine too, but you are an artist in Westchester County with three kids and a husband."

My mother looked at me and laughed,

"I know but you're my kid."

I hugged my mother, "I love you, Mommy."

Children from all over the city came to the Playhouse after school. We couldn't have the school buses drop the children off at the Playhouse for insurance purposes. Most children took the city bus and some walked. The children whose parents had vehicles came to pick up their children when they got off work.

We had three donated vans we used to drop off those members who didn't have a ride. Snacks and entertainment for the children were always present before they went home for the day. Things went smoothly.

After two months, we had a few young people who tried to fight, and there was some bullying of the younger children going on. Nonetheless, my security team handled the situation easily by asking the troublemakers to leave and not to come back. The Playhouse was vandalized two days later after the troublemakers were asked to leave.

What no one knew except for Siobhán and I was we had a state-of-the-art camera system that caught them vandalizing our Playhouse. Siobhán had become "friends" with some local street entrepreneurs (her term). She knew they had pulled into the neighborhood; she asked them to intervene on behalf of the Playhouse. The drug dealers liked the Playhouse because Siobhán let them play basketball on the outside courts after hours. The only rules Siobhán gave: they could not sell drugs or use drugs anywhere near the Playhouse, no weapons, and no fighting of any kind. They agreed, and it was a good relationship.

The drug dealers talked the vandals into coming to the Playhouse to talk to Siobhán. Siobhán told them she knew what they did, but she forgave them. She still wanted them to be a part of the center, but she needed to know they understood the rules of the center.

"The dealers told me the kids in their neighborhood needed a place they could go that was safe and focused on education."

"Why the hell would they give a shit about that?"

"Maybe they didn't have one, maybe they have brothers or sisters, or they just know what can happen if they don't have one."

"I guess."

"Anyway, they said if they treated it badly, they knew the center wouldn't last. They want it to succeed. They used a lot more curse words, but that's basically what they said."

"Come on. Tell me what they said."

"You just want to hear me curse with my accent."

"I do. Say it."

She squinted her eyes for me and said "These fucking kids in our neighborhood need a place they can be fucking safe. And we want these kids to fucking graduate."

I smiled at her. "Fuck you," she said. I started laughing.

"There was one guy who wouldn't come in. He told me it was 'fucking stupid, and what did some white lady from another country know about his life, anyway?'"

"I stared him in the eye and asked, do you think because I'm white I don't understand the ghetto? You don't know me. You think only black people are poor? Just cause I'm not black doesn't mean I don't believe in this neighborhood. He wasn't interested."

"So, what did you do with him?"

"I told him to leave, and he wasn't allowed back. He called me a bitch."

"That was it?"

"I guess. He didn't come back. I want to believe he decided we weren't worth the trouble, but he was way too pissed off about it. I asked his friends what happened to him, and they claimed they didn't know."

About four months after the Playhouse opened, I found employment. I was working part-time as a counselor for The House and Home, a place for abused women and their children. My degree in social work helped, but it wasn't easy getting my foot in the door. In my first interview, they hired someone else. I was devastated. I called my interviewer because I had to know.

"Hello, Mrs. King. This is Harrison McCuff. If you have a moment, I would like to ask a question."

"Good morning, Ms. McCuff. I have a few moments. How can I help you?"

"Social work is what I want to do, but I feel like I did something wrong in my interview."

"You didn't do anything wrong, Ms. McCuff. You have all the degrees, and you've had fabulous internships. I didn't hire you because the members of House and Home do not need saving. They already saved themselves by coming here. When I gave you a tour, you looked at the members and your eyes were filled with pity. They don't need you to pity them. Until you understand that these members need help not saving, I can't hire you."

I was silent.

"Are you still there Ms. McCuff?"

"Yes, I am. Sorry. I didn't know I was doing that."

"You are not the first, Ms. McCuff, and you won't be the last. I liked you a lot. Maybe you can volunteer here if you can afford to."

"Maybe. I will give that some thought. Thank you, Mrs. King. I appreciate the feedback."

"You are welcome. I hope to see you soon."

I was volunteering by the next month. I was there a few days a week and some weekends. I loved working at House and Home. The women were amazing, as were their children. And my interviewer was right. You can't feel sorry for them or treat them like fine china.

The women were beaten down in some form or manner and just needed someone to listen and understand them, protect them, and help them to take care of themselves. I couldn't imagine doing anything else. But I didn't believe I could save them anymore. I reserved that for the other jobs I had. I just wanted to help, and I hope I did.

Everything was coming together for me, and I couldn't have been happier.

Chapter 20

Patty, Siobhán, and I were still friends, but how often we saw each other tapered off. If Patty called Siobhán and needed something, Siobhán would call me, and we arrived with whatever was needed. There was no hesitation. But our days of hanging at bars, drinking guys under the table, and waking in the morning to Patty's pancakes happened less and less.

In July 2006, Patty was invited to a reception at the Sheraton Hotel for an artist and former student of SU, Richard Provone. His art was being showcased along with a couple of other local artists. Patty's professor invited two students to attend with him to network. Siobhán and I would have gone with her, but Siobhán was meeting with some investors, and I was out on a job.

Around 2 a.m., my phone rang. Patty was on the other end, crying, asking me to come pick her up. I didn't ask what was wrong since I could hear the fear in her voice. I told her to tell me her room number. The hotel was forty-five minutes away. I was there in about twenty-eight minutes.

When I walked into the Sheraton Hotel, there were two attendants behind the counter. The bar was shut down, all the shops were closed, and there were no other employees or guests around. I headed straight for the elevator.

I made it to the fourteenth floor and I knocked on the door of room 1426. Patty did not answer right away. I was about to give the door another knock until it came open, and Patty stood in front of me. A large white sheet was wrapped around her body. Her eyes were bloodshot and puffy. I noticed a large bruise above her cheek and Patty's hair was all over her head as if she was in a fight. I followed her into the room. She stumbled on her way back to the bed where we sat at the edge.

"Is it OK if I hold your hand?"

Tears were streaming down her face, causing her makeup to smear, "Yes."

"Patty, what happened?"

"I met this guy, Maxin Little. I think he works in music, but I can't remember." She placed her hand on her head and paused.

"We had a few drinks, and the next thing I remember was waking up in this room. I didn't have any clothes on, Maxin was nowhere to be found, and I could not remember how I got here.

"I tried to remember what happened to me, but I can only remember flashes of things. They don't make any sense. It's like watching movie scenes out of order."

Patty started crying. I wrapped my arm around her, and she placed her head on my shoulder. I was about to tell her we were going to the hospital, but she lifted her head and said, "Maxin was in the movie." I gave her a tissue from the nightstand as she continued, "But I don't know if he was in the room with me or if it was someone else." She blew her nose and sighed. "I remember having sex, but I don't remember with whom, or what I really did during sex. I called you 'cause I'm scared. I called Siobhán too, but she didn't answer."

Still hugging her, "It's OK, Patty. I'm here. I need to tell you what is going to happen now, okay?"

She nodded her head, and her tears became steadier, falling onto her sheet. "You are going to put your clothes back on, and we are going to go to the hospital to have you checked out."

"I don't want to do that, Harri."

"Patty, we have to go get you checked out."

"Everyone's going to know. I can tell you. I don't want other people to know."

"I can't force you to go, Patty, but you need to know what he did to you. Yes, the police will be called, and they will be as discreet as possible, but you need to know what happened."

"Maybe I don't want to know. I just want to go home and forget how stupid I was."

"Patty. You were not stupid. He did something to you. The fact that you can't remember means he did something to you. You did not do anything wrong."

"I just feel like that."

"I know. It's up to you Patty, but I think you should get checked out."

"You deal with this all the time?"

"I do, but that has nothing to do with this. What do you want to do?"

Patty was wiping her eyes with her head hung low. She then raised her head.

"I'll go. I don't want to, but I trust you."

I started gathering some of her things while she placed her clothes on. Patty and I made it to the lobby. She did not make eye contact with anyone as we headed out of the hotel. She didn't speak on the way to the hospital, and I didn't try.

When we got to the emergency room, there was not a lot of people waiting. I went right to the front desk.

"Hello, ma'am. I believe my friend was raped."

The woman raised her head up from what she was doing. She looked at me with these clear blue eyes, and threw some papers at me, "Fill those out."

"I can fill them out, but can we get my friend into a room?"

"We can, when one becomes available."

"Sasha, we have room three ready, I can take her back," a young black nurse replied to the desk nurse

"Melanie, there are other people ahead of her."

"None of them were brought in by ambulance, no one is bleeding and no bones are sticking out, Sasha. I'm taking her back.

Rolling her eyes at Sasha, she turned to me, "Ma'am, where is your friend?"

"She's over here," I took her to Patty.

"Miss, will you come with me."

Patty rose from her chair, drawing her clothes around her and dropping her head. We followed the nurse past the receptionist's desk to the back of the emergency room.

"My name is Melanie. What is your name?

"Patty," she whispered.

"Hi Patty, we will get to you as soon as possible, okay?"

"Thank you, Melanie," I said. "I know there are new protocols for assault victims, does Nurse Ratchet out there not know that?"

"She is a stickler for rules. That's why we are here to try and keep things moving. Your nurse should be in soon."

"Thanks again."

A nurse entered the room we were in after ten minutes. Her skin was the color of mahogany with a wide nose which offset her almond-shaped light umber eyes. She sported the same haircut style as Patty and was about the same size. There was a distinct burn mark exposed on her arm where the sleeve of her scrubs was bunched to the shoulder. "Good morning. My name is Daria. I am going to be your nurse. What is your name?"

"I'm Patty. This is my friend, Harri."

"Hello, Patty. Hi, Harri. Harri, would you mind stepping outside while I examine your friend?"

"No! I want her to stay."

"OK. You can have a seat over there, Harri," she said pointing at a chair next to Patty's bed.

"Patty, do you consent to me doing a rape kit on you?"

"Yes," Patty said with her voice cracking.

Daria gave Patty a gown to put on and closed the curtain around us so she could change. I got up to pull back the curtain when Patty was ready. When I sat back down, Patty took my hand.

"Patty, I am going to tell you everything that happens next. My colleague has called the police as we are required to do by law. You do not have to speak to them if you don't want to. I am going to do your rape kit. I am going to tell you everything I am doing as I do it. If you have questions or I'm hurting you, I want you to tell me. OK?

"Yes, ma'am."

"I am going to take samples and swabs from your body that will go to the lab. I am also going to ask you some questions as I collect everything. If anything makes you uncomfortable or you want to stop, you tell me. OK?"

"Yes, ma'am."

"I am also going to take some pictures of your body to help document what happened. Do you have any questions for me before we start?"

"What happens if I don't talk to the police?"

"They won't make a formal report. You won't get into trouble if you don't talk to them. I think it might help, but that is your decision."

"Is this going to hurt?"

"There might be some discomfort, but nothing should hurt."

Patty paused, looking at the wall behind the nurse. "OK. I'm ready."

Daria told Patty everything she was doing before she used any of the instruments. Her voice was calm and even. Every few minutes she asked Patty how she was doing. Patty didn't speak to me during the examination. She bit down on her lower lip, and her eyes were shut tight as more tears poured from the corner of her eyes while Daria collected her samples. There were also a couple of intakes of air when Daria inserted a swab into Patty and a couple of tight squeezes to my hand.

When Daria was finished, she checked in with Patty one more time.

"Patty, we are done. I am going to take everything with me. I have some clothes for you to put on. I'm sure the police are here by now. Have you decided if you want to talk to them?"

She wiped the tears from her eyes with the back of her hand. "I will talk to them."

"OK. You can stop anytime you want."

Daria exited from the room. Within a few moments, two police officers entered the room. They had on the same suit, one blue and one grey, and they had the same Ivy League haircut, one blonde and one brown. The taller cop had a strong chin and deep blue eyes. The shorter one had brown eyes that almost matched his hair.

They asked Patty the same kinds of questions as Daria. They were as delicate as they could be but the questions they asked, like "What were you wearing?" or "Did you go upstairs willingly?" seemed a little accusatory. There was also a rape counselor who tried to talk to Patty.

"Hello, Patty. My name is Lisa. I am a counselor here on staff. I'm here to see if you need to talk or if I can suggest someone for you to talk to?"

"I don't want to talk anymore," Patty answered.

"OK. Is there anything I can help you with?"

"No."

"Is there anyone else I can call for you?"

Patty turned to me, "Harri, I want to go home. I need to go home."

"Okay, Patty. Thank you for coming by, Lisa. I think she just wants to go home."

"I understand. Take my card for her in case she needs it. Take care of yourself."

I let Patty get dressed and I took her home.

A week later, Siobhán and I took Patty to the police station for the lineup, and right off the bat she picked Maxin. The rape kit came back a few weeks later negative for semen, her blood alcohol level was .10%, which was legally drunk, and she couldn't seem to remember the events of the previous night. Zolpidem was found in her system. She did not have a prescription, and Zolpidem was a known date rape drug.

They arrested Maxin but let him out on bail. The investigators told Patty they interviewed people who attended the party, hotel employees, and Maxin, the main suspect. Not one person recalled anything unusual. Two of the hotel staff did say they saw Patty with Maxin. Of course, he denied the rape even happened.

Patty hired an attorney soon after the lineup. The attorney started contacting the police and the DA's office to get an update on her case. After three months of stalling and informing Patty, they were still working on the case.

The District Attorney told her the case was weak. It was her word against his. The DA didn't feel it was worth his time to prosecute with the lack of evidence.

Patty cried all night after that phone call. Siobhán and I didn't want to leave her, but she said she needed to be alone. She eventually locked herself in her house and wouldn't take our phone calls or our knocks at the door.

There was usually something for me to do in these situations, but I didn't know how to help my friend. So, I started investigating Maxin Little.

He was a "record producer" who worked with a few marginally successful artists that came out of Upstate New York. He was thirty-eight, originally from New Jersey, and had a girlfriend who lived in Syracuse.

When I mentioned his name, both men and women knew who he was. They thought he was a good producer, he was always helping out within the community, and he let up-and-coming young artists from the neighborhood use his studio. Some women said things like, "he's all right," "only interacted with him once," or "I don't want to talk about it."

The mixed reviews were a sign I needed to do more. I started following Maxin Little around Syracuse. On the third night, I followed him into a bar. When the door opened "Right Thurr" by Chingy poured out of the bar. People were dancing on the floor, people stood at the bar while others sat at tables and drank. The place was a little crowded, but I could move around.

Maxin was sitting at the bar. He had beautiful high cheekbones and deep brown eyes that contrasted with his beautiful dark skin. He was fit, dressed in a nice suit, and carried himself as if he owned everything. Even his voice was smooth and deep when he spoke.

I sat a few seats away from him. We were there for about fifteen minutes when a woman danced over toward the bar. She ordered some drinks, and Maxin started talking to her.

"You seem to be having a good time tonight?" said Maxin.

"Oh, I am."

"My name is Maxin," holding out his hand.

"Jennifer," she said shaking his hand.

Maxin did not discriminate. The woman was white, blonde, and in heels looked 5'10". Patty was black, had black hair, and was not so tall. The woman sat and talked with Maxin for about half an hour. She only had one drink. When she had her second, one of her friends walked up to her to talk. Everyone in the bar was dancing, drinking, or talking. No one was paying attention to Maxin Little but me. He quickly slipped something into the woman's drink.

It took effect fast after she drank it. I now had an understanding of how Patty could have seemed drunk. Jennifer was slurring her words while grabbing onto Maxin. She spoke loudly, and almost fell off her stool. He tried to get her to leave, but her friends came and intervened. Jennifer was holding on to Maxin's neck as her friends tried to pull her way.

"Yes, baby, I want to go with you. You are so hot."

Two of her friends finally dragged her away, kicking and screaming. Everyone in the bar was watching them, but the three friends only paid attention to removing their friend from Maxin. He watched as Jennifer was pulled out of the door. He then turned around on his stool and slammed his hand down on the bar. The bartender came over.

"Sir, are you OK?"

Maxin threw some money on the bar. "Fuck you. I'm fine." He snatched up his jacket and stormed out of the club.

After watching him interact with this woman, I realized Maxin Little had been doing this to women for a long time. What he was doing was practiced, polished, and he was never going to stop raping women. When an individual has been committing a crime like this for a long time, and they haven't been caught, there's no way they'll stop on their own.

Ever always told me if I felt myself getting too involved, to distance myself from the job as much as possible without jeopardizing the client. I knew my plan for Maxin Little should never be executed because I was emotionally involved. This was no longer about me or Patty. I knew what would happen if Maxin Little was allowed to stay on the streets. The police and the DA's office wouldn't do anything without more evidence, which meant Maxin would hurt more women. I couldn't let that happen.

I thought about this for two weeks before deciding what to do. My focus had to be on the task and not on revenge, or I couldn't do this. It had to be about the safety of all women, not just Patty. If Ever knew, he still wouldn't be happy.

I called Maurice and explained what I wanted.

"I know some guys who can help you out."

"Who?"

"They are two guys I know. They can probably get this done in a week from start to finish."

"That would be great. I can do it, but it would be so much easier with help."

"It's gonna cost you."

"How much?"

"Twenty-five thousand."

"Seriously?"

"They cost 'cause they're good Harri. They are two brothers who don't speak."

"What the hell does that mean?"

"Just that they don't speak."

"How are we supposed to communicate with them, Maurice?"

"They seem to communicate fine. You meet them first, and let me know if you want them to work for you. They will contact you."

"How, Maurice?"

"They just will Harri."

Chapter 21

Business was not conducted from the house I lived in on Rugby Road. I used a beautiful loft apartment for that. No one knew about the apartment except for Maurice, and he never came here.

I was at the apartment checking some private accounts I had when I heard a knock on my door. I peered at the camera screen and saw two Latino men who looked to be older than me, standing in my doorway. They both turned and looked at the camera. Then my phone rang.

"Are they there yet?" Maurice asked.

"Who?"

"The twins?"

"What the hell are you talkin' about, Maurice?"

He laughed. "Are there two guys standing at your front door? Those are the twins; those are the brothers."

"How the hell did they know where I lived? Did you tell them?"

"No, they just knew. Let them in before they leave. I'll call you later."

After hanging up with Maurice, I reluctantly let them in. They were both dressed in suits I knew cost more than my rent. They were a beautiful dark blue, and they wore dark blue shoes that matched. I couldn't figure out what I was dealing with. Along with the suits, they were uncomfortably handsome. One had black hair, and the other twin's hair was blonde. They both had blue eyes, full lips, and small noses.

I offered them something to drink. They shook their heads no and sat down on the large windowsill. The only other furniture in the apartment was my bed pushed against the south wall, a dresser, an end table, my computer desk, and two stools at the other end of the loft that sat at my kitchen counter. Across the front of the loft were four bay windows.

I gave them the file on Maxin Little. They read it from back to front and didn't say a word to me or even look at me while doing it.

Then they stood up, came over to me, and one of them put their hands together, palms facing each other, opened them up, and offered them to me. "You want to know what I want?"

They nodded. Do not ask me how I knew that was what he meant because I had no idea.

I told them what I wanted to do with Maxin. They nodded again, wrote an address, a time, and a date, and gave the piece of paper to me. I asked them what I should call them, and they just looked at me.

"What, you don't have names?" I asked.

One of them smirked and then the other turned over the paper they gave me and wrote The Twins.

When I showed up at Shoppingtown Mall, the parking lot was still pretty full at ten thirty on a Saturday night. I'm sure the owners of the cars were inside the mall making their last purchases, buying tickets for the last movie, or eating their last French fry. Whatever they were doing, they were all inside, and no new people were arriving. The individuals who were coming out were weary and spent their day walking, shopping, and eating. No one was going to notice a Black woman getting into a gray van any more than they would a white woman getting into a red car.

I climbed into the bed of the van where there were two seats on either side. One twin sat in one seat and the other was empty. The other twin was driving, and Maxin was lying on the floor of the van. The twins were dressed in all black, and Maxin was unconscious dressed in jeans and a t-shirt.

We drove out of the parking lot onto Erie Boulevard towards the highway then the thruway towards Buffalo. It wasn't a long drive, but it seemed long since the twins didn't talk, and our passenger was incapacitated.

When we arrived at our destination, we were on the edge of Niagara Falls, near Canada. Supposedly, there was a very big culture in this area for what I had planned.

They parked us in front of a weird-looking structure. It looked just like the outside of a house I might see in New Rochelle, except it had four floors.

From the street, you could see the front door of the house, which was a dark color. There were huge bay windows on the first floor that seemed to go all around the house. On the second and third floors there were also windows that were half the size of the first-floor windows. Also on the third floor was a balcony, and then above that, there appeared to be some kind of attic. I had never seen a house so big. It wasn't only tall; the house took up an entire block.

I walked up the front steps with one of the twins and rang the doorbell. The woman who answered was at least 6'3". She was slender and had on a tight-fitting green dress that showed off her ample breasts. She had huge hands, a very light voice, and legs that went on forever. I'm sure if I had lifted her dress, I would've seen a big penis too. Her name was Stacy.

As soon as she saw one of the twins standing with me, she led us inside. She went behind what I assumed was the front desk. It looked to be made of granite, spanned the length of the room, and was three inches taller than I believe it should have been. There was a door behind the large desk on the right that I assumed went to the back rooms. Stacy was the only one there to man the desk.

We could see the living room to the left of the door and another room to the right. Both rooms had low lighting, and faces were hard to make out. I could make out there was kissing and caressing happening. There were a few couches and comfortable-looking seats scattered around the lobby, along with a coffee pot and a television. If anyone else had come into this house, they would have thought they were in the lobby of a hotel.

She asked what we needed, and I explained to her what I wanted. She was thrilled and said she was more than happy to take on extra help. The twin I was with went to signal his brother that Maxin could come in. I talked to Stacy more.

"Stacy, there's no need to dump him. We'll be back for him tonight."

"No problem. I'd do anything for those boys."

"How well do you know them?"

"Well, enough not to answer that question. They may work with you, but that doesn't mean they trust you. You ask them about it."

"Fair enough. Sorry."

"That's alright honey. If I was just meeting them, I would want to know everything I could too. They are mysterious and hotter than volcano lava."

I smiled at her. "There is just one more thing, Stacey. I don't want any pictures or videos taken of this guy. It needs to be completely anonymous forever."

"That's no problem. There are no cell phones allowed in my establishment. Not only do I pat people down, but we also have all cell phone signals and any other signals blocked in this area. Believe me, anonymity is important in my line of work."

"Great."

By this time, the twins were back with a very unconscious Maxin Little.

"Is it OK if I change his clothes?" Stacy asked, looking him over.

"Of course. Just make sure you leave his original clothing intact."

"Will do. Oh, he is pretty, isn't he? I might have a fight in here tonight over him. Hell, I might take him for myself." Stacy pressed a button behind her desk and two huge men dressed in t-shirts that said security across the chest, miniskirts, and Timberland boots came out and took Maxin away. "And how long will he be out?"

"We suspect he'll be out at least until the morning, but we'll be back for him right around four or four thirty."

"Oh, can't we have him till six o'clock?"

"No, we have to get back."

One of the twins gave a stack of bills to Stacy, which to me looked like twenty-five thousand dollars. She gave the other twin a set of car keys. We thanked Stacy again and left.

We got into a Honda Accord, drove to a nondescript motel, and waited for Maxin Little to feel some of the pain he had caused his victims. The twins stayed in a room, and I stayed in a room. I did some Tai Chi, meditated, and read a little. Who knew what the twins were doing.

Around four fifteen, the twins knocked on my door. We got back in the Honda and drove to Stacy's. When we got there, shadowy figures were still moving around in the side rooms. Now, people were walking around the lobby area with men who were caressing breasts and being caressed. The men who were here were from every walk of life: they were in business suits, sweatsuits, and jeans and tees. These men were black, white, and everything in between. None of them seemed to be embarrassed that we were standing there watching.

Finally, two big guys (different from the first two guys) came out of the back, dragging Maxin behind them and Stacey not far behind.

"Did he give you any trouble, Stacey?"

"Oh, no honey, he woke up at the beginning, but whatever you gave him was some powerful shit. He never fully regained consciousness, and my guys loved it. Some have even asked when he's coming back. They love virgin ass."

"We hopefully won't need you again, but if…"

"Don't even worry about it. The boys will get in contact with me if lover boy needs to become a guest here again. If not, it was nice meeting you, and thank you for bringing us some new meat. That always gets me some extra cash."

The twins picked up Maxin while I was at the door. We walked back to the van and headed back to Syracuse.

When we got back, the sky was the color blue just after night had given up, and the sun was starting to take over. The road in front of Maxin's house in the Sedgewick area was quiet. There were only a few people who were up on a Sunday morning at six thirty, and they were half asleep. The twins waited until they saw no movement and placed Maxin back in his car where they found him. They locked his car, got back in the van, and drove away. They dropped me off and went somewhere to rest. I hoped our little adventure would do the trick for Maxin, but there was no guarantee.

Over the next few days, I watched Maxin. When Patty was raped, the first thing she did was call a friend. If someone drugged me like we drugged him, and my asshole was one size bigger, I might not be walking around as if nothing had happened, but that's what Maxin Little was doing. He went to work on Monday. From what I can tell, he didn't hire bodyguards. He called no one to find out if they knew what had happened to him... nothing. I assumed he was embarrassed and didn't want anyone to know.

It was Thursday evening around 8:00 p.m. Maxin had two residences in the city. One was an apartment in the Eastwood area and the other was the house in Sedgewick. I knew his schedule and knew where he would be. When he came into his apartment, I was sitting in the kitchen. He kept trying to flip the light switch by his door, but it wouldn't come on. He couldn't see me from the small amount of light coming through the windows in the kitchen and the living room.

"Hello, Maxin."

"Who the hell is that?" Maxin asked as he spun around toward the kitchen.

"Stay where you are, and pay attention."

"What the fuck?" Maxin shouted. "Who are you?" He moved toward the kitchen. I shot the bookcase behind him with a nine-millimeter. The bullet made a thud sound when it hit my target. There was hardly any sound from the gun because of the silencer, but I saw him flinch as the bullet flew past his head. Maxin dropped to the ground.

"All you need to know is that I know what happened to your ass on Saturday night."

"You fuckin' bitch! Who the fuck do you think...?!"

I shot again, but this time I winged his arm.

"I didn't miss, Mr. Little. That was your last warning. Now, you're gonna turn yourself in to the police and confess what you've been doing to the women of Syracuse and the women of New Jersey. You know, the same thing that was done to you."

He didn't make a sound this time and remained still. I was happy about that because I didn't want to kill him.

"If you don't turn yourself in, the same thing that happened on Saturday night will happen again. Your choice." I got up and he shifted on the floor.

"I'm gonna leave now to let you tend to your wound, but I want you to think about what I said."

I went through the kitchen window. Like the punk he was, he didn't make a move to stop me.

I waited for a few days to see if Maxin would do what I told him to, but he didn't. He went back to his life as if nothing had happened. When he didn't turn himself in, I knew I needed to keep an eye on him until we took him again. I didn't want him to hurt another woman or try to run away. But I didn't have to worry about that. He didn't bother anyone, not even the willing participants, and there were quite a few of those.

I did notice that he had a shadow now. When Maxin came out of his house, I saw his shadow come from behind a hedge in the next yard. He didn't get into Maxin's car, he got into his own vehicle and followed Maxin around Syracuse. But his shadow would not help him. The shadow was good, but not good enough to hide from me. I informed the twins, and they "said" they would be ready to pick him up again whenever I was ready.

Chapter 22

I knew this lull would not last. Men like Maxin didn't give up their perversions. They couldn't. When we took Maxin the second time, it was uneventful. We drugged his bodyguard in his car and took them both to Canada. We left the bodyguard in his car once in Canada. Stacy was very happy to see us, especially since we were leaving him for a whole weekend.

When we brought him back, we left him in the gazebo at Higher Onondaga Park. We also left him in the lovely outfit that Stacy provided, a pink mini skirt, black fishnet stockings, no underwear, and a black tube top.

I wasn't sure what Maxin's response would be to the second kidnapping, but I hoped he would end his pain. He did not.

On Saturday night, I waited until his house in Sedgewick was dark.

I looked around quickly before I carefully cut out a part of the attic window. The only light came from the moon that was out that night. The window opened with little resistance. When my foot hit the floor, there was no creaking from the floorboards. I moved toward the steps, put my ear close to the door, and listened. When no sound came through the door, I pulled a magnet out of my pocket. The lock on the attic door was a simple slide lock. The magnet easily slid the bar away from the housing. I quietly opened the door.

The door squeaked. I stopped moving. If he was awake, he would have heard the squeak and would investigate. There were no windows to add light to the hallway. My position against the wall kept me hidden as I listened for movement downstairs.

He sounded like someone who was trying to be quiet and sneak up on someone. My breathing was slow and steady even though my heart was crashing against my chest. Although the hallway was a standard size for a house, it was still too narrow for a real fight, especially with someone who was bigger and supposedly stronger.

Maxin didn't see me standing in the shadows, and when he got to the second floor, he turned towards the attic door where I was on the other end. When he went to the door, I went behind his back and descended the stairs to wait for him. When Maxin came back downstairs, as he passed me at the bottom of the stairs, I grabbed him from behind and held him in a chokehold. He wasn't ready for me, but he recovered quickly and elbowed me in the stomach. I flinched but didn't let go.

The flinch let him have room in my choke. He got a hand between my arm and his neck. He was trying to pull my arm from around his neck. He was struggling to get away from me. The both of us were swinging around, and I knew what was coming. I let go. He flew into a coffee table, banged his knee, and stood upright quickly. He turned to look at me and asked who I was. I did not answer him. He lunged at me, trying to grab me. I punched him in the face. He dropped to a knee and came at me low, and we both fell to the floor; me hitting my head on a bookshelf. He tried to get on top of me, but I had my knee up before he could pin me. I flipped him over. His back was against the front of the couch, and I punched him again. I was about to punch him a third time when he grabbed me by the neck. I punched him anyway, but he didn't let go.

I could hold my breath for a long time, but I needed him off me. I put a finger in his eye and used my other hand to wrap around his neck. I don't think he knew what to do. I was getting lightheaded, so I knew he was.

He took his hands off my neck and grabbed my hand trying to remove it from around his neck. I took my finger out of his eye and punched him again. I took my hand from around his throat while I pulled my knife and put it to his neck. He stopped moving.

"Did you enjoy your weekend?"

Maxin struggled to breathe. "You fucking bitch. I'll kill you."

"No. You won't." I pressed the knife into his neck, broke the skin, and pulled it back without taking it off his neck.

"Don't make me keep doing this to you. I know what you've been doing to the women in Syracuse, and I'm not gonna stop because you're not gonna stop. If you die while I torture you, good riddance. Now, you are going to turn yourself in."

I pressed the knife back into his neck. He let out a tiny sound of pain.

"You're not gonna run because there's nowhere for you to hide that I won't find you. This is your only out. I'll make sure you don't get bothered in jail, but if you don't turn yourself in, you're not gonna have an ass when I get through with you."

I pulled back the knife again and got off him. He jumped up and sat on the couch. He touched his neck and looked at the blood on his hand. If you can believe it, he swooned. "I will not go to jail. I did nothing to those fuckin whores they didn't want."

I laughed, "Whores? You rape them and they're whores? You piece of shit. Look, I don't care what your problem is with women, but I will not allow you to keep raping women in this city. And you don't have to go to jail. But you will never have a moment's peace, even if you think you can run from me. Just so you know, I know where your brother lives in Virginia, your mother still lives in New Jersey, and you have an old girlfriend that you still talk to who lives in Hawai'i. You also have a friend you've known since junior high that lives in California." His eyes became big with recognition. "No matter where you go, I'll find you. Turn yourself in Maxin," I said pointing my knife at him. I turned and went back up the stairs, out the way I came in. He didn't say a word, and he didn't follow me.

A few weeks later I was getting ready to take Maxin again since he still had not turned himself in. But Patty saved me the trouble. Siobhán called me.

"Hello?"

"Harri, turn on channel five"

"Siobhán, what's the matter?"

"Just turn it on. And stay on the phone with me."

I turned it on. Patty was on my TV screen standing at a makeshift podium. I could see a window in the back with Mario's on the window in backward letters. A few people were standing listening to her, and there were cameras for all the stations in Syracuse. She had papers in her hands, her hair had grown out some, and she had on a nice suit. Her eyes were puffy and worn, but her look at the camera seemed determined. Before I could ask Siobhán what was going on, Patty spoke,

"Good morning, ladies and gentlemen. My name is Patty Huntley. About six and a half months ago I was raped by a man named Maxin Little. He drugged me, had sex with me, and then left me in a hotel room. Fortunately for him, I cannot remember a lot of what happened because of the drugs he gave me. He will not be prosecuted, and I will have to live with what he did to me for the rest of my life, probably seeing him around Syracuse.

"I'm holding this press conference because I want other women to know that this man is out there, and he is dangerous. Here is a picture of the man I'm talking about." Patty held up an 8 X 10 picture of him for the cameras.

"If you see this man, don't accept drinks from him or spend a lot of time alone with him. I will not be taking questions, and I will not be giving any interviews. I just don't want any other women to go through what I went through. If you've been assaulted, please contact House and Home at 315-555-2876, and they can help you. Thank you."

Reporters of course tried to talk to her, but a man I didn't recognize led her out of the restaurant. Siobhán spoke first.

"Did you know she was doing this?"

"No. Good for her. I have been so worried about her."

"Me too. You think she will open the door for us now?"

"I don't know, but let's find out. I'll meet you over there."

Patty opened the door and flew into our arms. We all cried with her for a while.

"I'm sorry I didn't tell you. I had to do this on my own."

"Who was the man on camera with you?"

"My lawyer. He suggested I do this to give myself some closure from this."

"I am very proud of you, Patty," said Siobhán.

"We've been so worried."

"I know. I'm sorry I cut you off, and I appreciate that you all abided by my wishes. I needed to do this."

"What's next?" I asked.

"Nothing. I can get on with my life."

Patty was going to see her boss to get back to work. Siobhán and I stayed with Patty. In the morning her lawyer called her,

"Patty, it's John."

"What's the matter?"

"Maxin's lawyer filed paperwork in court today to sue you."

"Sue me? For what?"

"According to the paperwork, defamation of character and libel."

"You can't be serious. Why do I still have to deal with this?"

"Don't worry about it. They won't win. He's just doing this so you will back down and take back what you said."

"I'm not doing that."

"I know. I'm going to come over, and we can talk about next steps."

"Okay."

The affidavit said Patty was making allegations that had no basis in fact. She had no proof that Maxin did anything to her. John told her what they really wanted was for Patty to take back what she said and say she didn't know what happened. He also told her he would represent her if they had to go to court. Then it all went away.

About a week after Patty held her press conference, five other women came forward to say he had done the same thing to them. All six women, including Patty, had been assaulted in the last three years. There were others, but the statute of limitations had run out for them. There was also one woman who came forward to Patty as she was coming out of the courthouse one day. She told Patty he had assaulted her before any of the women who had come forward.

Patty tried to talk her into telling the DA her story, but she didn't want to press charges. She just wanted to thank Patty for coming forward and making sure that he went to jail.

Maxin was eventually charged with six counts of sexual battery, six counts of rape, six counts of kidnapping, and six counts of unlawful imprisonment. There was no law on the books at the time for drugging someone, so they didn't charge him with that. All five women, as Patty did, went to the hospital and had rape kits done. None of them tried to press charges against Maxin when it happened to them. Patty was the only one who tried when it happened to her.

All the charges carried different sentences ranging from five years to twenty-five years. They made a deal with the District Attorney, the women involved, and Maxin, for him to plead guilty to six counts of rape. They tossed the sexual battery, kidnapping, and unlawful imprisonment charges.

Because of the rapes, the DA split the difference, and they sentenced Maxin to 20 years in prison. I was thrilled about the outcome because I knew what his fate would have been with me. I wasn't going to keep kidnapping him. Eventually, I would've killed him, and I did not want to do that.

Chapter 23

Two years after Patty was assaulted, I was still working all three of my jobs and started making shadow appearances at rallies and Take Back the Night events around New York State. What happened to Patty, and what I did to Maxin made me want to become an advocate for women who were assaulted. The time and visibility necessary for that were not possible for me. This was the next best thing.

I held signs, clapped at event speeches, and chanted their mantras. If you saw me on TV, it would be hard to pick me out among the rest of my sisters. However, if someone was looking for me, they would find me.

It was a normal spring day, and I was coming out of House and Home. It was sunny, there was a light breeze, and the temperature was 68º. For Syracuse, it was like summer.

I stopped at the bottom of the stairs looking around. I didn't feel danger, but I felt a presence. I saw a woman leaning against a small dark green car. She looked about 5" 3', weighed probably 120 pounds, looked to be in her late thirties, had on little makeup, and her hair was pulled into a bun. Her stance and the way she held her body didn't look like she could fight, but that could have been a trick. When she saw me, she moved towards me, looking me right in the eye. What the hell was this?

I balled my hands into fists as I walked. "Can I help you?"

"I hope so. Are you Harrison McCuff?"

People who knew me called me Harri. Whoever this was, she didn't know me, and there was no reason for her to know my name. I almost put her nose in her brain, but I didn't see fear or hesitation in her eyes. "Who are you?"

"I'm Cara, and I wondered if I might talk to you?"

"About?"

"I want to talk to you about an opportunity."

"What kind of opportunity?" I didn't see anyone hiding, and no cars or vans were driving by. I recalled thinking to myself, "I think she's alone."

"Can we go somewhere more private?"

Chuckling. "Listen, lady, I don't know you, so I'm not going anywhere with you."

"Ms. McCuff, please. I know you could probably kill me with one stroke of your arm. You are in no danger..."

I grabbed her by the neck and slammed her against the car.

"Who... the... hell... are... you? If you don't tell me who you work for right now, <u>I will</u> kill you." I loosened my grip on her neck so she could talk and took half a step back.

"I work for an organization that believes you can help us with our mission," she said, slightly out of breath. I stepped forward to tighten my grip on her neck again when one of my co-workers came out of the house.

"Harrison, are you OK?"

I turned around. It was Judy. She was a nice short old lady who wore polyester pants and flower shirts, with her hair teased high. She was nice but was known to be in everyone's business.

"I'm fine, Judy. Just giving this lady directions. Thanks."

"OK." Judy slowly went back into HH, but I knew she was looking out the window. I turned back to Cara rubbing her neck where my hand had been wrapped around her throat. Before I spoke, she said,

"Ms. McCuff, I'm not here to hurt you. I hope you can help us. I would just like to present what our organization does and let you decide."

"What is this organization?"

"I can explain everything if you come with me."

"Why can't you explain here?"

"My boss would like to speak to you, and she's at a remote location. We would essentially need to go to her."

"Fine. Bring your boss to the public library. I would rather be in a more public place, and they have..."

"No. To keep our privacy, we need to do it in our van."

"In your van?"

"So we can block any signals and prevent people from finding out where she is."

I was beginning to like these people, but I couldn't go on my instincts alone. It was too weird.

"I need to know who you are first."

"You won't find anything about us through the usual channels, and those who have heard the rumors don't have solid information. I can give you what you need, Ms. McCuff."

"Look, we have to do this my way. You want to meet with me and be all mysterious and shit, fine. Meet me at this address in an hour. You're not there, I'm gone, and if I see you again, you'll be dead before you see me."

"Fine, Ms. McCuff. We'll do it your way."

I called Maurice and asked him to meet me at the top level of the new parking garage they were opening on Monday. The structure was previously an office building in downtown Syracuse, right near Armory Square. A garage company bought the space, tore down the building, and built a parking lot in its spot. They installed cameras on each of the levels, but they were not operational yet. The top level was outside and higher than most of the surrounding buildings.

Maurice didn't even ask what was going on when he showed.

"What do you need?"

"Some woman approached me today about her organization. She wants me to join them."

"What's the organization?"

"I don't know, but that's what we're here for. I am going to meet them here to discuss this. I just wanted a little backup."

"They? I thought it was one woman?"

"It was, but we are meeting her boss here tonight. She wanted to do it someplace I don't know. I thought this was safe. I did some recon, and I didn't see anyone. We just have to be cautious when they show up."

"Why did you agree to this?"

"Because when I grabbed her around the neck, she didn't seem scared and because of my instincts. I always listen to them, and they're telling me she is not a threat."

Maurice parked his car at the farthest end of the parking lot from the entrance. I stuck an assault rifle in the back seat. In my waistband, I had a nine-millimeter, an ankle gun, and my knife.

When Cara arrived, she was in a gray van with what looked like satellite dishes on the top. She had parked two spaces from Maurice's car. She got out of the van and opened the sliding door.

When I looked inside the van, there was a bank of computers, some machines I didn't recognize, and three small box structures I assumed were seats. Cara and I got into the van while Maurice stood outside. She didn't even ask who Maurice was.

She started a bank of computers along with the other machines. I found out later that they were more sophisticated versions of some tracker and jamming equipment I own.

When all the machines came on, Cara told me we were waiting for her boss to arrive. A few seconds later, a woman's silhouette came on the screen.

"Hello, Harrison. My name is Maybelinne, and I run an organization that helps women and children get away from abusers."

Not only was she hidden from me, but so was her voice. It was computer generated. I liked the directness.

"There are lots of those around. We have a few of them in Syracuse."

"Yes, but none hide better than we do. No one sees them again when we do it."

"Isn't that kidnapping?"

"Perhaps, but if it saves a woman and/or child from dying, it's worth the risk."

"Why would you think I would be interested in something like this?" Maybelinne said nothing. Cara answered instead.

"We had you vetted and…"

"Vetted? What is this fucking congress? How would you even do something like that?"

Maybelline answered, "She means we checked out your background. We needed to know if we were right about you. We found out your name after a lot of digging. It wasn't easy."

"You're serious? Look, this is bullshit. I don't know who you people are…"

Cara raised her hand. "Harrison, please hear us out. I know this is a lot of information. If you let us explain, you will understand why we think you might fit with us. After that, if you want to leave, we'll forget about you, and you can forget us."

I didn't say a word. I was pondering if I wanted to continue. I was intrigued. "What did you find out?"

"We know about your family in New Rochelle, your friend from childhood who was killed, your relationship with the pimp (she jerks her head in Maurice's direction outside), your involvement with a friend's attacker, just to name a few things.

"Holy shit."

"There was no other way to do this. We needed to know if we could trust you in the organization.""How come I've never heard of this organization? I've worked with women and violence for years. How have you never been caught?"

In unison, Cara and Maybelinne said, "We're good."

I sat there thinking. "What am I supposed to do with this? Just say 'Oh yeah, I'll come work for you?' I don't even know what you want from me."

Maybelinne said, "We wouldn't expect you to just say yes. We know you want to know more about us."

"How do you know I won't go to the police or FBI?"

Cara answered, "Because you would have left already. And what are you going to tell them? We haven't given you any real information."

"So, you trust me?"

"No, we had you vetted like I said and know your personality, your morals, and your beliefs. We've watched your behavior, especially what no one else pays attention to. That's what's important in choosing allies."

I sat there, considering all of this. Fear wasn't the issue, and I didn't feel threatened. I needed to know more. "OK, ladies. I'm here. Tell me exactly what it is you do and what you want from me."

Chapter 24

"The organization is called The Collective. As I've already told you, we hide women and children who are being abused from their abusers, and sometimes we help them begin new lives."

"How did you find me?"

Cara smiled. "We are always scanning newspapers, websites, and new programs from all over the country looking for agents to help with our cause."

"Most people listen to what people say. What they should be doing is watching the rest of the body and paying attention to their behavior."

"In the videos and articles, we saw you were in the back and didn't say a lot. You would disappear and reappear in videos, and no one seemed to notice. You were everywhere and no one was paying attention."

I was a little impressed. These ladies were better than the FBI, CIA, and Congress combined with their vetting process.

"I told Maybelinne about you after a few months. She decided to have this go to the next step. The process took us months because we had to be thorough."

"Who did you talk to? No one in my family mentioned being questioned. Friends never said anything. How do you know this information is accurate?"

"We have ways of finding information without including the family. They are a great source, but they tend to talk a lot. The information we received is accurate."

"Ok. And what do you want from me?"

"We want you to be an agent for The Collective. You would be helping to transport the women and children to safety."

"That's it? I can do that. Now, what are you not telling me?"

Cara didn't answer me. She looked towards Maybelinne.

"What we do is dangerous. What we are doing can be considered kidnapping. We have a very tight-knit network, and we want to keep it that way. That means you have to be careful; you can't tell anyone about us, and you will not have a lot of information except for what you do. If you can handle that, I think you can be an asset to The Collective."

I didn't know what to say. I didn't know what I thought she was going to say, but I was not expecting that. "Wow. How long do I have to think about this? I want to be sure this is what I want."

"You can take all the time you want," Cara answered handing me a phone number. "You can call us at that number if you are interested. We will get in touch with you."

"I'll think about this, ladies. I'll call you."

Maybelinne thanked me and was gone. I thanked Cara and left the van where Maurice was still waiting for me.

"Didn't need to kill anybody?"

Cara was pulling out and leaving the garage. "No, I didn't need to kill anyone."

"What do they want?"

"My services."

Cara was right. I could not find anything about The Collective through regular channels. Even the people who were underground had very little information for me. They have been around for a while (no one knew exactly how long), no one knew who anyone was in the organization, and if somehow someone were to get caught (which happened years ago), no one ever talked.

The information I gathered and after meeting the ladies, I decided to say yes to the job.

"Can I speak to Cara please?"

There was a pause on the other end. The feathery voice that answered the phone answered, "May I say who is calling?"

"Harri"

"Is there a last name?"

"No."

There was a pause. "Hold on please."

A few minutes later, "Hello, Harri."

"Cara. I would like to accept your offer."

"Great. We need to meet to talk about specifics. We have a phone for you and some instructions. We do not need to meet in Syracuse again. Let's meet in Ithaca."

"Okay, let me know when and where."

When I began working for The Collective, I kept my job at House and Home for a while. After a year, I couldn't do both jobs effectively, so I had to quit one. The Collective won.

I told Kathy, my boss, my old professor wanted me to help him with some research, and I needed to do it full-time. She tried to convince me to work temporarily, but I explained I couldn't. I needed flexibility. I loved what I did at House and Home, but I knew the work for The Collective was more important.

There is no information on why or how Maybelinne started The Collective. I did know that by the time I was a part of the organization, The Collective had been around for over thirty years.

They ran a smooth operation with few problems or issues as far as getting caught. One of the main reasons this was possible was our tracker and researcher, Magus. The things he did with a computer were incredible, and he defined many of the protocols The Collective uses today for communication and investigation.

He was one of the top hackers in the country. I didn't know how they found him or how he found them. Magus's fact-finding skills were impressive. When I started working with him directly instead of having Cara as a buffer, Magus hinted that he knew about Senshijutsu. I'm sure it was Ever who told him, but I could never confirm.

For five years, I worked for The Collective and the Playhouse with little or no fanfare. I wasn't at the Playhouse consistently, so they didn't miss me if I was gone for an extended period. My friends thought I was working on securing funds for the Playhouse, which I was, but only when I wasn't doing my other job.

The majority of my clients for The Collective I met through my Outsider connections (a person who assists the organization but had no direct association with The Collective). There were only a few women I came into contact with through the police. So, in the beginning, the authorities were not paying attention to me or what I was doing. They didn't know I existed.

This is how it worked: someone would recognize a woman in trouble and find the right time to approach her about getting out for good. Most women didn't believe we could help, so we never pushed; we might nudge, but not push. There were others who didn't want to go with us at all. If they used our services, we moved them to a local safe house. This was what the police and other authorities knew about.

Over the years, there were a lot of questions asked about what I was doing, and the cops even arrested me a couple of times, but I never stayed long.

None of the cops disliked me except one. His name was Sergeant Anthony Costillio. He was an old-school cop who grew up in a new time world. I think he was a cop like his father before him, who was a straightforward Italian cop. Costillio was originally from Brooklyn and moved here with his parents and his eight brothers and sisters when he was three. They started out on the Northside of Syracuse and now all lived on the Westside in a three-block radius. He had a wife, five boys, tried to play by the rules, and he hated me.

Costillio thought I was an obstructionist (my word) and a pain in the ass (his words). He didn't like my involvement in police business. He believed the abused women were victims for the police to deal with, and I shouldn't be involved at all. It pissed him off even more that he couldn't catch me doing something wrong. At one point I had to go to the police chief, with my lawyer, and ask that the harassment by Sgt. Costillio cease and desist. Costillio continued to tail me, which was fine, but it got harder to lose him.

I could not have imagined this was going to be my life. When I told Ever all those years ago, I knew there was something I needed to do, this was not what I was thinking about. Using my skills in this way was what Senshijutsu was about, and Hajime Ino would have been proud.

Chapter 25

When I told Ever about The Collective, it was one of the only times I saw him smile. It was more than a smile. His whole face was beaming. I wanted to fly into his arms and hug him forever. I didn't realize until that moment how much I wanted him to be proud of me.

Although my work with the Collective was where I put all my energy, Ever still sent me on jobs. Over the years I continued to go home for training sessions. Keeping my skills sharp was even more important since I needed different skills for my two jobs. I didn't use a lot of violence with the Collective, but I used planning and critical thinking in both jobs.

My brothers still lived in New Rochelle. When I came home, my mother had all her children with her. During this stay, I was home for two weeks, didn't have any jobs coming up, and had no other obligations. All I had to do was eat and train. This suited my mother. She cooked for everyone and knew everyone's schedule.

Ever took me to the shooting range, practiced my hand-to-hand skills, made me meditate, and we even did some boxing. Ever was getting up there in years, but he could still hold his own. I was better, but not by much.

I had a few days left and Ever wanted rest days to be a part of my schedule. He told me to meet him for lunch at New Rochelle Mall. It was eleven o'clock on a weekday. The food court was filling up. Ever ate at Sbarro's, and I ate at the Chinese restaurant. We got our lunches and sat at a table away from other patrons. He asked me about JC whom I had not seen in years. I knew he was asking me how I was doing without him since we never talked about it. He also asked me about Maurice. It was nice to talk to him about nothing and everything. Now, when I talked to him, it was like talking to a friend. While he was talking, I looked up at him and thought, "My God, this is Ever. He's a real person. I'm having a conversation with him." At that moment I couldn't have been happier.

"Harri? I want to know why you're holding yourself back from your responsibilities?"

"What do you mean?"

"You're not honoring your skills, Harri."

"Yes, I am. You know what I do."

"Yes, I know, but you are holding a piece back. You are forgetting this is about people."

"I know that Ever."

"Then why no children?"

How did he always know everything? "I help children. I have to with the work I do."

"You do it by helping their mothers. That's not what I meant, and you know it, Harri. Why?"

I knew what he meant, but I didn't want to talk about it. This worked for me for almost four years, so why did I have to change it now?

"I help them, Ever. I do it in the back."

"That is not our way, and you know it. You've been avoiding it. I thought you had worked through all of this already. She wouldn't want this for you."

Pushing my food around my plate and not looking him in the eye, "You didn't even know her. You don't know what she would want!"

"I didn't know her, but I know you. You cannot be a master and not be fully committed. What happens when someone needs you who doesn't fit your criteria?"

"I'll find someone to help them. I always do."

"Yes, but you are the best, Harri."

"Nothing has happened so far. I know what I'm doing."

"I'm telling you, you're not being a master. They will need you one day, and you must be there, Harri."

I didn't say anything else. Ever changed the subject to my family. He said what he said, and now it was up to me. He was right. I hated it, but I knew he was right. Every time a kid in need of my help was shuffled off to another agent, there was a deep pang. The pang was pushed and twisted until it was a dull ache I could ignore and move on from. No one challenged me. Now Ever had shined this huge light on it and it couldn't be ignored. I had a choice to make.

Ever and I didn't come together, but we parked our cars in the same area in the underground garage. This was probably the last time we would see each other for a few months. I recall I had to force myself not to cry. The boxing, the gun range, and the lessons in my shortcomings were usual. Having lunch and talking about life made this day special. These types of days don't happen often with us. It was a fantastic day.

I saw them out of the corner of my eye at the same time Ever saw them. The garage was surprisingly vacant--no one was coming or going.

We were standing by Ever's car. My vehicle was about three rows away from where we were. The lot was at full capacity.

"Harrison?"

"Yes, Sensei?" I did not take my eyes off the five men coming towards us.

"I want you to get in your car and..."

"No, Sensei? You know I'm not leaving."

He paused. "Remember your training. Breathe and think."

"Yes, Sensei."

The men kept exchanging looks with each other and then back at me as they advanced. Two of them came towards me and three went towards Ever. They should have made it the other way around.

When the first guy came towards me, I kicked him before he could react. The second guy saw what I was about to do and jumped out of the way. The first guy was crumpled on the ground, but I knew he wouldn't stay down long.

Ever was holding his own with the three guys. I brought my attention back to the guy still standing. He smirked at me and lunged. I moved out of the way, and he slammed into the trunk of a car. He smashed his hand on the trunk, turned around, and came for me again. His friend was off the ground but dazed. The second guy caught me in the face with a punch, but it was a mistake. I grabbed him by the throat, started squeezing, and punching him in his jaw.

I got three good shots before he realized what was happening. He chopped down on my arm for me to release his neck. I spun out of the way and glanced at Ever. One of the guys was on the ground. I had to end this.

I kicked my guy in the chest as hard as I could. He stumbled back and came for me again. I punched him right in the nose. It broke; he yelled out and used both hands to try to cover the blood spurting from his nose. I hit him again in the head until he was on the ground. When the first guy came for me again, I hit him in the throat and then hit him in the head with my hands, and I think I kicked him until he was on the ground.

As I turned to go help Ever, one guy pulled a knife. I could see anger on his face. His partner tried to stop him, but it was too late. He stabbed Ever twice in his side before Ever knew what had happened.

"Nooooo!" I ran to him. The two guys picked up the guys on the ground and took off. People were leaving the mall. Some were passing the garage, and some were walking into the garage. I could hear someone calling the police.

"Ever! No, please."

"It's OK, Harri."

"Ever!" I had both my hands over his wound. Blood was seeping through my fingers onto his shirt, my shirt, and my pants.

He grabbed my arm. "We don't have a lot of time. They were after the gym. I recognized one of the men who came to the gym. Don't let them get it. We need that gym." His voice was fading.

"Ever, please! Hold on, I hear them coming. Please."

"Tell Maurice that I love him. Tell all the kids." He closed his eyes.

"Ever! Ever! Ever!!

The ambulance arrived but Ever was gone. I couldn't stop the bleeding, and Ever didn't regain consciousness.

They had to peel me off him. The cops asked me questions, but I told them nothing except descriptions of the men; bad descriptions. They asked about his next of kin and I told them about Maurice.

I couldn't let him hear about Ever from the police. I tried to keep the tears out of my voice when I called him.

"Maurice?"

"Harri? What's the matter?"

"It's... It's..."

"Where are you, Harrison?"

"I'm in New Rochelle."

"I'm coming. What happened?"

I couldn't hold it back. I burst into tears. "Ever is gone, Maurice."

There was a pause. "What happened, Harri?"

"Some men attacked us at the mall. I tried Maurice. There were too many of them. I tried to get to him, but I couldn't get to himI couldn't get to him, I..."

"Harrison! Take a deep breath. You're going too fast. I'm coming right now. I want you to go to the gym. I'll come there. I'll see if I can get a flight."

"I have to go to the police station and look at mugshots. Maurice, I'm so sorry. I tried to save him."

"Do you know what they look like, Harrison?"

"Yes. This was about the gym."

"How do you know that?"

I paused, "Ever told me before he died." I started to cry again. "He also told me to tell you he loved you, Maurice."

I didn't hear anything. "Maurice?"

I could hear tears in his voice this time. "I'm here. Don't tell the cops anything. I know who this is. It started before I left. And Harrison. I know you did everything you could to save him. I'll be there soon. I have to call my brothers and sister, okay?"

"OK."

The police took me to the station. On the way, I called my brothers. They met me there. My parents were out of town, but Day called them.

At the police station they let me wash Ever's blood off my hands. They offered to give me some clothes to wear, but I refused. I needed his blood on me right now.

The police wanted to go over my story again. I told them the same story I told them the first time and again, I left out what Ever told me. When they thought they had got it all out of me, they had me look at mugshots. That was what I was doing when my brothers arrived.

When I saw them, I burst into tears. I tried to hold it in, but I could not do it. We stood in the middle of the squad room in a sister-brother sandwich while I bawled my eyes out. I could feel all the cops watching us. I didn't give a shit.

Keenan pulled my head off his chest and kissed me on the forehead. I placed my face back on his chest and cried some more. When my tears slowed, the mug books were waiting for me. My brothers sat next to me, holding my hand and rubbing my back.

There was one guy I recognized. His name was Mark Lavelle. He was the one who had a broken nose because of me. I didn't tell the cops I knew him. After three hours at the police station, they finally let me leave. We went back to the mall to retrieve my car and then to the house to take a shower. I stayed in the shower for thirty minutes. The shower took three minutes. The other twenty-seven were spent crying over my Sensei and what I let happen.

Maurice texted me to let me know he was coming in at seven o'clock. He was lucky his flight was landing at Westchester County Airport instead of having to go to LaGuardia or Kennedy. I told him I'd meet him at the gym.

I explained to my brothers what happened, but I didn't tell them what Ever said. That part of my life had nothing to do with my brothers. I wanted it to be, but I wouldn't do that to them.

My brothers came with me to the gym. We talked about how I was doing about Ever and about my life in Syracuse while we waited for Maurice.

When Maurice arrived, I broke again. I saw the hurt and pain in his face. He hugged me tightly for what seemed like a long time. He told my brothers he needed to talk to me. They were reluctant at first, but I told them it was OK.

I delivered the entire story to Maurice. He listened with his head down and didn't say a word. I apologized over and over, and he then ultimately looked at me.

"Harri, please stop apologizing. I know you tried to help. You could have left him there, but you didn't. It's not your fault.

"The developer's name is Maxwell Washington. He came to see my father about a year before I left. He wanted to buy this building and all the buildings along this block. My father wouldn't sell to him.

"Washington offered my father three times what this building is worth. My father knew the game. If he offered that kind of money, it was worth way more than that.

"He was harassing my father, coming around all times of the day to talk to him about the gym. I guess he thought my father would give in, but you know Ever."

Maurice had tears in his eyes and stopped to compose himself.

"I know where this guy is. I made sure I knew where his office was and where he lived."

"Give me the information. I will take care of the rest."

"You are not doing this alone, Harrison."

"You're right, Maurice. I am not. I'm gonna need your help, but you will not help me with hurting these men."

"He was my father."

"I know that. But you're upset, and you will be in the way in this state. Plus, Ever trained me for stuff like this. Not you."

"I want to see their blood run, Harrison."

"You will. By my hand with you watching."

"OK. So, what's the plan?"

Chapter 26

The next evening, Maurice's brothers and sister arrived. They went to identify their father's body at the coroner's office. Maurice always made it seem like his sister and brothers didn't know who their father was, but when I told them what happened, none of them asked a lot of questions or seemed surprised.

The funeral was going to be a small ceremony. The size of the funeral was not comparable to the number of people who knew Ever. Maurice said Ever never wanted a big funeral. He said if anything happened to him Maurice should call his brothers and sister, me, my family, and to contact a man in Columbia.

They held the funeral a week and a half after his death. People who didn't come sent flowers. The funeral home staff had to put the overflow of flowers in the lobby. The casket was a plain wood box. No ornaments, no gloss. There were four older gentlemen I did not recognize, and they all spoke Spanish. Everyone else was either family or a friend, but there were still about twenty-five or thirty of us in the funeral home. The casket was closed, and there was a picture of Ever in the gym on top of the casket. He did not want his body viewed like that.

The service was nice and short. His daughter, Nesta, gave the eulogy. She said a lot of wonderful things about him and talked about his life as a teacher. I saw each one of them cry about their father. It was like the realization of his death hit them one by one and tears would flow. As they cried, the others would console them.

At the wake, in Ever's house, everyone was telling me how sorry they were. People were in his living room, his sitting room, his kitchen, and in his den. I wanted to shout, "Get the fuck out of his house," because they were in his space. He would not like everyone in his home. And their words of condolence did not help. I only thought about how I had failed him. How I could not save him?

After the funeral, I went back to my parent's house. I stayed there doing nothing for three weeks. After the third week, my mother wanted to know why I was there.

"Harrison, you have a life in Syracuse. Ever would not want you sitting in my house moping around," she said as she followed me into the living room.

"Mom, I just need time to think and some breathing room. I'm going to go back to my life, just not this second."

"Well, which second will that be, Harri?"

"Mom, I don't know. I just know I need some time right now."

Even my brothers got in on this and told me I could not stay there forever. I told my brothers to mind their business. My mother accepted my explanation, but I knew she wouldn't forever. Even Maurice came to shame me.

Sitting in my room, "Do you plan on staying in this house forever?"

"I don't know."

"You have work to do, Harrison. We need to put our plan in place. I don't want too much time to lapse."

I had not even gotten out of my pajamas. It was 1:30 in the afternoon, "Maurice, can't you do it? I was wrong to cut you out of this."

"Stop feeling sorry for yourself, Harrison. Ever's death needs to be avenged and you are the person who can do it. You did not kill him, Harrison. My father lived a life that should have had him dead a long time ago, many times! You didn't stab him, and if you weren't there," He paused. "I don't think they were there to hurt him, Harri. I think they were going to take him, and you were a surprise. Now get off your ass and help me get the motherfuckas that did this to you and my father!"

"I need more time."

"Time for what?"

"To just live and not think. I don't need this right now. I need to mourn, too. Now get out!"

"No. Don't tell me to get out!"

"I'm not gonna fuckin' help you, Maurice! Get out!"

"Oh yes, you are because you promised me. My father taught you better than this"

"I don't care! I can't do this, now get the fuck out!"

He glared at me, jumped up, and left.

I couldn't think straight. I needed to relax and get out of my head.

I went to a bar where I knew no one would pay attention to me, and no one knew me. Anthony's is a house they converted into a bar on the South Side. It was illegal, but the cops and the neighbors let it go because there were no fights, and no one complained.

When I walked in, there were a few people at the bar. The bar was at one end of the house, which could be where the kitchen should have been, and there were tables and chairs set up in what could be where the living room should have been. I moved over to the corner and ordered a rum and coke. I ordered three more, but I was drunk after two.

I knew I drove home, but I didn't remember driving. When I woke up, I couldn't move. Thankfully, my parents weren't home. I finally dragged myself out of bed after an hour. I took a shower and got some food. My brothers came in, took one look at me, and started screaming at me.

"What the fuck, Harri? What are you doing?" asked Day.

I was holding my ears from his shouting and my head was on the table I was sitting at, "I'm fine. I just had too much to drink last night. Mind your business. It's not like I haven't seen you two do worse."

"That's 'cause we were stupid guys. You have never been that person, Harri. What is going on? I know your friend..." said Keenan.

"He was more than my friend, and this is not about him!"

"Then what's it about, Harri? You've been here for almost a month, and you aren't doing a thing except lying around and now getting drunk. We can help."

"No, you can't cause there is nothing wrong. I just need a little break. Why can't everyone just let me grieve? I'll be fine. Leave me alone," as I hurried out of the kitchen and upstairs. This was about Ever, but I didn't want to talk about it with them. I always went to my brothers, but this time was different. I couldn't tell them what they didn't know.

My drinking didn't stop, and my brothers kept my drunkenness from my parents. Unfortunately, my parents knew exactly what was going on. We had talked about it. We had discussions, and then we had fights about it. Finally, my mother could not deal with it or me anymore.

We were sitting on the couch in our living room, "Harrison, you will not keep behaving like this in my house. I had hoped this would stop, but it hasn't. It's been six weeks. ENOUGH!"

"I'm grown. You can't tell me I can't drink," I said standing up.

Then she stood up, "I can in my damn house. I don't know who you think you are talking to, but..."

"I know who I'm talking to. My mother. I'm not trying to be disrespectful Mom, but I have to do this my way."

"Your way is hurting you, Harri. I thought you had learned tools to deal with..."

"This is different. It's my fault..."

"Harrison..."

"No. I need some more time to get my head together and if you can't..."

"Don't even finish that sentence. You need to leave Harrison. You can't stay here anymore. I love you with my whole soul, but I won't watch you hurt yourself. I can't."

I stared at her for a few seconds. Moving past her, I went upstairs and packed my stuff. I didn't want to be who they needed me to be. I wanted to not feel, and not think about anything.

I was not going back to Syracuse, and I did not want to talk about it or explain it. I wanted it all to be over. I had money. Siobhán could have The Playhouse, The Collective could replace me. I wanted to be free from it all.

I moved to Mount Vernon, near the Bronx, and spent six months living in a small house there. I would stop at little bars to drink all night, get into fights, and lived as if no one mattered. Not even me. Every night I would find myself crying when I was sober enough to cry.

My parents tried calling me, my brothers came over to my house, Cara tried getting in touch with me, Patty and Siobhán tried to reach out, and Maurice tried to call me. I responded to none of them. They even sent the cops to my home to do a wellness check. Fuck them. I didn't care.

I woke up one morning with my eye hurting, lying in my clothes, my head hurting, and feeling like a cat died in my mouth. I knew I had been in a fight, but I could not remember where or with whom the fight took place.

I could barely move, but I got in the shower, put on some clothes, started walking down the stairs, and I almost fell. The twins were sitting on my couch watching TV. They were both dressed in sweat suits, their hair neatly cut, looking as fine as they always did.

"What the fuck are you two doing here? How did you even find me?"

They exchanged looks with each other and turned to me. "We're taking you home," one said. I plopped down on one of the stairs, staring at them.

"What is happening?" I said through tears.

The other twin walked over to the stairs and knelt in front of me, "You have work to do. You can't stay here. You're gonna come with me and Ramón."

I started crying. "Why are you both talking to me? You don't speak. His name is Ramón? What's your name?"

"Orland."

"We talk when we want. Most times, we don't need to talk. You need us. Orland, get her something for her head. I'll make you something to eat. Then we're gonna pack, and we're gonna go."

Orland went upstairs, and Ramón went to the kitchen. I couldn't move. It was too much, and I started bawling, my head in my hands. Orland came back with aspirin. Ramón brought me water. I took the aspirin, and they led me to the kitchen to sit. Ramón made us breakfast. We ate in silence with my tears in my eggs and grits.

After breakfast, I cleaned the dishes while Ramón and Orland started packing my stuff. I told them to stop.

"I am going to go with you, but I need to talk to my family. Where is Maurice?"

"He's waiting at home for you. He got in touch with us," said Orland.

"Can you give me a couple of days? I have some explaining to do, and I need to get this alcohol out of my system."

They both looked at me and at each other, talking to each other the way they did. "OK. We'll stay here while you do what you need to do," Ramón responded.

I smiled and went to make some phone calls.

I wasn't sure how bad my withdrawal would be, but I had been drinking as if I was trying to put out a fire. For more than eight months, I was only somewhat sober when I was asleep.

On the second day of no alcohol, I started throwing up. I couldn't keep any food down. When I stopped throwing up, I could only eat soup and water. The shakes started at the same time. By the third day, I could eat more solid food and the shakes stopped, but the headaches started. Aspirin did nothing for it. That first week, I wanted to drink so bad, but Orland and Ramón would not let me out of their sight. I could not see anyone for three weeks.

When the pain, headaches, and nausea passed, I attended meetings, which didn't work for me. I went to a few and never went back. I called Maurice, who told me he loved me, and he was waiting for me. He told me he was disappointed in me that I did this to myself and proud that I made it through to this side.

I called my family. I needed to apologize and say goodbye to them. When they showed up, I introduced Orland and Ramón as friends from The Playhouse. They were here to take me back to Syracuse. When my father questioned them, they had answers to what he wanted to know. I should not be amazed by them, but I am. Standing in my living room, they took every question.

"What do you do for the Playhouse?"

"We help with security, sir, and we do what Harrison needs."

"Where do you two come from?"

"We are originally from Columbia, but we have been in the US since we were nine."

"And your parents?"

"Our parents died when we were teenagers, sir."

"I'm...I'm sorry to hear that."

My mom moved to my father's side, "Davis? Stop interrogating those men."

As she dragged him away, "Thank you, mom. I just want to say that I have been in a bad place for the last eight months. I needed to work some things out, but I did a horrible job handling this. I'm sorry if I scared you or made you all worry."

"Sorry! You know damn well you scared us and made us worry! Why wouldn't you let us in, Harrison? We talked about everything together. I don't understand," she said sitting on my couch. I sat next to her on the couch. I held her hand.

"This was different. I lost him."

"That was not your..."

"I know Mom, but I couldn't see that at the time. My pain was greater than my need to let you or anyone else comfort me. I'm sorry for how I handled this."

She hugged me with my face on her neck. She still smelled of lavender and cocoa butter. I soaked her neck with tears. After about thirty seconds or so, I raised my head and looked at my brothers.

"I'm sorry for the way I treated both of you. You two have always been there for me, and I'm sorry I pushed you away. Please forgive me."

They both came over to hug me in our brother-sister sandwich. "We forgive you. We were just worried about you," Day said.

My father didn't say a word while I was groveling for forgiveness and telling them my plans.

I couldn't say anything to him. I knew how hurt and angry he was with me, and I didn't know how to fix it with his silence.

We all talked for a little longer and had dinner together. When it was time to go, my father stood up and came to me as everyone was getting their things to leave.

"You scared me." Everyone stopped what they were doing.

"Dad, I'm…"

"No! No talking from you," he said pointing to me. "Your whole life I have watched you be this little version of your mother. To witness you lose that and for you not to let us help kept me up at night and worrying during the day."

I placed my head low. "I… I don't know what to say, Daddy."

He raised my chin, "I don't want your sorry or your hugs or your kisses. I need to know that you are OK. I need to know that this will never happen again. And if it does, you will reach out. I need to know that, Harrison."

I took his hands. "Dad, this won't happen again. I am going to see someone, and I will be OK. I won't give you my apologies. I will tell you I won't let myself fall down this hole again. I don't like the look I see in your eyes right now, and Ever wouldn't be too happy with me either." I lowered my head and tried not to burst into tears. I lifted my head. "I'm OK."

He kissed me on the forehead. "Good. I believe you, and I know you mean it because if you don't, I will be very disappointed with you," he said looking straight into my eyes.

"Yes, sir."

"Have a safe trip back, and call your mother when you get there."

"Yes, sir."

On the way back to Syracuse, the twins told me Maurice had found the faces of the men who killed Ever. Even with all my bullshit, he still put our plan into action. I hoped he still wanted my help because it was what I needed to help me heal.

We knew Washington had a state-of-the-art surveillance system at his office and we were sure the guys went to him on the same day or the next to report to him.

Maurice called his friend to find out if he could hack into the system. It took him a couple of hours, but he got in, and we got pretty good shots of all five guys. He sent over the information, and I sent it to Magus.

Magus got back to me in a week and had the names, addresses, and some of the history of these men. One of them was local. The other four were from out of town. Magus told us the four who were from out-of-town left two days after Ever was killed. The local was still in New Rochelle as far as he could tell, but not at home.

Maurice and I looked for Mark Lavelle for a week. I told my parents I was in New Rochelle to help Maurice and the family decide what to do with the gym.

Mark was not a professional. If I were him, my space in New Rochelle would have been burned, and I would have left everything behind. Instead, he came back. I assumed he thought it was safe. No professional would think that.

I watched him for a few days to see if I could pick up his pattern. He stayed in the house a long time, but when he ventured out, I could tell he was nervous and cautious. But not enough I couldn't follow him, not once did he see me. If he did, he was hiding it well.

I knew enough about him that I could plan how to do this and where. I didn't tell Maurice when I was going to kill him or where I was going to do it. If the police figured out Mark Lavelle was involved in Ever's murders, I didn't want Maurice to know a thing. Maurice and I would be the first questioned, and Maurice didn't have to lie about what he didn't know.

Mark Lavelle lived on a side street in Camillus, New York. Woods surrounded his house on two sides. He had no curtains on the windows and usually kept the shades raised. The houses next to his, although close, also had a lot of foliage coverage, which made it easy to stay hidden from them.

The twins got me five sniper rifles that they would get rid of for me. They drove to New Rochelle to bring me the first one. They came to the gym when it was closed.

A few days later, I went to the woods behind Lavelle's house. There was a high point about two miles away from his home. I set up my rifle, checked my wind, my sight, and my position. Then I waited. I waited for two hours, and Lavelle pulled into his driveway. I could see him through my sight. He fixed himself something to eat and sat in front of the television. His couch faced away from the window.

I checked my wind again, my sight, and my position. I inhaled and exhaled a few times, closed my eyes, breathed out, and opened them. His head was in my sight. I pulled the trigger. The bullet hit him on the back of his head and then hit the television. His living room was lit up like a fireworks show for about one second and then it was shrouded in darkness.

I exhaled again. I picked up my gun, put it in my case, moved the leaves and sticks around, and listened to see if there were any movements around me. I only heard the rustling of leaves and small movements among the branches. Then I moved back down the hill and to the car, which was parked in a clearing at the bottom. I placed the case in the trunk and drove home. One down and five to go.

Chapter 27

When I returned to Syracuse, I needed to continue my work with The Collective, but I told them I needed to slow down a little, just at first. My main goal was to make the men who took Ever, my sensei, from me, but my other goal was to stay clean. Admitting that I was an addict was the hardest thing I have ever had to do in my life. And although meetings were not for me, I could not do this alone. I was lucky. I found a sponsor and a therapist. They both have changed in all the years I've been sober, but I still have a sponsor and a therapist today.

The twins did some research on the best places to kill these men and helped me develop my plans. They brought me weapons to each location. It was my job to bring it back. I tried to pay them for their time, but they wouldn't allow it. This was personal and they didn't charge anything that was personal.

I didn't have to focus on what my sensei told me with my focus on these men. I could still hear Ever's voice, "You know what you have to do." The work I had been avoiding for years was going to need attention.

The second guy I went after was Wilson Dean. He was in Florida. The third guy, John Wiscnoski, was in Montana. The fourth guy, Quinn "Larry" Rotan, was in Ohio, and the fifth guy, George Charles, was in Georgia.

There was only one place I had to go where I was doing double duty. I was dropping off a charge in Florida and would get rid of Wilson Dean at the same time. All the other kills were independent of my work for The Collective.

Each kill was completed at night, except for the Ohio and Florida jobs. I chose to do those during the day because of their locations and to make them look different from the others. Wilson Dean was a creature of habit. His need to go to the swamp to hunt made a wonderful cover for me. I'm not sure if anyone even found his body. As for Larry, he lived in a secluded part of Ohio. There weren't a lot of other houses around and minimal people in the area. There was one road to his home. There were woods on both sides of the road to his house that went for miles on both sides. Instead of trying to keep quiet in the woods or find a quiet way down his street, I arrived the day before while he was out. I waited in the woods for him. When he drove into his driveway and got out of the car, I put a bullet between his eyes. His wife and child were inside the house. I could hear his wife screaming as I made my way out of the woods.

Every single hit was a clean one, or as clean as I could make it. All of them took one shot to the head except for George Charles and Larry Rotan. I tapped both of them twice just so the kills did not look too identical. I knew they were in different parts of the country, and no one would make the connection, but that was how Ever raised me. When I finished a kill, the twins and I met at different locations, and I gave them the guns. The twins destroyed each of the guns I used and not by throwing them in any body of water.

Maurice took care of Malcolm Washington. A Columbian drug dealer who was picked up and charged with felony weight told DEA agents he had a bigger person for them. He gave them Malcolm Washington's name. Not only did Malcolm have multiple trips back and forth to Columbia on airline records, but Columbian dealers corroborated the prisoner's stories, and dealers on the street who were picked up in stings were asked about Malcolm Washington. They mentioned they heard of Malcolm Washington but never met him. Malcolm was supposedly crying in front of investigators, trying to explain to them it wasn't him. He was just a real estate developer.

Washington's fiancée left him, he lost all his clients, and all his assets were frozen. He ultimately got thirty years for drug trafficking. He was ultimately killed in jail during a prison fight.

"Maurice, why did you have him killed? He would have died in prison or been old when he got out."

"That was my plan all along. I didn't want his death to come back on you or me. No one will suspect."

"This was a lot of work, Maurice."

"It was, but it was worth it. You told me I couldn't do it. You didn't say I couldn't have it done."

Maurice never told me a lot about how he pulled this off, but I'm sure it involved a lot of money and a lot of connections. I suspected his brothers and sister helped him. In all the time I'd known Maurice, his brothers and sister did not talk to him. Months before Washington was killed, the four of them were together all the time and I didn't think they were just visiting.

When Malcolm Washington was dead, Maurice and I went out for a drink. I drank Pepsi. We toasted to Ever and reminisced about our time with him. He told me stories I had never heard, and I told him some he had never heard. Ever would not have liked what we did, but he would have been proud that the two of us were moving on from it.

While working on my side project, I didn't have time to think about what Ever said to me. I didn't have to deal with fixing what I knew was broken. When I finally settled back in Syracuse, I still didn't want to do what Ever told me I should do. I knew I was holding back a part of myself from Senshijutsu, but it was not in me to do.

I returned to work with the Collective and resumed moving people to safety. Now and then I could hear Ever's voice in my mind telling me I wasn't being true. I increased my work with younger children by interacting with the children in HH. It did not silence the voice of Ever. When I was called to The Playhouse, I should have known what was coming.

#####

I got off my knees and asked myself, "Why am I acting like this?" She'd been gone for so long, and I'd made my peace with it. Sensei. That's what was wrong.

I did not want to do it. My entire career, I stayed away from older children. They were always around, but I didn't have to be close to them. Cara and Maybelline always gave cases with older children to someone else. If they were under five, I had no issue. And the children at House and Home, I didn't have to interact with them much. I wasn't a counselor, I worked in the kitchen sometimes, I didn't do intake, and I did not come to any functions. I would talk to them when they came in and help the mothers comfort their children. But that was it.

I always listened to my instincts, and they were telling me this was not just some guy. I saw the look of disgust, hatred, and murder in his eyes. I was going to have to keep them safe. That meant I had to be involved; I had to be a part of their lives, and I didn't think I could do it. I went to the kitchen and ate my stew while I thought about what I was going to do.

This was what he was talking about. Damn it. Even when he was dead, I could not ignore him. I knew Sensei was right. The piece I was closing off to the world was not allowing me to be who I am truly supposed to be. My protective guard was protecting nothing inside me. As soon as I saw a doll, I almost fell apart.

I went back to Grant's on their second day to find out if Mona wanted to go into hiding. Mona had been through this before, and women in her position were not always ready to make the move to leave. Most people did not comprehend what it meant to go into hiding properly. It was nothing like it was in the movies. Every time I saw a movie about witness protection, I wanted to throw something at the TV or the movie screen.

To properly go into hiding, one must go off the grid completely. Anything even resembling the old life can no longer exist. Friends, family, and acquaintances are all dead to that person. Names no longer exist and who that person was must be buried.

When children are involved, the change has to be simple. They have a hard time with details. Both Braxton Jr. and Ledawnia could make a mistake easily.

There was a widely held view that one could make secret phone calls or sneak in and visit people from their old life, and it was not at all accurate. Unless they were being chased by someone who did not know what they were doing. They would eventually find that individual if they weren't cut off from everyone and everything they used to know.

When I arrived at the house, I didn't see anyone inside, but I heard their voices and laughter. When I glanced through the open doorway into the backyard, I was shocked.

Ledawnia was running around the huge Elm tree in the middle of Grant's backyard chasing Deanna's son, James. Deanna was sitting on a blanket, reading, and watching the two other children. I stepped out of the house onto the back porch and saw Mona sitting at one end of the porch. She seemed to be in serious concentration on something. She was looking at her daughter and looking past me to the other side of the porch. When I turned to the other side of the porch, I saw Braxton Jr. sitting in Grant's lap, sucking on a bottle, and playing with his foot.

Mona stood to her feet with a radiant smile. When Ledawnia saw me, she ran over to me, hugged me around the waist, and then went back to play with Deanna and James.

"I haven't seen my children this calm in a long time," Mona stated, still watching the same scene as I was.

"I'm glad. I see that Ledawnia has taken to me. She hasn't said two words to me since we met."

Mona chuckled. "I couldn't get any sleep last night because she kept talking about you and what you did. She's nine, but I think she thinks you're a super-hero. I think it took her a little while to process it."

"I'm no superhero, but I am glad your daughter has some peace. Is it OK if we go inside and talk for a little bit?"

She looked at her children for another moment. "Sure."

We sat in the den on one of the couches facing a big, curtained bay window. The room on all four walls was bookshelves filled with books.

"Mona, do you know what your goal is for you and your children?"

"No. I haven't thought about it. You told me he would never find us, but how would we live? Would we stay here forever?"

"No, but I can make sure your husband never finds you, but is that what you want?"

She gave it a moment to think about it, "Yes, I would love that but..."I held my hand up. "Do you know what it will mean for you and your children to disappear?"

"I think so."

"What?"

"It means I am leaving everything behind."

"That's right. If you go into hiding from this man, you must leave Syracuse and New York State. You will never see any of your family or friends again. Your children will have to forget who they are because they will have a new name and will have to forget their old life. That is not an easy task for children.

"You will have to become someone new. You can never tell anyone who you used to be, not even people you've come to trust and love. Your entire life will become a lie, and not only will you live that lie, but you will have to be that lie in your mind. It's not just about changing the name on your ID or getting another social security number for you. That's easy. The hard part is becoming the new identity we formed for you."

Again, she didn't say a word right away.

"The man I'm married to has been torturing me and my daughter since before she was born," Mona said, her voice cracking.

"I've been away from him for two days, and the two children in that back-yard," she points to the backyard. "Are not the children I raised. They are the children that I should have raised." She stood up and stood by the window, looking out. She started to pull back the curtain and stopped herself. "It has only been two days. I feel safe here, but I'm still scared he's going to show up." She paused for a long time.

"Do you know I've thought about going back? Even with my children being so happy, even though I had the most hours of sleep I've had in years last night, I still think I should go back." She didn't say anything. Tears started to run down her face.

"Even though my daughter was safe from his hands and his body for the first time in years." She stared at the curtained window for a few seconds and then turned to face me. "I love him. I know, to someone like you, you think I'm some weak woman, but he has been my whole life for eleven years. What do I do without him?"

I remained sitting and waited for her to continue. "Can you keep us safe?"

"Yes," I reassured her.

"I will do what needs to be done if it means I don't have to go back to him. You just tell me what we need to do."

I stood to my feet and strolled over to where she was, "If you want to do this, our journey begins with another move to a new house."

"This is not a safe house?"

"No, this is just a stop. I just needed to get you somewhere safe. I wanted to make sure you really want to do this."

"I just want to know if he will not come and get me. Can you guarantee me that?"

"Yes. I can. If you trust me and you want to do this, I will move you and your children to a safe house. You're not gonna have contact with anyone except the woman who you will stay with. You will hardly have contact with me. I'm assuming you want to testify against your husband?"

"I don't know. If I can leave and he'll never find us, why do I have to testify or put my daughter through testifying?"

"You can, but the man I saw yesterday won't stop looking for you. At least if you put him in prison, you'll know where he is while you disappear, but this is totally your call. No matter what you choose, I'll help you."

Mona dropped to the armchair nearest the window and placed her head in her hands, "I don't know what to do."

I rushed and placed my hand on the tip of her trembling shoulder, "You think about it. We have a few more days here, but you do need to decide if you want to testify or not."

Grant came into the den and closed the two sliding doors. "I listened to the messages on Mona's phone yesterday before I got rid of it. There was a message from the Assistant District Attorney that said she wanted to talk to Mona and it was urgent. She didn't say what it was, but she wants her to call or better, come in."

"How did you get my messages?"

"Magic," Grant answered.

"Grant?" I squinted at him and shook my head a little. I turned to Mona. "Do you want to call her, Mona? Or do you want to go down and see the ADA?"

"I don't know. What do you think I should do?"

I put my hand on hers. "No one has to tell you what to do anymore, Mona. You can decide what is best for you."

"I know, but I don't know what that is. How do I decide?"

"Well, do you want to see her, or do you just want to talk to her?"

"I don't want to leave. I'll call her."

"OK. Grant will show you the phone to use."

Mona followed Grant into a small alcove off the kitchen. He then came back to the den while she used the phone.

"Go top to bottom with her if she's gonna go out on her own. She knows nothing. She is in a worse spot than Deanna was, and she was pretty bad. That's a lot of work."

"I know, but I knew what I was getting into. Besides, it's not like I don't have the time. I think this is bad, and she's gonna need me."

Mona walked back into the den and closed the sliding doors. "The ADA said that Braxton made threats against my life, and they want to put me in protective custody."

"Protective custody? For a woman beater and child molester that's in jail?" I asked.

"That's what she said, but I told her I was safe where I was. She wanted to know where I was, and I told her I couldn't tell her. That was right, right?"

"Yes," I answered again.

"She tried to talk me into it, but I told her no, thank you and I hung up."

"This will not end well," said Grant.

"What?" asked Mona.

Again, I squinted at Grant and said, "Grant!" I turned to Mona. "He didn't mean anything, Mona. You did fine. Don't worry about the ADA. In the meantime, we need to discuss you going into hiding."

"I'll go check on the kids and my sister," Grant said as he left and closed the doors.

"Where are you going to take us?"

"I don't have that information. I won't until we are ready to go. First, we will be going to the safe house."

"What about my children? Will they be safe with me?"

"Yes, of course. Your kids will be safe with you."

"No one is going to come to take them from me because I took them away?"

"No. No one is going to find you. Ever."

"What am I going to do for money?"

"You will get a job. We will find something for you."

"I don't know how to do anything."

"We will figure that out."

"Am I asking too many questions?"

"You can ask as many questions as you want, Mona. What else do you want to know?"

For the next hour, Mona and I discussed the beginning of her new life. I think the phone call rattled her because she was nervous and jumpy as we talked. No matter how safe someone told you they were, I guess when a psycho threatens them, they couldn't help but be worried. She did, however, seem open to changing her entire life into something else.

After our talk, I told Mona she would not see me for a few days. When I came back, she would go to a safe house.

"You need to think about everything we discussed. If you have any reservations, then I won't move you to the safe house."

"What will happen to me and my children?"

"I will keep you here until after you testify. Then you can go wherever you want."

"I have nowhere to go. My friends are all here, my family doesn't want anything to do with me. Where would I go?"

I smiled at Mona. "Mona, your family may surprise you. Don't count them out. But we are getting ahead of ourselves. Think about it and I will see you in a few days."

"OK."

Chapter 28

The next day, I was leaving the house I lived in on Rugby Road. There was a black Crown Victoria parked in front of my home. Detective Anthony Costillio got out along with his partner, whom I didn't know. He looked as though he was in his thirties. He had dark brown hair that fell in his eyes, was taller than Detective Costillio, and was built like a football player. His green eyes were such a contrast to his dark brown hair, it made him look very mysterious.

A black and white car was also there with two uniformed officers who exited the car and stood on the passenger side as Costi and his partner walked to meet me at the front of my steps. I couldn't imagine what I had done for all these cops to show up at my house.

"Detective? What can I do for you?"

"You can get in the car, Ms. McCuff. The ADA wants to see you."

"The question is do I want to see her?"

"Are you going to make me force you?"

"You would love that, wouldn't you? Don't threaten me Costi, I don't have to go with you if I don't want to, but I will."

When I arrived at the ADA's office, Rochelle Rown was sitting behind her desk with her hands folded. Her short blond hair would have made her look like a man if it wasn't for the lashes, lipstick, and dangling earrings. She had a huge rock on her left ring finger and six gold and diamond bracelets on her arm.

Sitting at the edge of her desk was ADA Todd Felder with his arms crossed. The suit he had on looked like it cost more than all the clothes in the room combined. The rest of him, his two-dollar haircut, the cheap ring on his finger, and his cheap cologne made him look ridiculous. They asked me to have a seat and Detective Costillio and his partner stood behind me on the back wall.

"Hello Ms. McCuff, my name is ADA..."

"I know who you are."

"Oh, how is that?"

I leaned back in the chair. "Ms. Rown, I'm sure you didn't call me down here to go over our mutual friends list. What do you want?""I understand you have Mrs. Lancer in hiding."

"I don't have Mrs. Lancer in anything. Costi is making assumptions."

"You understand her husband has made threats?"

"Yes, I'm aware."

"And you think you can protect her better than the police and the District Attorney's Office?"

"No. I know I can."

"So, you think you're better than the cops?" Costillio said indignantly.

Turning around in my chair, I glared at him and said, "Yes Costi, and you know it."

"Look Ms. McCuff," said ADA Rown, trying to bring the conversation back.

Turning around to face her, I leaned forward and said, "No, you look. I'm not giving her to you. If she wants to come in, fine. But I'm not giving her to you."

"She needs protection."

"Yeah. I know."

"I can arrest you for obstruction."

"You can do whatever the fuck you want, Ms. Rown, but Mona will be gone. I will not send another woman to her death."

"That was not our fault!" said Costi from behind me.

I turn around again. "Really? Whose fault was it? As soon as she was with you, she died. Shit, you guys didn't even see that psychopath coming for Mona!"

"How do you know he's a psychopath?" ADA Rowan asked.

I turned, but I didn't answer right away, "His... face was a kaleidoscope."

"A kaleidoscope?" said Costi.

"Yes. A kaleidoscope. The toy makes different pictures when you turn the bottom. Sometimes with different colors. Sometimes it just moves the existing colors around to make a new picture."

"I know what a kaleidoscope is," replied Costi.

"Good. 'Cause that's what his face did. I watched it actually change shape as he went through his emotions. Along with that, he was going to attack her in a room full of cops while handcuffed? I don't know who this guy is, but he's not just some pedophile woman-beater. He has serious issues." The ADA said nothing. She stood, staring at me, then glanced to the ground.

"That's what I thought. No. I'm not telling you where she is. If Braxton Lancer gets a hint of where she is, he will burn down this city to find her."

"Oh, so now we have leaks too?"

No one responded to Detective Costillio's comment. "We want to at least talk to her. We want to go over her testimony. Can we at least do that," said ADA Rown.

"What! You're not gonna hold her?"

"What the hell do you want me to do, Detective? I don't know if he would burn down the city to find her, but from his jacket, Ms. McCuff is not that far off. She hasn't broken any laws, and I think she's willing to bring her in."

"I will if she's willing to come in."

Detective Costillio raised his voice again. "I don't believe this. She's hiding a vic in one of our cases. We should take her to jail."

I turned around in my chair again and playfully said, "Why do you hate me so much, Costi?"

"Stop, calling me that! Because you interfere with police business and act like you're above the law."

"I don't think I'm above the law. I just don't have to work within its confines. I never broke the law."

"This is bullshit!" And with that, Costi slammed the wooden door open and walked out of the office with his partner following behind him.

"Why do you call him that?" Todd asked.

"Because he hates it."

"I don't want to fight with you, Ms. McCuff," said ADA Rown. She stood up and came to the other corner of her desk. The dark blue dress fit every contour of her body. It looked as though it was painted on.

"I know you give these women a safe place to go. We just want to make sure the women and children are safe and that they're not being held against their will."

"I understand, Ms. Rown, but I didn't say what I said just to annoy Costi. I can do things the authorities cannot. I never make anyone go with me who doesn't want to go.

"I've only worked with five women who came to the police first. I know you know the story, but do you know how many women left me because they thought they would be safer with the police? Three. Two came back, and one stayed. I'll give you three guesses who's dead."

"I understand what you're saying. I don't disagree with you. The women always come to their court appearances, and sometimes what you give is what others cannot do. I want to work with you. We will work to keep you all safe."

"Uh, huh? I'll talk to Mona and get back to you about when. I want to help because we need to get him off the streets."

"You have no idea."

When two weeks had passed and Magus had not returned any information, I had to find something to keep myself occupied. If Magus doesn't call in two weeks, it's going to be a while. I eventually went on some jobs with the twins. Even though I worked for The Collective, I still found time to have a second job with them. I knew Mona and her children would be safe with Grant, but I didn't go far, just in case. The farthest I went was Canada. The jobs were never more than one day, and mostly consisted of reconnaissance, but once I did have to assassinate someone.

When I worked like this, I didn't sleep a lot. It was fine while I was working; however, when I was done, I crashed hard. I tried everything to change this, but it was the way my brain and body worked together, and there was nothing I could do about it. I learned to live with it, and it made my work easier, especially doing surveillance.

When I called to check in with Grant, he informed me the kids and Mona were getting restless. I went to see them.

Ledawnia was happy to see me, but Mona was enraged.

"Why have you been gone for so long?"

"This is what I do to keep you and the children safe."

"I thought something might have happened to you!"

"Grant would let you know if something happened to me, Mona. Look, I know it's hard not having contact with the outside world and I'm your only lifeline, but you know that everything I do, I do to keep you and the children safe."

"What if he showed up?"

I walked over to where she was standing in the hallway, which is where she ambushed me.

"He doesn't know where you are, Mona. I've been monitoring you and the house this whole time. I would've known if he showed up. I told you I would not let anything happen to you."

Mona crumbled to the floor and began sobbing. I realized I'd made an error. She was exhausted. She had been worrying for a month about what would happen to her and her children. Probably during every waking moment. She was on alert, with no skills on how to protect anyone if anything happened. I knelt down and apologized to her. She hugged me as if I was all she had in the world. I never made that mistake again.

I didn't go home that night. I ended up staying in the loft. Locking my door, I turned on my computer and took a shower while it booted. By the time I was out of the shower, my computer was up and waiting for me.

I typed in the address to Ask the Geek.com. It was a website for people who had questions about computers, hardware, and software. The questions were answered quickly and accurately. If an individual was not computer savvy, they had never heard of the site; they would probably go to Microsoft or Apple forums to find their information.

When the page loaded, at the top of the page was a moving banner with pictures of personal computers from the Programma 101 and the IBM SCAMP to the current PC and Apple Macbook. I clicked on the computer from 1973 made by IBM and was on another login page where I entered a username and password provided by Magus. The password changed regularly, but not on any particular schedule.

The login page looked like the regular login page. If someone stumbled upon this gateway page by mistake, they would have had two attempts to enter the username and password. Thereafter, it took them to the "real" forgot password page.

The gateway was an entrance to a server set up by Magus. No one could download a thing and they would not be able to print anything. An individual could view all the items Magus placed on the server.

I logged in; an interface loaded that looked just like a Windows interface. When I clicked on Windows Explorer, it looked just like the filing system on anyone's computer, except there were only files, no destinations. I located the file on Braxton Lancer and read:

Braxton Lancer is the oldest boy of six children, born on October 15th, 1983, in Savanna-la-Mar, Jamaica. His brothers and sisters from oldest to youngest are Lisa, Donnell, Beverly, Newton, and Zyed. None of the children born after each other are more than two years apart.

Braxton was a smart kid all through school until he was in eighth grade and his grades slipped. He did not graduate high school, but when he came to the United States, he got a perfect score on the math, writing, and science sections of the GED. There is a rumor he has an eidetic memory. There is no confirmation of this.

Braxton's father, Neville Lancer, was a cruel and sadistic man. He was an assassin for a gang called the Parliament Gang. They ran drugs, women, and gambling. They were ruthless, and it was unending. Trench Town was their hometown. It was a place where you had to fight to keep your space. Anyone who got in their way was eliminated, and Neville was excellent at what he did. The difference between him and some of his gang family was he brought his brutality home with him.

He used the girls in his family as sex toys. It is said that the father thought women were born to cook, clean, and have sex, and none of them did that well (which is confirmed by multiple sources). His wife was not even his wife, but the woman that he had children with (as well as others). He did, however, call her his wife. Why he never married her is unknown. He never married anyone else either.

When Neville's sons turned 14, he brought them into the gang. The other gang members loved having Neville's sons around to do errands and groom them for the life. 14 was also the age he started raping his daughters. It is believed there was some kind of sexual abuse going on before 14, but it definitely happened after 14.

The first time he went to Lisa's room, Nina (Braxton's mother) tried to attack him, and he beat her, telling her these were his children and he could do as he pleased. Cops came, nothing was done, and the abuse continued.

When the boys turned 16, they formally joined the gang. Braxton, Newton, and Donnell had all dropped out of school. Zyed graduated from high school and even went to college. He received a bachelor's degree in business administration and Information Technology and a master's degree in computing.

When the boys formally joined the gang, the head of the gang made Braxton's two brothers, Donnell and Newton, finish school. For some reason, they did not do the same for Braxton, and I could not find out why.

Neville Lancer died when Zyed was still in college. Braxton was with his father when he died. There were a lot of groups trying to take over what the Parliament gang had. This time, the rival gangs made a very aggressive push for their organization and eventually killed Neville. It is believed the goal was to weaken the organization, and Neville was specifically targeted.

By this time, Braxton was just as ruthless as his father, so it was easy for him, after his father's death, to step into his place in running the drug part of the business. No one believes he took more than one day to mourn his father's death.

Braxton was mean, ran his part of the operation like a dictator, and had a lot of women. Anyone who got out of hand in Braxton's eyes was dealt with, which sometimes meant death or worse. There is another rumor that he killed someone at 17, but cannot confirm.

I think the other brothers had the same reaction. They went back to work fairly quickly. People said it was odd because all four boys seemed to really love their father, but when he died, they went on with their lives. Nothing changed in their lives except for retaliation against the men who killed their father. That was the focus for a little while.

They also continued to terrorize and abuse their sisters. Their mother thought she could stop them because they were not their father, but she was wrong. When she intervened, they beat her; not as severely as their father had, but enough.

A year after Neville's death, Newton tried to stop his brothers from raping their sisters and abusing their mother, but his brothers attacked him. Braxton killed him (confirmed). I do not know what they did with the body, but people knew Braxton did it. He went to the U.S. shortly after that. I do not know if he went because he killed his brother or if this was something that was planned because they wanted to strengthen the connection between New York and Jamaica.

Right before Braxton left, his oldest sister, Lisa, killed herself. This did not seem to affect Braxton and his brothers. None of them attended the service, and no one knows who paid for everything. It always seemed, according to various sources, that Donnell and Zyed were as ruthless as Braxton, but about six months after Braxton left, his mother and younger sister Beverly left. Everyone believes that if Braxton was in Jamaica, they would not have been able to run away. I have looked for them and cannot find them anywhere.

When Braxton came to the United States, he went to Brooklyn, where there was a faction of his gang. He took over the gang when he arrived, killing the leader who did not like the fact that Braxton was coming to the U.S.

He gained his reputation quickly and it was not much different from the one he had in Jamaica. One year after his arrival, lower Brooklyn belonged to him from Coney Island to Flatbush and all points East and West between. He also had police and City Council members on the payroll. Three years after that, he had added judges, DAs, and a DC FBI agent to his ranks. Cannot confirm he ever had mayors working for him, but cannot deny the allegation either. Some things happened in Brooklyn the Mayor must have known about, but cannot find evidence of.

Braxton's female consumption did not change when he got to the U.S. He had two other girlfriends when he met Mona Montclair. Mona met Braxton at a club in New York City with her girlfriends. She grew up in Lansing, Michigan. Her mother was Black and her father was White Canadian. Her former friends say that he knew which one of them to pick. She was 21, and he was 26. Mona had little experience with men and Braxton was handsome, had an accent, and was interested in her.

About six months after they met, Mona stopped hanging out with her girl-friends. They tried to stay in touch with her, but he was controlling. About six months later, they were married. No one knows what happened to her after that because there was no further contact. The next time she came up on the radar was when they moved to Syracuse. Braxton traveled back and forth between Syracuse and Brooklyn, but Mona never left Syracuse. Do not know how he controlled her with his traveling. The rest of it, you know.

End Of Report.

After I finished reading it, I said to myself, "I knew I would need Maurice's help." I went to sleep, and the next morning it began.

Chapter 29

The next day, I started preparing. I called Lisa and Cora to create papers for Mona and her children. They were two of the best forgers I'd ever seen. I knew Cora's father was a forger who did time, but I didn't know where Lisa learned the skill.

I also stopped by Xavier's to see Maurice. It was seven in the morning when I arrived. The day was just ending for them. There were two girls sitting at the back of the bar. The rest of the girls were probably making their way back. I sat across from Maurice, who looked exhausted.

"Remember the woman and her daughter I told you about? They're being harassed by her husband? I have her in hiding, but her husband is a psychopath, and if I want to keep them safe, I know I'm gonna have to do some things that require more than just me."

"How bad?"

"If even half of what I learned is right, it's bad."

"I'll call them, but I have to try and find them. You know how they are?"

"I do. Please try to find them. I might not need them anyway?"

"Why would you want me to call them if you don't need them? You've handled things worse than this?"

"I don't think so. This is bad Maurice. I can feel it. Plus, I work the long game. I need this over quickly. If this goes on for an extended period, I think a lot of people are gonna die."

He looked at me before he spoke again, "Alright. I'll let you know."

I left Xavier's and drove to a diner for breakfast. This was my day to myself. At this time of the day, patrons were coming and going. It was constantly filling and emptying. So busy no one paid any attention to me. Not even the wait staff.

I sat in the diner for a few hours, read some newspapers, and relaxed. Then I drove to downtown Syracuse and parked behind The Galleries. I strolled past the travel agency, walked up the stairs, past two other businesses I cannot remember, and arrived at the public library. I enjoyed going to the library even though I didn't have time to read a book. I loved knowing that books were available if I ever had time to read. My To Be Read list was long and ranged from three-year-old fiction to the latest biography.

After the library, I walked around downtown. I did this occasionally to help hone my observation skills. There were so many activities and so many people downtown that it took a lot of focus to distinguish what each individual was doing. It was an easy way to help keep my skills up.

I walked into Rite-Aid on the last leg of my trip to buy a soda and some candy. When I came out, I bumped into Jerome; a wannabe bad guy who took it upon himself to be Maurice's servant. I don't know how he got into this life. He was average height, with bronze skin, gray eyes, and full lips, and was built like a Mack truck. His shirts were always tight, and his ass filled out any pants he wore. People always made the mistake of thinking because he was pretty, he was a punk. It was a huge mistake.

Maurice and Jerome had a strange relationship. Jerome made sure all the girls got where they needed to be, he ran menial errands for Maurice, and he would kill anyone Maurice told him to.

He was not like most wannabes who didn't have the stomach for this life. Wannabes want to associate with the people in the life and not actually participate. They hoped people would think they were a ruthless motherfucker by association. I called Jerome a wannabe because he was a wannabe pimp. He was more than capable of being a ruthless motherfucka.

"Harrison?! What are you doin' walkin' around? It's freezing out here." He stepped in to hug me.

"It's not that cold yet. Plus if there's no snow, we go outside," we both chuckled. "I just wanted to be among the people, Jerome. Why aren't you with Maurice?"

"He said he wasn't gonna need me till later on this afternoon. I take time for myself when I can get it. That man is demanding…"

I heard what he said, but I could feel something was wrong. As Jerome finished his sentence, I turned to my left and back and saw a couple of men standing on the West Fayette corner, staring at me. I turned to my right and saw three guys across the street standing, glaring at me. I knew what was going to happen. I turned back to Jerome.

"Harrison is something…"

"Jerome, call Maurice and tell him to meet me on South Salina Street near the Red Cross. Tell him to come right now! Call him Jerome!"

I put my bag in Jerome's hands, and I started running. I went back into Rite-Aid, through the aisles, and out the back door. I was on Bank Street and crossed over to Warren Street. Thank God I had a gun on me today. I usually did not carry on these days, but I was planning to go to the range. With Braxton in the mix, I felt I needed to keep all my skills up. I answered my Bluetooth when it rang.

"Yes?"

"Where are you?"

"Running towards you. I'm almost at the Red Cross," a shot rang by my head.

"I'm parked in front of the statue in Billings Park. How many are there?"

"I counted at least seven, only see four right now, and we're comin' in hot," another shot rang around my head. I didn't return fire because I couldn't see what I was doing and run at the same time. I wasn't running in a straight line. I prayed for the rest. "I really hope you have a gun on you."

"Why would I come with no gun? I see you. Damn, they are comin' from both sides."

"Shit."

By this time, I was almost at the car Maurice must have stolen because it wasn't his car. He was parked on the South Salina Street side of the park. There were people everywhere, but most of them ducked or ran when the gunfire started. Maurice got out of his car with one gun in each hand and shot one of the guys behind me. I shot the first guy coming to my left in the leg. As I got to the car, I turned and focused on the men shooting at me and we both took shots at the guys on the left. They were returning fire, but I was better than them. They wounded Maurice in the arm and grazed my ear. Maurice shot two more, while I killed the rest. It was a miracle and a testament to my training that Maurice and I only got an arm and ear wound.

I learned everything there was to know about guns when I was training with Ever. I took a gun apart and put it back together so many times, I could see the pieces in my mind. Ever taught me how to shoot, but the twins taught me precision.

For four months, every day, they made me practice. We stayed at this place in Canada, went out during the day and sometimes in the evening. They used stationary and moving targets, and I wasn't allowed to go in for the day until I had completed all the lessons with precision and accuracy. I was exhausted every day, but when the four months were over, not only was I an excellent shot standing still or on the move, but I was an excellent long-range shot. They also taught me to never shoot what I could not see.

The twins used me sometimes for sniper work when they had to be somewhere else. They would send me the job, I would let them know if I could do it, and they would pay me. We never talked about it, and I never told anyone, including Maurice.

When the last guy was shot, Maurice and I jumped in the car and drove away. Back then, there were no cameras in that area, but there were a lot of people. Lucky for us, they were hiding behind buildings or running and didn't get a good look at us. They gave descriptions of us and the car, but no one saw us clearly.

When we got to the bar, Jerome was there, as were all the ladies. Maurice told Candy to get rid of the car. Jerome took care of Maurice's arm and then my ear. When we were all patched up, we had a drink. We were both sitting at the bar.

"Maurice, thank you for coming..." Then Maurice stood up and slapped me hard across the face.

"What the fuck is wrong with you? You're never careless... ever! How could you not know they were following you? You don't make mistakes like this, Harri. What the hell is goin' on?" Maurice's chest was visibly moving in and out. I stood while Maurice was yelling, let him finish his tirade, and then I punched Maurice in his face and heard and felt his nose break.

"Don't you ever put your hands on me again, Maurice. You're like my brother, but if you ever fuckin' touch me again, I'll kill you." I walked out of the bar.

When I left Xavier's, I could hear sirens going to the scene Maurice and I had created, but I couldn't care less. I was angry, embarrassed, and my ear was hurting. I didn't even know where I was going, and then I remembered my car. I didn't notice Jerome walking next to me until he gave me a jacket to put over my shirt so no one would see the blood on it. I made it to my car, got in, and left Jerome standing on Warren Street.

I drove and when I stopped driving, I was in front of Sicily. One of my professors brought us to Sicily's in grad school when we had a particularly hard clinical day. The restaurant was located twenty five minutes outside of Syracuse and the food was spectacular. I started going there on my own after I went the first time. It's run by a whole family. From the mother to the grandchildren, they all worked in the restaurant. The head was this little Sicilian woman who stayed in the kitchen cooking most of the time. She didn't like the people so much, but she loved feeding them. She started talking to me when she realized I was coming in by myself. Then one day, I was helping her cook. I learned how to make a proper lasagna and a proper cannoli from her.

I knew they were getting ready for the evening crowd. I went in the back door of the kitchen, and the only person in there was Mrs. Uccello. The rest of the family was in the dining area eating. I could hear them all laughing and talking.

"What has happened to you?"

"Nothing Mrs. Uccello. I just wanted to see how you and the family were doing."

"You do not have to lie to me. You can say it is none of my business. Besides, that ear is not nothing."

I chuckled. "I just wanted to see all of you. It's been a while."

"No, you came here to escape. It is OK. I need help with dishes. I'm making cookies today."

"Oh, goodie."

She smacked me on the butt. "Hey, you don't be fresh. Now get the dishes so we can cook."

"Yes ma'am."

When I took my jacket off, she looked at my shirt with blood on it but didn't ask any questions. She went into the back and gave me one of her grandson's shirts to wear. She threw my shirt in the garbage.

I worked my butt off at Sicily's for four and a half hours. I washed dishes for twenty minutes and then baked cookies with Mrs. Uccello. We also made two pies. Then I went to a hotel to sleep.

While I was working in Sicily's kitchen, I realized they must have been watching me. My house was not a secret, it would have been easy enough for them to find me. I should have known, and I should have seen them. But I knew they weren't there. Maybe someone had finally got me. Damn, I needed to step up my game.

I slept through the night and most of the next day. I rolled out of bed and went home. I paid attention this time, and I didn't see anyone following me. Of course not. Maurice and I shot them all. I had to keep in mind they were probably going to regroup. I checked the house as I would if I were a client and found nothing.

I went to check on the Playhouse. Siobhán was doing well after all the excitement with Ledawnia. The Playhouse went back to normal, and she didn't tell anyone what had happened. She wanted to know what I did with the family. I told her about the safehouse after what happened at the police station. I also told her it would be best if she didn't know more than that.

Siobhán let me know people were asking about Ledawnia, and she told them she was sick and would not be back for a while. When I asked her what she told the staff, she said she would tell them at the next staff meeting.

When I woke up the next day, I called Grant to check in and went to the house to make an appearance.

When I got to the house, Ledawnia was sitting in the living room cutting pictures out of magazines. I went in and sat on the couch with her.

"How are you?"

"Good."

"Where is everyone? Why are you in here by yourself?"

"Are you a superhero?"

I chuckled. "No. I just know how to take care of myself."

"Oh."

"Do you like it here?"

"Grant is teaching me to cook." She grabbed my hand and started dragging me to the back of the house.

"He is? So, what have you learned?" We were standing in the kitchen and she started to show me around as if it were her kitchen.

"I've learned how to use the blender, how to choose the right vegetables, and what spices to use. Tonight, he is going to let me help him make the sauce."

"That's great. Where is your mother?"

"She's in the back with Grant. Is my father coming to get us?"

I stopped walking and looked down at her. "Do you want him to?"

"No. Mommy says you're keeping him away from us. But my daddy is strong."

"He might be, but I'm smarter," she giggled at that. I knelt down in front of her. "Listen to me, the only way that he's going to get to any of you is if Grant and I are not here. Otherwise, we will stop him, but he can't find you, anyway. Don't worry, okay?"

"OK. But are you sure? He found us before."

I was hurt and angry at myself. If the men I shot in downtown Syracuse just followed me and didn't attack, they would have found them. I had to hold back tears.

I underestimated Braxton even with the information I had. I didn't take the time to find out what he had here in Syracuse, but I should have expected what he was capable of from the information I was given. Thank God I was smarter than him. I never would have attacked me. But he underestimated me too.

My phone rang. I answered,

"Yes."

"She wants to talk to you."

"Okay." I look at Ledawnia. "He may have found you before, but he knew where to look before. He doesn't know about this house. No one knows about it. Now, go back to cutting your pics and I'll be in soon, okay?"

"Okay," and Ledawnia went back into the den.

"How are you, Harrison?"

"I'm fine, Maybelinne. A little scratched up, but nothing more."

"Does he know where you are?"

"He knows where I live, but he doesn't know where I am. I wouldn't be talking to you if he did."

"I do not want you to get killed."

I chuckled. "Neither do I. I'll be fine."

"We cannot jeopardize the Collective."

"I know, Maybelinne. Nothing will be compromised."

"Is any of what I read true?"

"It seems that way. I think the authorities think it's true because they wanted to put her in protective custody. They only know I gave her a place to stay."

"If this gets to be dangerous, you need to get them out and then yourself."

"You know that's not gonna happen, Maybelinne. The important thing is to protect The Collective and to protect them. I'll be fine no matter what happens."

"Please take care of yourself, and call if you need us."

"Thanks."

I went out back and told Mona that in about a week, it would be time to move her and the family. Mona seemed sad about the news. I knew she felt safe here, but Grant was never a permanent solution. No one stayed at Grant's for this long. And I felt bad for Grant because I think he fell in love with Junior a little bit. Yet it was time.

A week later, everyone packed the few things they had. Everyone was hugging and saying goodbye. Mona thanked Grant, Deana, and her son. Grant had been holding Jr. throughout the goodbyes. When Mona tried to take Jr. out of Grant's arms, Jr. started screaming like someone was killing him instead of trying to remove him from Grant. Grant asked Mona to stop.

Grant took Jr.'s coat off and walked him around the house for a few minutes talking to him and rubbing his back. Jr. had his head on Grant's shoulder, sniffling and glaring at Mona and me with murder in his eyes.

When Grant thought he was calmer, he told us to get everything, and he walked out to the car with Jr. in his arms. Jr. still screamed when Grant tried to hand him to Mona, but he let Grant give him to his mother. He kissed Junior on his head twice and walked back to his house without saying goodbye to any of us.

Braxton Jr. cried the entire time to the safe house. When we got there, Mona had to give him a bath to calm him down and then he finally fell asleep.

"I knew Jr. liked Grant, but I didn't know he was that attached to him. That boy has never screamed like that before. I was a little nervous. I feel awful I had to take Grant away from him and take Braxton away from Grant."

"It's okay, Mona. Braxton is young. He will be OK. Grant will be too."

"I know, but I suspect Grant doesn't get a lot of baby love. That's special."

I introduced them to Norma, whom they would stay with until their final move. Norma was fifty years old, lost her husband when she was thirty-five, never remarried, and didn't have children. She was five feet tall, had blonde hair, weighed about 130 pounds, hailed from Puerto Rico, and punched harder than I did. She was also going to help them get settled into a kind of normalcy. We talked for a while about the next step.

After that, it was time to make some amends and start getting some things ready. Along with deciding she wanted to move, Mona had decided she was going to testify as was Ledawnia. That decision was both brave and dangerous. Braxton was going to find out we were going to the DA's office. I underestimated him before, and I wasn't doing it again.

There was no one following me. Someone told him where I lived. I needed to plan how I was going to keep them alive. I had to plan as if he knew.

Chapter 30

It had been a week and a half since I'd seen Maurice. When I arrived at Xavier's, Maurice wasn't there. I didn't even go back to talk to Candy. She must have been mad because she didn't come to speak to me either. I sat at the bar and waited. When Maurice walked in, I saw his nose was still swollen and it looked as though one of his eyes was black and blue. I hopped off the stool and walked over to him, then threw my arms around him. He hugged me and picked me up.

"I'm sorry Maurice. I should have been more careful, and I wasn't." He put me back on the floor.

"I shouldn't have hit you, Harrison. I was scared and mad at you. I know Ever taught you better than that."

"You're right, you shouldn't have hit me, and Ever did teach me better than that."

"Aren't you going to apologize for punching me?"

"No. You deserved that."

Holding up his hand, "You're right. Just tell me you're gonna be more careful. This guy is really gunning for you."

"I know. When do the twins get here?"

"They said they would be here in a few days."

"Good."

The next two days of waiting for the twins turned into four days, so I did research while I waited.

Braxton was downtown and being held without bail. He had an expensive lawyer from New York who made more in an hour than most people in Syracuse make in a month. Braxton didn't have any connections in Syracuse or the surrounding area that I could find, so the men who shot at me must have been from out of town.

Three days later, the twins were sitting in my living room looking out my window. My apartment was huge, but the living room, bedroom, and dining room were in the same room along with the kitchen. The only room that was its own room was the bathroom. They both had guns in their hands.

"I told you two the last time you did this not to do it again. It took me three days to fix my alarm system the last time. You know I can't call anyone."

I rolled out of bed, went to the bathroom, took a shower, and changed my clothes, and they never moved. I logged on to my computer and the website. The two of them came over and read all the information I had about Braxton. When they were done, I said,

"This guy will not stop. I think he tried to kill me because he didn't know I had his family. I can't understand it. Maybe they jumped the gun, and his orders were not to kill me. I don't know. All I know is that he thinks I'm just a stupid woman, which is to our advantage. He won't see us coming. I know he had to re-group over the last few weeks, but I am sure he's going to try again. Our only goal is to make sure that he doesn't get to his family. He must never know where they are.

"Mona and Ledawnia need to go see the ADA She wants to talk to them, so they need to go to the office. We need a plan. The cops will have a plan when I tell them we're coming, but I have no confidence in them. I want to make sure they're safe, do you understand?" They both nodded their heads.

"Listen, I know this is different from what we usually do, but I hope you're both OK with this."

"We're OK with it," Orland said.

"Just tell us what you need," Ramón stated.

"Good, because I'm not sure I can do this one without the two of you."

I got a copy of the schematics of the building, including renovations that had been completed recently. I also received a layout of the streets, the traffic lights and traffic patterns, the surrounding buildings, and what other offices were in the buildings. The plan we devise cannot get anyone hurt.

I called ADA Rowan and told her we were going to come in on Monday morning. She told me she would have all the security we needed just in case, but Braxton was still in jail; there should be no problems. With his ability to do what he did to me in a few days, I was sure that was not true, and I would not take a chance--not again.

For the rest of the weekend, we worked on our plan. On Monday, we went to pick up Mona and the children. I knew no one knew where my safe house was, but we still made sure we weren't being followed.

Only Norma was awake in the house. She went and woke Mona and her children. I spoke to Mona alone first.

"Mona, there are two guys outside who are going to take us to the courthouse. They are here to help me protect you."

"You think Braxton is going to come after us like he came after you?"

"Yes, I do. I am treating this as if Braxton knows we are coming."

"Why didn't you tell me this before?"

"Because I didn't want you to think about this for weeks. That's my job."

She paused. "You are not going to let him get us, are you?"

"No. He will have to kill all of us for that to happen. And we're really, really good. I'm telling you this now because I don't want it to be a surprise if anything happens. No matter what, do exactly as I say, OK."

"What about the two guys? Do I listen to them too?"

"They don't talk, so no. Just me."

We loaded Mona and her children into the black Lincoln Town Car and drove to the courthouse.

When we pulled up to the courthouse, two cops were standing by the double doors, waiting for us. I was impressed. The twins stayed in the car. When we got out and moved toward the open doors, they drove away.

The hallways of the courthouse were empty at this time of the morning. There were a few police around. All the office doors were closed with their lights off. The only open office we saw was the one on the third floor that belonged to the ADA

We were escorted to the ADA's office. She greeted all of us and asked Mona and her family into her office. I waited in the outer office with the two officers from the front door and Costi. Costi stood in a corner with his partner, David Sean, glaring at me. I took out a book and did some reading, trying to ignore the anger coming off Costi. After over an hour, Mona and the children came out of the office. Mona and Ledawnia had bloodshot and puffy eyes. Mona was holding onto Ledawnia as she walked to the stairs. I made sure they had everything and waved at Costi. He did not wave back.

At the front of the courthouse, the car was there waiting for us. When the policemen opened the doors, we walked out and took two steps toward the car. A shot rang out that missed us and just missed one of the policemen. The cops pulled their guns and started looking around for the shooter. Another shot rang out and a man fell off a roof across the street on the right of us. Cops were running towards the body.

In the chaos, I got Mona and the children in the car where Ramón was waiting for us. As soon as the door shut, he took off. Mona and the children were crying and holding onto each other. Ramón was moving fast.

When we were three blocks away from the courthouse, I noticed a black Lincoln Navigator chasing us. We got to the highway and Ramón took 81 North. We knew the highway would be pretty empty and less of a chance of people getting hurt. They started shooting at us and it started snowing a little. Mona screamed, and the children cried harder. The back window shattered. I could hear bullets hitting the side of the car. I told them to get on the floor of the car.

I pulled my nine-millimeter and started shooting. I was hitting the car, but not hitting my marks. The Navigator had a guy hanging out the passenger window shooting at us.

There were four people in the car: two in the back, the driver, and the front passenger. Ramón looked at me, and I nodded to him. He slowed down by five miles. I hung out the passenger window, shot the front passenger, and then shot out the front tires.

The truck spun out 180º, flipped over twice, and stopped in the middle of the street. A car swerved around the wreck, and I saw two more cars behind it. Ramón took my gun and gave me his colt. I saw he was bleeding from his arm. He smirked at me and nodded his head. I went back to my post, and I started shooting at the lead car. Ramón slowed the car again, but the lead car was weaving. I realized the second car was fighting for position with the third car.

The shooter in the lead car shot the left-hand mirror and caught me on the side. I put a hole in the driver's head and got back in the car and braced myself because the car chasing us was about to collide with us. I could see the passenger trying to steer and brake. They pulled off to the side. The second car was hit with a pit maneuver and landed on its roof. The car behind them drove past us. It was Orland. I could hear the sirens in the background.

I couldn't let them take the twins. I kept Ramón's car, and they took the other and drove off to the rendezvous. I kept Mona and the kids with me.

The shooters had the same idea. They tossed out the guy I shot. Everyone got in one car and drove off. The cops chased them. Two cop cars stopped in front of our car. They had their guns drawn on us. Fucking assholes. Told all of us to get out of the car with our hands up. They didn't even notice the two scared, screaming children. When we were all out of the car and they were handcuffing Mona and me, Costi arrived.

"What the fuck are you doing?"

"They were identified as the people shooting up..."

"Uncuff them, you morons. They just left the courthouse. They are the victims!" yelled Costi.

"Sorry, Sarge."

They took the handcuffs off me and Mona. She reached to comfort her children. Costi admonished them a little more and sent them on their way. He had the EMTs look at us, who decided we all needed to go to the hospital.

As soon as we were all seen, Costi and his partner came to see us.

"Where is the guy driving your car?" Costi asked.

"I don't know what you mean," I answered by repositioning myself on the bed.

"You know what I mean, Harrison. You were not driving that car when you left the courthouse. Now, where is the driver?"

"I don't know."

"How about I take you all in?"

"Just because I don't know what you're talking about?"

"No, because you're lying to me."

"Then take us downtown, Costi. I don't know what to tell you."

He stood glaring at me. I knew he wanted to take me downtown, but knew it was more of a hassle than he wanted to deal with. With two cars turned over, the few witnesses, and the other car they were chasing, I was the least of his worries.

"Fine. When they release you, we go downtown."

I guess I was wrong. When we were released, he brought all four of us downtown. He gave Mona and the children a place to lie down and proceeded to interrogate me for two hours. By the time we were done, it was 6:00 a.m. I would not tell them where the twins were. I could not tell him who the men were who were shooting at us, and I could not tell him why this was happening. I had a guess about all those things, but I couldn't tell Costi. Somehow, they knew about our plan. I would not tell him anything.

Costi wanted to keep Mona and the children there to keep them safe, but Mona would not stay. She said she was safer with me. He offered me a ride since the car I was driving was impounded. I told him no, and I called Grant.

I took Grant to a hotel and I left Mona and the children with him. I tried to go to the rendezvous, but Costi had someone following me. She was good. It took me a while to lose her. When I finally made it to the rendezvous, the twins were waiting for me when I pulled up. Orland had tended to Ramón's arm.

They already ditched their car. I apologized for losing the other car. They said it wasn't theirs anyway.

We picked up Mona and the children, then we drove back to the safe house. I texted Norma to give her a heads-up about what we were bringing back to her. When we got out of the car at the house, Mona hugged me.

"Thank you. Who were those people?"

"I assume, friends of your husbands'."

"This will never stop, will it?"

I looked at her and decided to tell her the truth. "No. If your husband is who I think he is, he's not gonna stop until you're dead."

She didn't say anything at first. "Maybe I should just go back. He'll stop, and it wasn't so bad when he wasn't so mad."

"That's up to you Mona. I can't tell you what to do. I will tell you I think your husband is so mad, he would probably kill you as soon as he sees you. I know you're scared, but when you go into hiding, he's not gonna be able to find you. I promise. I'll keep you and your family safe."

As I was finishing my little pep talk, I noticed that Ledawnia, who was hugging me right along with her mother, was no longer hugging us. I thought she went into the house. But she was walking over to the twins, who were standing by the car in the driveway. She motioned for Ramón to kneel and motioned for Orland to do the same. She hugged them both and whispered something to them. The twins exchanged looks and whispered back to her. She whispered again, then they did, and then the three of them touched foreheads together with Ledawnia's arms around their necks.

I stood and stared. I couldn't believe it. They never spoke to anyone. Even though they spoke to me now, they said very few words. Orland got shot once when we were working on a job together. He didn't make a sound as the bullet went in or when I took the bullet out. As close as Ramón and Orland were, you would think that Ramón would have cried out for his brother when he got shot... nothing.

"I thought you told me they didn't speak. I wonder what they're saying to Ledawnia?" said Mona.

"They usually don't. I was wondering the same thing."

"Ledawnia rarely takes to people this quickly."

"Neither do they. Your daughter is something else."

I went into the house with Norma, Mona, and her family. I sat and talked with Mona and Norma for a while. It was early, and I hadn't slept, but before I left, I needed to talk to Mona. I knew she was exhausted, but I wanted to prepare her.

"I'm leaving now, and I won't be back for a while. I need to make sure that you and the children are safe. No one knows about this place or that you're here. Norma knows how to get in touch with me if she needs me, but she won't.

"You're safe here. I know this is scary for you, but I promise that when I come back for you, this will all be over. You will need to go to the Grand Jury, but after today, I don't know how that's going to work. I will let you know what I find out. Please listen to Norma."

"How long is a while?" said Mona.

"I don't know. It depends on how long what I need to do takes. It could take a few weeks, or it could take months. In either case, if Norma does not hear from me in a month, she knows what to do."

I hugged everyone, gave some final instructions to Norma, and walked outside to the twins. "Listen, this is gonna get bad. This guy tried to ambush us at the courthouse. We need a plan."

"There must be a mole," said Orland.

"I know. I think I know who it is, and I think I have a way to be sure, but we're still gonna need a plan. I know the two of you didn't sign on to any of this. I'll understand if you don't want to move forward."

They looked at each other and nodded their heads at me. We got into the car and drove away from the safe house.

Chapter 31

Ramón, Orland, and I went into hiding. I made two trips to Syracuse to make sure Mona and Ledawnia made it to the Grand Jury with no problems. The twins didn't come with me because I didn't want them seen.

The DA's office was not happy about what happened at the courthouse. They tried again to convince me to bring Mona and her family to the police. I told them no and DA Waters informed me he was going to throw me in jail for obstruction of justice. Costi was standing there, watching, with a big grin on his face. I told the DA to go fuck himself, and he threw me in jail. I was out after a few days.

When I came out of jail, they tried to follow me and put a tap on my cell phone. Magus alerted me of the tap and the tail—could have been wearing neon signs.

Once I took care of all of that, I went back to the twins to decide what and how we would deal with Braxton Lancer. I talked to Maurice. He was my ears on the streets, and I needed to know if they were out there. He said he had not heard anything about it. Even though what happened on the highway was a big story, there were few witnesses to what happened, and they didn't see much as they didn't stop to look with all the bullets flying.

The twins and I went into planning mode. This time our plan was going to be on a bigger scale. We were gone for two and a half months and in that time, two things almost derailed what I knew I had to do.

The twins and I went to a house they own (I do not know how or when they purchased this house) in Cortland, NY. It was December and there was some snow on the ground. Snow was a good cover for people who did the kind of work we did. It was so much easier to see someone coming in the snow.

The house was a huge farmhouse with six bedrooms and lots of land around it. The next house was at least three blocks from us (if we were in the city), so there was a lot of privacy. We had to light the fireplace most nights because it was cold. One of us was always freezing since we took turns patrolling the perimeter of the house.

The first thing happened about three weeks after I got out of jail. I called Maurice for a weekly check-in when Candy answered.

She was sobbing and talking. I couldn't understand a word she was saying. "Harri, ...for Maurice. He's ...hospital and he is really... and I'm trying to...they killed...and..."

"Candy. Slow down. What happened? Take a deep breath."

I heard Candy intake air and let it out. "Three guys came here today, and they wanted to know where you were. Maurice told them he didn't know. They grabbed Meghan and said if he didn't tell them, they were going to kill her. Maurice tried to get to her, but two of the guys were holding him. Maurice told them again he didn't know." She paused and I could hear her crying again. "They shot her in the head."

"Oh, God."

"The two guys started beating him up. Maurice was trying to fight back, but there were two of them. They were punching and kicking him. Then one guy pulled out a knife and the other lit a cigar. They started poking and burning him asking where you were. The third guy put the gun to my head, and he yelled that he wanted to know where you were. He said he didn't know, but he could call you. They let him off the ground." She was crying a little harder now. "He was bleeding and his eyes were starting to swell. He could barely stand up. That's when Jerome came out of the back. Jerome blasted them all and took Maurice to the hospital."

"Do you know how he's doing?"

"They broke his ribs, his hand, puncture wounds on his back, and burn marks on his legs, arms, and chest," Candy told me he wouldn't tell them anything. I didn't have the heart to tell her he didn't have any information to tell. I didn't even have the phone with the number Maurice had for me; I tossed it when I came to Cortland so he couldn't contact me.

I apologized to Candy, and she replied,

"This is the game, girl. I knew what I was in for and so did Daddy. He'll be happy that you called." I thanked her and hung up. I told the twins what had happened. I thought for a second I saw concern in their eyes, but then dismissed it as their urgency to have this done quickly.

Almost around the same time, my mother came out of a store on Fordham Road. Two white guys jumped out of a van and tried to drag her into the van in broad daylight. My mother pulled out her pistol (yes, her pistol), and shot one in the arm so he would let go of her. The other man who was dragging her let her go when she shot his accomplice. She shot into the van and shot out a window and thought she had wounded the driver.

The two guys were already in the van and all three of them drove away. There were no cops on Fordham Road that day, and there were no bodies left at the scene. My mother blended into the crowd with a few people staring at her, but no one stopped her. Everyone went back to their shopping, and my mother went home.

When Maurice found out what happened to my mother, he called my brothers. He told them he was sending bodyguards to watch over the family. My brothers wanted to know what was going on, and Maurice told them he didn't know, but he needed to keep the family safe because that's what his father would have done. They called me. I acted surprised and told them I was not sure what was going on, but that they should take the help. They reluctantly said OK.

I guess my mother was where I received my assassin skills from. I didn't know my mother owned a gun, let alone knew how to shoot one. My mother told me she was never so scared in all her life, but she knew what she had to do. When I asked her how she knew how to shoot a gun, she said, "Your grandmother."

I almost went off track because of those events, but I knew I couldn't. My mother could obviously take care of herself, and Maurice could take care of himself. My focus had to be on Mona and her children. The rest would have to wait. As I said, I was smarter than Braxton. He thought he could make me peek my head out of the rabbit hole before I was ready.

The last piece we needed to complete our plan was the mole. I read the file Magus put on the server about my suspicions. I was right. We continued working on our plan, and I made a call to Detective Costillio.

"Hi, Detective."

"Ms. McCuff. What can I do for you?"

"Well, I heard through the grapevine that the DA wanted to question me again about the attempt on Mona's life?"

"I've heard that as well, but no one can find you."

"I've been out of town. I will be back in a few days and the DA can meet them then."

"I don't know why everyone is always giving you these passes. You think you're special. You think you don't have to follow the rules like everyone else, and you think you are above the law."

"Costi, you know that the way I do things is necessary for the safety of the women and children since the police couldn't handle it."

I smiled and stifled my laughter for the tirade I knew was coming. "Goddamn it, Harrison! Stop blaming us for what happened! We didn't do it on purpose, and we follow the law and do what we have to do. None of those women should be dead and maybe if you worked with us instead of against us she would be alive! You are a fucking pain in the ass, and if I had my way your ass would be in jail right now so you can't be a menace to police work!"

"Oh, Costi, stop yelling. I know it wasn't your fault. I promise we will be in the day after tomorrow."

"Fine and stop fucking calling me, Costi." He slammed the phone down. I chuckled to myself and glanced over at the twins; they nodded and so did I. We knew tomorrow was it.

At 2:45 a.m., Orland woke me and gestured with two fingers pointing at his eyes and then pointed out the window. He was holding a gun for me. I jumped up, grabbed the gun, put my shoes and coat on, and rushed out on the porch with Orland. About three minutes later, we saw cars and a van driving up the street and turning onto the road toward the house. It was dark, as there was not a lot of lighting on those streets.

Orland and I pulled our night vision goggles down. There were no lights from the vehicles as they made their way to the house. They thought they were going to surprise us.

Before the three cars and the one van even stopped, three men in each vehicle jumped out and started shooting at the house. We shot back. Ramón was on the roof, shooting from above. He took out two of the men in the first car and one in the van. Orland and I were taking heavy fire from all the guns but took out the drivers from both front vehicles.

There was a lot of confusion on their side. They didn't know where to shoot. One of them started shouting "Encender las luces, Encender las luces." (turn on the lights, turn on the lights.) Orland and I pulled up our goggles. Someone turned on the car lights, but by this time, five of their guys were dead. They sprayed the house again. The two cars in the back weren't able to move any closer to the house because the car and the van were blocking the way and had no drivers. This gave Orland and me time to take more strategic positions.

These men were better than the men Braxton had used in the past but still not as good as us. They spread out across the property but had not taken care of Ramón yet, which caused them some issues. There was a man who went across the property to a tree to try to take out Ramón, but I took him out first. A guy did manage to climb into Ramón's position. There was a scuffle on the roof and shots were fired. The man flew off the roof and hit the ground.

Orland and I knew there were men in the house trying to surprise us by coming from behind. The problem was, they didn't know where we were.

Orland was on the west side of the house, and I was on the east. As they moved across the curtainless windows of the house, we shot two before they realized what was going on. Now there were eight men left.

Orland and I couldn't see them anywhere and knew they were waiting for us. I could see Orland through the window on the other side of the house, and we both held our positions where we were. They must have decided they wanted this over quickly and came out of hiding.

Two men came around from the back of the house to the west and east. I was low on the ground, waiting for them. Orland and I moved back to the front of the house. We were signaling our kills through the window, so we could keep count of who was left. There were five in the house and three outside the structure house. As soon as they saw us, we started exchanging fire.

When we got back to the front of the house, two more men were dead. They shot Orland in the arm, and I took a bullet in my leg. As I was fighting off the men coming from the east side of the house, in my peripheral vision I saw a man coming from the west side straight for me. I took out another man. I turned to take care of the man on my side, and he was on top of me with a knife, not a gun. I realized the man was a woman going for my face. I was not expecting her to jump on me, and she threw me off balance. I fell to the ground, and she went with me. She was trying to shove the knife into my cheek and said, "This is from Braxton, bitch."

The gun blocked her from slicing me to bits. I kicked her off, and she landed on her feet. She rolled a few times trying to get away from me, and I shot her in the chest and the back as she was trying to roll away. Then a a loud boom and a flash happened behind me, close to the trucks. There were three men left, along with Orland and me. We all flew backward, and I felt something hot hitting my skin. After that, I remembered nothing.

I learned later that Ramón came off the roof after taking care of his wounds from his own private shootout. He was surveying the area and preparing to get us and leave. He heard sirens, and they were close.

The man who threw the grenade was in the truck throughout the entire fight. He must have been their contingency plan. He shot Ramón in the shoulder, which knocked him down, but not before he shot and killed the guy hiding in the van. By the time the authorities got there, it looked like a scene from a war zone.

Chapter 32

I opened my eyes to harsh lighting. The sun was blinding. I could not figure out why they had left me outside all night. I could not think because I felt pain washing over me. I looked to my right and saw white walls, flowers all over, cards, and pictures hanging up. On the other side, Costi was sitting in a seat. A door, a lot of tubes, and machines were making noises. I could not speak or move.

I saw Costi go through a door. The next thing I remember was a doctor talking to me. A nurse was looking at a machine. I could hear him, but I could not respond. I did not know how long I was awake, but I must have gone to sleep because the next thing I remembered was waking up again. My mother and father were talking to the doctor. Keenan and Day were sitting on either side of me. I looked at Keenan first.

"I need to see Costi!" Everyone in the room turned toward me and started talking to me or grabbing my hands. The doctors were trying to move people out of the way to get to me.

"Shut up! I'm sorry, but I need to see Costi. Please."

The doctor would not let anyone come in until he had examined me. He practically shoved everyone out of the room. He then ran tests for my brain function. He took blood and checked my vitals. I do not remember what he did or what he asked me. I remember I was in a lot of pain. I asked the doctor what was wrong with me. He said I had broken a rib from a grenade blast, and I had three bullet wounds: one in my leg, another in the arm, and one in my side. As soon as he said that, I felt the pain in those places. He said I had some cuts and bruises too, but the other serious injury was to my head, which had a huge bump on it.

When the doctor was done, I told him again I wanted to see Detective Costillio. Costi came in a few moments later and sat next to my bed.

"How long have I been out?" Detective Costillio didn't say a word. "Costi, how long?"

"Three weeks."

"Three weeks!"

"You had a concussion and were in a coma."

"Jesus. Where are the twins?"

"Gone."

"Gone!" I said, half sitting up and then falling back down.

"No, not dead." He half raised up out of his seat. "They left. Do you know where they might have gone? We still want to speak to them."

"No, and even if I did, I wouldn't tell you. You won't see them again. Hell, I probably won't see them again. What happened?"

"One of the twins was recovering from a huge hole in his shoulder. They kept him sedated for a while. When they took him off the sedation and he woke up, he and his brother just left. You know, if you had just told me where you were, I could have helped you out."

"How did you know I was in the hospital if you didn't know where I was?"

"They airlifted you and the twins from Cortland to University Hospital as Jane and John Doe. They always call the police when there's a Jane or John Doe. An officer recognized you and called me."

I looked at him. "Costi? There's a mole in the department."

"A mole? How did we get to a mole?"

"They knew where I was. No one knew where I was, Costi."

"How do you know it's the department?"

"Because I called you."

"What are you saying? It's me?" He was getting angry.

"No, Costi. You wouldn't do that."

"Then what are you talking about?"

"I called you on purpose that day and stayed on the phone long enough for them to trace my call. I had an idea who it was."

"Who do you think it is?"

"David Sean."

"Bullshit. How did you come to that?"

"I looked into him."

"Looked into him? How would you even do that?"

"That doesn't matter right now. Look, he has a bank account in Canada listed in the name of his dead brother. He's received payments to the account over the last few months, and the money traces back to Jamaica where Braxton's from."

"That's circumstantial. You have no real proof it was him?"

"I know it doesn't seem like a lot, but when I called you, he was there, wasn't he? He's the only new person in the department. Does David Sean look like he should be receiving five-thousand-dollar payments from Jamaica? I know it's all circumstantial, but I'm not wrong. I wouldn't tell you this if I was wrong."

He sat there thinking about it for a few minutes. Then he got up, went to the door, and looked out. "Fontaine?"

"Yes, sir?"

"Arrest him," he stated, pointing at Detective Sean.

"Sir? What?"

"You heard me. He tried to have her killed."

David Sean tried to run, but the cops caught him. Officer Fontaine threw him against the wall and handcuffed him. "Take him to the station and put him in holding."

Detective Costillio watched for a few moments as Detective Sean was being led away. He closed the door and went back to the seat beside my bed. I let him sit for a few seconds. "Where's Braxton?" I asked.

With his head held low, "He's still in jail. The DA put someone on him since he made the attempt on our witness's life. David never visited him. We've been monitoring his visitors."

"He gave David Sean information somehow. I would look into it. I also knew it was him 'cause he never talked much, but always seemed to pay too much attention to me. When I looked into everyone who was involved: you, the ADAs, the two cops who were waiting outside for us; David was the only one whose finances appeared weird. You need to find out how Braxton was exchanging information with him, Costi."

"We will. You investigated me?"

"Yes. Are all the people who tried to kill me, dead?"

"No. Two guys tried to escape as cops and ambulances arrived. They're in the hospital and there are four others in a hospital in Cortland. One of the guys you killed was Braxton's brother."

"No shit!"

"Yeah. It doesn't look like any other family members were here, but you might want to lay low for a while. I'm going to put an officer outside your door till you're released. After that, I can put someone on your house."

"Don't do that, Costi. I don't need you guys looking over my shoulder while I'm trying to heal. Plus, I think I'm going to go home."

"OK. I'll think about it. It's not like you can fight Harrison. You need someone to help you out." He paused again, looking at the floor. "I have to go to the station. I need to deal with David Sean. Think about the details. We'll talk later."

Grabbing his hand, "Thanks Costi." He looked down at me for a few seconds, put his hand on mine, and said, "Stop calling me that."

Chapter 33

I was discharged from the hospital two weeks later and went back to New Rochelle with my parents. My mother could not understand how working with women and keeping them safe turned into me getting a grenade thrown at me. I always suspected she thought there was more to my job than I was telling her, but she never pushed me.

I had no idea why my mother didn't pry because she always pried. I was grateful she didn't because I didn't want to lie to her, and I would have lied. My mother told me before she died, she wasn't sure what I did, but she was sure it wasn't just helping women and children. She told me there was a long line of that in our family, starting with her grandmother. She said she was proud of me.

My father and the rest of my family accepted my explanation about protecting a mob boss's girlfriend, or at least I thought they did. I told them this had never happened before and probably wouldn't happen again.

I stayed with them for six months and then went back to my life. During those six months, I worked out a little at the gym. It wasn't the same, but I did it anyway. Jeremiah was in charge. He had nine kids in the gym learning to box and three of them were girls. He also had a woman boxing coach. He didn't box anymore. "The gym is my life now," he said.

I went back to Syracuse and was off for another six months, then went back to The Collective and my side jobs.

When I got back to Syracuse, Maurice was at the airport waiting for me. I missed him. I jumped into his arms and hugged him hard. He took me back to Xavier's for a party. All the girls were there as well as Jerome. He wasn't just the errand boy for Maurice anymore. Jerome was a full-fledged part of the team. He was sending girls out on jobs and making sure things were running smoothly.

While we ate cake, I asked Maurice about the twins, and he said he had not heard from them. I didn't inquire too much about them after that because they disappeared for a while and popped up when they felt like it. After a year, I wondered what had happened to them. I didn't think I upset them, and it never crossed my mind they were dead. So, I asked Maurice about them again.

"Yeah, they called me."

"What do you mean, they called you?"

"I mean, I got in contact with them."

"Since when did they call you?"

"I just meant..."

"No. You've always said you contact them; you tell them what you want, and they show up."

Maurice looked at me. "I just made a mistake!"

"You don't make mistakes like that Maurice." He continued to stare at me. "Maurice!"

"All right! Look, don't get upset. They talk to me."

"OK."

Maurice hesitated again. "They're my brothers."

"What?"

"Ramón and Orland came to live with us when I was nine. They were thirteen. Their grandfather was Ever's boss back in Colombia. When the cartel started coming after Mr. Delgadillo, their father, he sent his boys to Ever. No one really knew about Ever because Delgadillo kept him in the background. They grew up together, and everyone just thought they were family. Some of his men didn't know Ever worked for him, so his boys were safe.

"When they came here, they didn't speak to anyone. About eight months later, they started talking to me. When anyone else would speak to them, they wouldn't respond. It was weird.

"At seventeen, they left. Didn't say goodbye, leave a note, nothin'. I asked my father about it, and he said they would be back if they needed us, and if not, we should be happy we had the time with them we did.

"I didn't hear from them for a year and then I got a postcard with my name and address on it in their handwriting. I knew they were OK."

"Holy shit!! Why didn't you tell me about this before? They didn't come to your father's funeral!"

"It wasn't mine to tell, Harrison, and yes, they did."

"When? I didn't see them."

"You weren't supposed to see them. They do what they always do, stand in the background. They came to the house after everyone left, and they were with us when we put the rest of his ashes in with my mother."

"Then why are you telling me now?"

"I think they're ready for you to know." He paused, "They're in love with you, you know? But I'm in love with you too."

I just looked at him for a few seconds. "You don't fucking love me."

"Yes, I do. I have for years."

"Really? So, you're gonna give up all your prostitutes, Candy, sleep with only me, and stop being a pimp? Bullshit."

"I would give it up."

"No. You wouldn't. We've been together since I was fourteen, Maurice, and you never once indicated giving up any of this for me. You may want to fuck me, but you do not want a relationship. You would stay with me for a while, but after a quick trip down this road, you would take one of the forks that lead back to Candy and this life."

I got up, kissed him on the forehead, and said, "You're my brother, and I'm your sister, and you're a depraved fucker for hitting on me. I love you. I'll see you later."

Maurice eventually married Candy, had four kids, opened a shelter for women, and employed his prostitutes in the shelter. Yeah, I know. It was ridiculous.

After what happened with Ledawnia and her family, Maybelinne tore me a new asshole. I brought too much publicity to myself and the family, even if it was local publicity. Thank God local news sucks at reporting stories. They were good at investigative reporting but not telling a current one.

The story they told went something like this: *Eleven people were shot and killed tonight in what can only be described as a massacre in Cortland, New York. Nine men and women were also wounded during the shootout at a farmhouse on State Route 41. There are no indications as to the motive or who lives in the farmhouse at this hour. The police will hold a press conference at one o'clock this afternoon with more information on this story.*

They did a few more stories, but all the people involved would not talk to the press about what happened, so the story died.

Authorities decided it would be better for all involved to never release anyone's name. Although Braxton was in jail under twenty-four-hour watch, they didn't think they could trust that he could not corrupt someone else.

They also wanted to keep this out of the press. The press could not be trusted to keep this confidential, so our names were also kept off police reports for the same reason. Maybelinne was still pissed and said I needed to be more careful. I wasn't.

Taking chances didn't seem like a big deal to me anymore. I did not think of immortality, but there was a sense that I could take whatever they gave. Maybelinne got tired of yelling at me. I was going out on my own to go after people I thought might be a threat, and I was looking into the history of people, which wasn't even my job. I did not want to be surprised by anyone again.

She stopped using me because of my antics. I was down for almost a year and thought she wouldn't let me come back to The Collective. She finally gave in, but she had Cara come to speak to me.

We were sitting at Stella's eating pancakes and waffles.

"You have to stop being reckless, Harrison."

"I'm not being reckless. I am trying to help."

"No, you're not. Look, I can't imagine what you went through with Ledawnia and her family."

"No, you can't."

"That's right, but that doesn't mean this can be your reaction to that. This isn't just about you, Harrison. You are not just protecting your charges when you are out here, you are protecting us."

I thought about what she said. "You're right. I do."

"I know how strong you are, Harrison, but if you don't cut the shit, Maybelinne is going to ban you permanently. Please don't let that happen. We need you."

I heard her, and I listened. I took my detective hat off, and I went back to just being an agent. I slowed down...a little.

Once I left The Collective, we lost contact on purpose. They didn't want to know where I was, and I couldn't know where they were. I had been out of the business a long time. I missed it terribly.

The Playhouse became more than I ever expected. Siobhán was still running the center, but we added some things over the years. We added a couple of therapists to the center, opened up the third floor for art and some martial arts classes. Siobhán stayed with the Playhouse for fifteen years. She went back to Ireland to open a Playhouse of her own. She took Patty with her and both of them are still there now working at The Playhouse Too. Before Siobhán left, we hired someone to take her place. The original is still standing today.

Costi kept his word and looked into how Braxton was supplying information in and out of jail. He was a good detective. Braxton's lawyer was receiving information from Braxton and either giving it to Braxton's brothers in Jamaica or to David Sean. He even had a guard on his payroll. After the shoot-out, they put Braxton into solitary confinement in Rikers, and two guards were guarding his cell. The DA handpicked them from another prison, and they took turns watching Braxton every six hours.

His lawyer was arrested, as were David Sean and the guard. From the testimony of Mona, Ledawnia, and the guard, they got an indictment for rape, molestation, aggravated assault, bribery, four counts of attempted murder, and attempted murder of a police officer.

The lawyer and David refused to talk to the police about anything that happened. David's money was seized, and they ultimately convicted him of conspiracy to commit murder and bribery. He was sentenced to twenty-five years to life. The lawyer lost his license and was also convicted of conspiracy to commit murder and bribery. We suspected Braxton had eyes on both of them, even from afar. David Sean was a cop in the general population and never got a scratch on him. He died in prison, but it was a brain aneurysm. The lawyer died of a heart attack, but after he had been in prison for twelve years.

Mona and the children were moved from the safe house. They stayed long enough to make sure that Braxton went to prison. The DA offered him a deal, but he wasn't interested. I thought he would take the deal since his lawyer had been arrested, but no, he just got another one. He wasn't just a psychopath; he was a wealthy psychopath.

The ADA in Syracuse must have received a file from Brooklyn on Braxton Lancer. I saw a similar file, and I understood why she thought Mona and her children should have been in protective custody.

The Brooklyn police had been following Braxton for years, and what they saw wasn't pretty. The empire Braxton Lancer built for himself was built on top of blood and torture. What I have written here is mild compared to some things he did to gain success. Mona and her children were terrorized for years by this man, and they were not the only ones.

Braxton Lancer hung men who disobeyed him in the middle of the street from light poles, beat and/or raped women who had the audacity to tell him no, and maimed or killed family members of people he felt wronged him. Braxton was believed to have killed a child or two to get what he wanted.

He had cut his way through Brooklyn by making a river of blood with his footprints in it. Everyone knew who he was, and no one tried to cross him. He did not only kill people he thought wronged him. He killed fellow criminals, his own men, the police, and anyone else who got in his way.

There were no girlfriends. There were plenty of women who wanted to be with Braxton, but Braxton only used women for sex, and most of that was non-consensual and depraved. If a woman was with Braxton once, she never wanted to be with him again, not even sex workers.

They convicted Braxton of the rape, molestation, bribery, and attempted murder of a police officer. With everything he'd done, the DA wanted to go for the death penalty, but because of some technicality with paperwork, they couldn't. He was sentenced to Southport Correctional Facility for one hundred years.

A lot of men went to prison during my tenure with The Collective, but sending Braxton Lancer to prison was the greatest triumph in my twenty-seven years.

Epilogue

Shortly after Maybelinne had me start working for The Collective again, I asked Magus to find JC for me. I could have gone to JC, but my work wasn't done. Even if JC was single or divorced, my going back to him would disrupt his life, and I couldn't do that to him. He was the only man that I ever truly loved, and I wanted him badly.

Magus found him, and JC did exactly what I told him to do. He got married and had four beautiful children, three girls and one boy.

The girls were Jesenia, Maximilla (my middle name), and Lùz. The boy's name was Javier III. JC was married for ten years until breast cancer took his wife. He became a single father and never married again. Magus kind of kept tabs on them and found out that Milla, the youngest, was good at sports, very smart, and beautiful. Lùz should have been named Jesenia because she looked exactly like her, and Jesenia looked just like Laila (JC's mother). Javi, the third, was a genius. He became a member of Mensa at twelve.

JC had a heart attack just after he turned fifty-three. He was alive for a few days, but he never fully recovered. I didn't go to the funeral. Trying to explain to people who I was to JC was too much for me. Plus, there was a big concern in my heart that I would completely break down. Seeing his children would have filled my world with gladness, but they didn't need me. I needed them. It was selfish, so I didn't do it.

Ramón and Orland took me away again after JC died. I woke up one day, and they were in my apartment. They had packed my things and didn't even tell me where we were going. I cried a lot, and they let me. After a few weeks, I was ready to leave. They said no. They would tell me when I was ready. They brought me back five weeks later. That was when I realized how they felt about me.

About a year after JC died, a woman I had worked with for six months was ready to move to her permanent location. When the van pulled up, two women got out. I escorted my charge to the van and one of the women walked right up to me.

"Hi, Harrison."

I recognized the voice immediately. "Ledawnia?"

"Yup, it's me, but it's Rochelle now." We hugged.

"I can't believe it. You are all grown up." Ledawnia was about 5'10", slim, and she looked exactly like her mother. The only difference was that she was a little darker than her mother. She wore her hair in a ponytail, and it hung down just past her shoulders. "What are you doin' here?"

"I work for The Collective."

"You're too young. Maybelinne would never allow that."

"It's a long story, but I have worked unofficially for them since I was fifteen. Maybelinne found out what I was doing and said if I promised to stop, I could work for The Collective after I graduated high school."

"Are you eighteen?"

"Yeah, a few months ago."

"I can't believe Maybelline agreed to this. But you do look so grown up. How is your mother and brother?"

"My mother is great. She works for a college professor as his assistant, and she loves it. She's even taken some classes. And my brother is still in high school. He doesn't remember much, but Mom and I told him everything last year."

"How did that go?"

"OK. He was a little shaken at first to hear his history. He asked about Grant."

"Grant?"

"Jr. didn't know his name, but he described him. We told him we didn't know where Grant was."

"I can't believe he remembered Grant. He was only sixteen months old when he was with Grant, and he only stayed with him for a little over a month. I don't know where Grant is. Now I wish I did."

"It's weird because Jr. didn't remember our father." She paused and looked down at her feet. "He's dead, you know."

"I know. You all must have been relieved."

"We were. My mother breathed for the first time in twenty years," she paused again. "The guy who killed him wrote to me."

"You're kidding."

"No. You want to read the letter?"

"You have it with you?"

"I carry it with me."

"No, I don't want to intrude."

"Read it, Harrison," she said, shoving the letter at me.

I opened the envelope and pulled out what seemed like ten sheets of paper.

Dear Mr. Lancer's daughter,

My name is John Bob Foster, and I killed your father.

I don't want your praise or for you to thank me. I thought you should know who killed your father and why.

I have always been a criminal and have been in and out of jail and prison since I was 11. It started with kid stuff, but when I got away with that, I graduated to bigger and better things. I robbed my first store at the age of 14. By the time I was 17 I had done three stints in juvenile hall, been in 6 foster care homes, and was no longer going to school.

In Nacogdoches, Texas, where I'm from, it's a lot harder than in other places when you get into trouble. They take that stuff seriously.

My sister Crissy Jo and I were extremely close and I tried to stay out of trouble for her since Dad was not around and Mom was a drug addict, but I couldn't do it. I loved her, but I wanted things, she needed things, and no one was going to stop me from getting them for her.

When Crissy Jo was 16 she met this guy Landon Pierce who became her boyfriend. This happened during one of my times in prison and it was one of the longer ones. He got a chance to get his claws into my sister. When she was 18, they moved to New York. She never visited me in prison, so I didn't know he was abusing her. She tried to get away from him, but he always found her and beat her up. From what I understand, she never tried to leave him again except for one other time.

Some woman came to her and offered her a hand. The woman convinced her that she could help her. My sister wrote to me for the first time in years, asking my advice. She told me she didn't know if she would stay with this woman because she was afraid that Landon would find her again. I told her to do what she needed to do so she would be safe.

Somehow the police got involved and she felt she would be safer with them. Landon found her. I was told he killed the guy guarding her, and dragged her away. They found her the next day in an alley next to a liquor store.

When I got out, I found out she was with this woman for about a month before she went to the cops. I think she thought a woman couldn't keep her safe because the last time Landon found her, he not only beat her up, but beat up a female friend who was helping her.

I tried to find the woman, but no one knew who she was. So, I focused on Mr. Landon Pierce. I looked everywhere for this man. I was in Syracuse for three months. Found out he did not have a lot of friends. When he came back from being out of town three people called to tell me where he was. I found him at a bar. I asked if he was Landon Pierce. He said who wants to know and I proceeded to beat him to death while I told him the story of who I was.

I don't know why people didn't stop me at first, but they eventually pulled me off of him. By the time the police arrived, Landon was unconscious. They took him to the hospital where he died later that night. He is the reason I am in prison right now.

When your father came here, I didn't think anything of him until his crimes started to float around the prison. He was bragging about it. When he mentioned Upstate New York and a woman helping his wife, I started to pay attention.

I overheard him talking about trying to kill your family and this woman again and I knew what had to be done. I didn't know if it was the same woman who tried to help my sister, but it was close enough. I will be in prison for the rest of my life. I can live with that. I didn't save my sister, but I helped someone like her and I hope that's enough to make amends and for her to forgive me. I hope that you and your family are safe. Good luck and goodbye.

All I could say was, "Holy shit! Holy shit!"

"Is he talking about you in the letter?"

"Yeah. His sister was the only person I lost in the almost 30 years I've been doing this. I knew about her brother, and I knew he was looking for me, but I couldn't expose myself like that. The pain he must have been in."

"I knew it was you somehow. I'm sorry if I upset you, but I thought you would want to see the letter."

"No. You were right, I wanted to see it. And I'm not upset. Did you write him back?"

"Maybelinne did. She didn't want me exposing myself, so she sent him a postcard with thanks on it."

"Then how did he find you?"

"He didn't. He sent the letter to the Syracuse police station. As I understand it, your cop friend found someone who knew you and asked them to get the letter to me. I don't know who."

"Was the letter sent to you?"

"No. Maybelinne gave it to me."

"She never mentioned any of this. I'll have to ask her. Are you OK? This is some heavy shit."

"I'm fine. I was shocked when I read the letter. I didn't know how to feel. I wasn't sad at all, but I wasn't happy either. I guess I just felt safe. I haven't felt that for years. I knew no one was gonna find us because you said they wouldn't, but I didn't feel safe until he was really gone. Hey, how are the twins?"

I smiled. "They're fine, I'm sure."

"I would love to see them. Is there some way to get in touch with them?"

"I can't give that out."

"Why? I won't tell anyone."

"Do you remember after your father tried to kill us at the courthouse when we went back to Norma's?"

"Yeah."

"Do you remember the conversation you had with the twins?"

"Yes."

"Do you want to tell me what the three of you talked about?"

"No. I can't."

"That's right. Because it's private and they never told me what they said. I can't betray them like you can't. If they wanted to see you, they would see you. Besides, they've probably been watching you this whole time."

"They told you that? How would they find me? No one knows where I am."

"They're the twins. That's how they would find you, and they wouldn't tell me if they were watching you. I will tell them you said hello and miss them though."

"Tell them I love them."

"I will."

The van horn honked. "I gotta go."

"Does Maybelline know you and I were seeing each other?"

"No, and she is going to be pissed, but I had to see you. I wanted you to know that we were OK. I know you don't get to see who you saved again. You and everything that happened then were a big part of my life."

"It was a big part of my life, too. I'm really glad you came to see me. Take care of yourself, Ledawnia."

"I love you, Harrison." She hugged me one last time and held on for a long time.

"I love you too."

After seeing Ledawnia, I decided I had to see JC's kids. I couldn't do it then because my life was still too dangerous, but after I left The Collective, I got up my nerve and made the move. I planned to tell them I was an old friend of their father from when we were kids, and I wanted to pay my respects in person since I couldn't come to his funeral. They didn't need to know who I was.

I also talked to Maybelinne. Maurice gave her the letter. I had no idea how Costi found him or how Maurice found The Collective. I never gave the three of them information about the others.

JC started his family in Boston. When his son was two, he moved back to New York and raised his family in Scarsdale.

I thought I would start with the oldest child, so I went to Jesenia's house. If she wasn't happy to see me, there was no need to go to the others.

I should have called, but I wanted to look her in the face. A phone conversation was too easy. I needed to be near them.

The whole time I was making the four-hour drive, I was practicing what I was going to say. I was nervous and thought about turning around a couple of times. But I stayed on the road to Scarsdale and made it to their house in three and a half hours.

I stood on her porch for a few minutes hoping none of the neighbors called her to tell her some crazy woman was pacing on her porch.

I rang the doorbell and waited. I thought no one was home and rang again. The door came open with a young man standing in the doorway.

"H... H... Hi. Is your mother home?"

He stood staring at me. Then he said, "Harrison?"

Then, I'm staring at him. "You know me, kid?"

"Yes, Harrison. My mother and my aunts and uncle talk about you all the time."

I had to hold on to the frame of the door and almost bent over because I was having trouble breathing.

"Jesus, who's at the door?"

A young lady came around to see who he was talking to. Her mouth dropped open when I lifted my head. Her son then said, "It's Harrison, Mom."

"Oh, my God. Oh, my God. We half thought he made you up. Oh, my God. Please come in," Jesenia said.

I walked in as if I was struggling through mud. She was saying something to me but I couldn't make it out, and her son went somewhere else in the house.

She sat me on the couch and was still talking, but I couldn't hear her. She then placed her hand on my shoulder.

"Miss Harrison? Are you OK?"

"How do you know who I am? I don't...I don't understand."

"I'm sorry, but I need to call my sisters and my brother. They will never believe this. I'll be right back."

She disappeared into another room and left me alone in their living room. I glanced around. She had high ceilings and art on the walls. Her living room had two parts to it. The lower part I was in had a blue couch in front of the fireplace, a red one on the back wall behind me, and a flower pattern love seat on the side. To the right was another room, not as big, but it also had a black couch and two green chairs in it. Both rooms were painted a deep beige.

Above the fireplace were a bunch of family photographs. I recognized Jesenia, Maximillia, Lùz, Javier, and JC. The others I did not recognize, but they looked like family. One of the pictures was a picture of me, JC, and Jesenia. I had forgotten all about the picture. It was the first time I beat Mr. Corrales at Canicas. No one in the house had ever beaten him, not even Mrs. Corrales. Their mother took the picture. There was another picture on the mantle of Jesenia and me just before she was killed. And a picture of me and JC together when I was in college. Tears started rolling down my face.

When I refocused my attention, it felt like fifty people were in the house. Everyone was talking at once, and I still hadn't wrapped my head around the fact that they all seemed to know who I was. Jesenia told everybody to shut the hell up and find a seat, which they did.

"We are so happy to see you. We have so many questions."

"You have questions? How do you all know who I am?"

Jesenia looked around, so I looked around. They were all smiling and smirking at each other.

"We know about our father's history. He told us when Tres was a teenager."

"Tres?"

"Javier. He told us about our grandfather and what he used to do, how they had to run, our aunt's death, what happened to our grandfather, and about you.

"He told us about those stories until the day he died. But it really started when we were kids. We wanted to know who the pretty girl was in the picture with him and our aunt. He told us you were his first love. Even our mother knew that."

"But it's like you all have been waiting for me?"

In unison, "We have."

"When he was dying, our father told us that you might show up one day. He said not to be disappointed if you didn't 'cause you might decide not to disrupt our lives," Jesenia answered.

"How did he know I was going to show up? I didn't even know I would come here."

"I don't know, but he did."

"Why didn't you come when he died?" asked Javier.

"I didn't know you all knew who I was, and I didn't want to disrupt your grieving process. That would have been selfish on my part."

"Why did you come now?" asked Maximilla.

"Because I wanted to grieve your father with you, and I could do it now. I also wanted to meet all of you. JC's children. I had a whole story planned about being a friend of the family when we were young. I didn't know you all would know who I was." They all chuckled.

"Dad always talked about you and our aunt Jesenia."

I glanced around the room and saw faces I recognized from my childhood. I couldn't believe it. I turned to Jesenia. "Tell me about your mother."

"Our mother?" asked Jesenia.

"Yes. I want to know about the woman who was an important part of your father's life. What was she like?"

"She was loving."

"She was generous."

"She loved her family."

"Our father told us he never thought he would love another person besides you, until he met our mother. She was in love with him. Every day she made his lunch, ironed his shirts for work, and went to all his boring parties."

"But it wasn't just her. Dad set up the coffee in the morning, even though he hated the smell of coffee, he helped get us ready in the morning, and once a month was date night. He never missed out.

"She was kind, but she made sure we stayed in line."

"Remember the time she caught Maxi sneaking in after curfew?"

"I never saw her so mad. She yelled at Maxi for twenty minutes about lying to her, what if something happened to her, and she wanted to kill her right now."

Everyone laughed. "Sounds like my kind of woman," I said.

"Yeah, she grounded her and took her off the softball team."

"Yeah, I was heated, but I better not tell her that."

They all laughed, including Maximilla.

"Our mother was a pediatric nurse, volunteered at the homeless shelter, and picketed for women's rights. We had dinner every Sunday and if we missed it there better be a good reason and there was no good reason. She was a great mom. When she died, the only reason our father went on living was for the four of us. She must have been a great wife too."

I wanted to hear about her, but I had conflicting feelings about him finding love after me. Another woman capturing his heart was unthinkable to me, but I was thrilled he found love and she loved him back.

"What about Dad? He was a great father. Came to a lot of my games, helped with homework, and any hobbies we had, he was in."

"When he died, it was such a hard blow for us. He never got to see us become successful, get married, or have children. We miss him."

They introduced me to their kids and then they wanted to know about me.

I told them as much as I could, leaving out what I thought they didn't need to know. We spent the entire afternoon together and most of the night. I knew they were my new family.

That evening, after the kids went to bed, and they sent their spouses away, we got intimate.

"Was our father your first love?"

"He was. I have loved your father since I was twelve and your father was fifteen. I was crushed when he left me at fourteen. He had to, but it still hurt."

"What was he like when he was younger?"

"He was smart, handsome, funny, and serious. He was all about his grades and doing well. I never saw him with girls when he was in high school. All he wanted to do was study."

"What was Jesenia like?"

"Jesenia was the best friend I ever had. She was creative, loyal, and fierce. If she thought something was wrong, she was gonna fight about it."

"Did you ever look for our dad?"

"I didn't have to. I knew where he was."

"Did you know he was married? Is that why you didn't come to him?

"I knew he was married, and it was part of the reason."

We talked for hours getting to know each other. They were all so successful and family-oriented. JC raised some great kids.

When I went there, I didn't know what I was going to do with the rest of my life. I was done with The Collective, and Maurice didn't need me anymore. The twins retired way before I did. My parents were gone, and my brothers had families of their own. I could stay with the twins, but I didn't want to come between the two of them. I needed something, but I didn't know what.

Then I came here, and I saw a place for myself. A place JC had left for me. How did he know? I knew they weren't my kids, but I could have a place here if they wanted me, and it seemed they did. Maybe I could live a piece of the life I always wanted with what JC left for me. A new journey in my life.

THE END

Acknowledgments

There are so many people I want to acknowledge who have helped me on this journey.

My sister, Tina who read my first couple of chapters a loooong time ago and told me what was right and what was wrong.

My first mentor, Aigner Loren Wilson. Your guidance made me leave my comfort zone and made my story work. I am not sure I would be where I am if it was not for you. Thank you.

My publisher Inspiring Jreams. Ashequka Lacey, I could have done this without meeting you, but I would be about 20 steps back. Love you.

To Miss White. The most avid reader I know. Her critiques and suggestions gave me the confidence to move forward.

To my other early alpha and beta readers, Joanne Stephens, Cody Maggi, Marlena Daher-Rahman, Courtney Zaryski (kinda), and my mother, Catherine.

To my critique partner Tamara. You and I both know this book would not be where it is if it wasn't for you. I love you, but more importantly, I appreciate you.

To Mykayla Bryant who created my beautiful logos. Every time I look at my them I smile. They are so perfect. Thank you so much for giving me so much.

To Tamira K. Butler-Lively, Phd, my editor. Thank you so much for all your help. There's too many commas in these sentences, aren't there?

To Ceylan Ozguner my proofreader. I couldn't see my mistakes anymore. Thank you for your eyes.

To TJ Manrique. I know you said thanks is not necessary, but it really is. Thank you so much for getting me through formatting. Your information was invaluable.

To The Tribe. When Eli B. put the group together, I knew I was going to love it. I know I wasn't there all the time, but all of you inspired me. I wanted to write more because of you and I wanted to be better because of you. Thank you for being on my writing journey with me. I love you.

To my Twitter Family. So, many of you have helped me on this journey. I would name each one of you, but not sure you want your names in print like that. Some of you may not even know you helped me, but you taught me something either indirectly or directly. You all gave me a place to vent and feel safe to tell you about my writing woes. Thank you for the encouragement and praise.

To my Thread Family. We have not been a family long, but it has been a beautiful ride with all of you. Our community is what a writing community is supposed to look like. Thank you for giving me that.

Finally, to Horrible Writers Writing Support Group on Facebook. Even though it was for a short time, you all are the reason I became a published author. I don't have enough words to thank you and 'thank you' isn't enough. The anthology you created gave me the ability to believe in myself and realize I could do this. The micro-short story I wrote will eventually become a future novel.

If I forgot anyone, I'm sorry. I love you all.

Call to Action

Thank you for reading The Life of a Collective Warrior. Please leave a review on Amazon and Goodreads.

Visit me on Instagram: writercdpulley

Visit my medium page: medium.com/@CDPulley

Visit my blog: womenareeverything.wordpress.com and cdpulleyblog.wordpress.com

and visit me on Threads at writercdpulley

About the Author

CD Pulley's love of reading fiction, mysteries, crime novels, and sci-fi is the reason she creates stories in multiple genres. Attending college, getting a job, and earning a second degree was the direction life took her instead of becoming an author. When CD's stories began calling to her, she was older and becoming an author had changed. The entire writing world had changed. CD realized she could self-publish her books and that she wanted more than ever to write stories about people who looked like her. A current administrator in adult education, CD lives in New York State with her husband. When she isn't writing she is cross stitching, creating DIY projects or working on her blog.